Buy the CHIEF
ᵃ Cadillac

Buy the CHIEF
ᵃ Cadillac

a novel

RICK STEBER

CARROLL & GRAF PUBLISHERS
NEW YORK

BUY THE CHIEF A CADILLAC

Carroll & Graf Publishers
An Imprint of Avalon Publishing Group Inc.
245 West 17th Street
11th Floor
New York, NY 10011

AVALON
publishing group incorporated

Library of Congress Cataloging-in-Publication Data is available.

ISBN-13: 978-0-78671-639-5
ISBN-10: 0-7867-1639-8

9 8 7 6 5 4 3 2 1

Interior Design by Jamie McNeely

Printed in the United States of America
Distributed by Publishers Group West

For Edison Chiloquin, the only true hero of termination. He refused to sell his heritage for a fistful of the white man's money.

1923–2003

The white man has made many promises. He kept but one. He promised to take our land and he took it.

—Spoken by Red Cloud, Sioux Chief

Foreword

On October 14, 1864, representatives of the United States government signed a treaty with several Indian tribes of the great interior basin of south-central Oregon, including the Klamath, Modoc and the Yahooskin band of the Snake Indians. By this treaty the Indians relinquished 20 million acres of territory and in return were granted more than a million acres of reservation land, including a vast forest of ponderosa pine.

Ninety years later, under the Indian Termination Act, the federal government purchased the reservation, incorporating it into the Winema National Forest and Fremont National Forest, and revoked the tribal status of the Indians. The motive for this act was to reduce federal spending while conducting a social experiment to force assimilation of the Indians into white culture. In 1961 each withdrawing tribal member received a cash settlement of $43,000.

Buy the Chief a Cadillac is a novel based on the facts of the U.S. government's termination of the Klamath tribe. Any specific incident, or resemblance of any character to an actual person, is purely coincidental. There is no town named Chewaucan. There is no U.S. West Bank. And there are no such things as greed, indulgence, tyranny, social injustice or racial prejudice.

Testimony

We have been wards of the government for 82 years. I am ready for something better or ready for a settlement. We can handle it a little better than what the government tried to handle it for us; and I don't think it should be the intention of the Government to keep the Klamath Indians corralled up for the rest of their lives. We should be turned loose and let us shift for ourselves. (Testimony of Eddie Cookman, tribal member, before the Subcommittee on Indian Affairs of the Committee on Public Lands, U.S. Senate, 1947)

★ ★ ★

To carry out the termination legislation of the Klamath reservation as now constituted would be a serious mistake and result in irreparable damage. In support of this contention, I offer the following information:

1. *Court records indicate a substantial majority of adult Klamath Indians living on the reservation have been arrested and convicted for offenses more serious than traffic violations. The number of convictions range up to more than 100 per individual.*
2. *The reported number of desertions, illicit unions, illegitimacies, and extra-marital relations far exceed that of the rest of the public at large.*
3. *Two thirds of the able-bodied male Klamath Indians on the reservation, between the ages of 18 and 63, either do not work at all or work only sporadically.*
4. *Almost 50% of the adult Klamaths living on the reservation were not considered competent to handle their own funds.* (Testimony of Robert Chandler, publisher of the Bend Bulletin, before the Subcommittee on Indian Affairs of the Committee on Interior and Insular Affairs, U.S. Senate, 1957)

★   ★   ★

We cannot compete with the whites and never will. Now, I want you people to understand, both whites and Indians, I have not got very much to say but what I say I want you people to carry it home, think about it a little while; if it ain't no good to you, drive it away.

I want to tell you this, we should keep our reservation. Don't let boneheads influence you and throw the reservation over. That will be all. (Testimony of Watson Tupper, tribal member, before the Subcommittee on Indian Affairs of the Committee on Public Lands, U.S. Senate, 1947)

★   ★   ★

The Klamath Indians, each man, woman, and child, has been getting per capita payments from selling their timber. Tax free money. These per capitas are the worst damn thing there ever was. The Indians don't have any incentive. They know they're gonna eat anyway. They've been brought up that way. The best thing would be to sell the timber to the government and let the Indians have the money to spend. After they've spent it they'll have to learn to work—or go hungry. (Testimony of Bert Albert, Klamath County resident, before the Subcommittee on Indian Affairs of the Committee on Public Lands, U.S. Senate, 1947)

★   ★   ★

For the past 30 years I have been associated with law enforcement in Klamath County and I think all the Indians here will agree with me—there have been certain Indians in and out of the county jail two or three hundred times, they are in and out and are going to be back again. I can only recall one killing on the Klamath reservation where liquor was not involved. If the reservation is liquidated, and if the payment is made and the Indians can go out and buy what they want, we have a class of Indian who is just going to get drunk and stay drunk. They will go out and lose all sense of judgment and kill someone. (Testimony of L. L. Low, Klamath County Sheriff, before the Subcommittee on Indian Affairs of the Committee on Public Lands, U.S. Senate, 1947)

One

Soon the government money would flow, gunshots would crack along the sharp spine of the ridge, and Indians would die. But for now, all was quiet. Pokey Pitsua sat on a basalt ledge, legs dangling in space, watching as opposing angles of light and shadow shrank and stretched in response to unruly clouds blowing across the face of the sun.

Below him the thin ribbon of the Chewaucan River twisted lazily in its bed. Hard by the river was the town of Chewaucan, nothing more than a drab collection of shacks, abandoned automobiles and junk strewn across the landscape. Overhead a turkey vulture spun lazy circles. It seemed to Pokey as if that bird had been hanging up there forever, waiting for the opportunity to sweep down and clean up the reservation mess.

Pine trees shuddered in the wind. Pokey slowly opened his left hand, the hand missing parts of two fingers. The sun pierced through shredded clouds and particles of light danced across the delicate fractures of the obsidian that lay in his palm. Pokey again made a fist around the perfect arrowhead. The weight of it was insignificant but caused him to contemplate an ancient brother who had chipped and formed the glass. Was it a weapon to hunt a deer or elk? Used in self-defense against a raiding tribe? Shot in anger at a white man? The arrowhead tied him to the past.

Others might see him as only a bastard half-breed, but in his heart, where it counted, Pokey thought himself pure Indian. He was out of high school and worked now and then buckarooing for local ranchers, but most of the time he was off having fun; riding saddlebroncs at All-Indian rodeos, playing All-Indian basketball, hunting, fishing and dancing at an occasional powwow.

Pokey's father was a white man. From him Pokey received his pale skin, the same tone as brain-tanned buckskin. His Indian blood had given him black hair, which he wore in braids, strong cheekbones and brown eyes flecked with gold. He was tall, well-muscled and graceful.

As a light rain began to fall, Pokey felt the knot in his gut torque tighter. In a few hours he would play in the championship game of the All-Indian basketball tournament. Big games always gave him stomach butterflies. But his foremost concern was termination. Tomorrow the U.S. government was annihilating the Klamath nation and stealing their million-acre reservation. The last battle had been fought and the Klamath tribe was surrendering. And for what? A cash settlement of $43,000 to each man, woman and child, quarter-blood or better. How could people sell their heritage, identity, birthright? And what was money? Nothing but printed paper traded for alcohol and fast cars.

Alcohol made you stupid. Fast cars killed you. As far as Pokey was concerned, it would be better to take the $43,000 and scatter it on the wind.

★   ★   ★

The big spring storm of 1961 was approaching, blowing hard across the broad plain of the Pacific Ocean, sucking moisture as it came. Brackish clouds slammed inland, dumping rain on the Coast range and snow on the high Cascades. Wind bullied its way over the mountains and dropped down to the mile-high level of the Klamath Basin where, out on the flat turquoise sheen of Klamath Lake, the reflected image of mountains and sky dimpled, danced and broke apart into whitecaps.

On the flank of Sun Mountain that same west wind shoved at the Trailways bus snaking through the curves of the narrow, yellow-striped road. Pine trees flashed past. The driver chewed a frayed toothpick while glancing in the overhead mirror, trying to make eye contact with the girl seated directly behind him. "Weather report says there's a series of storms, one right after another, just waiting to come in. Gonna be a wet one. For sure."

The girl did not respond. She seemed lost in her own world, staring out the window. The driver stole a quick peek at the road to reassure himself it was still in front of him and then looked back to the face in the mirror. With her long dark hair and youthful good looks, this girl was a beaut. He recalled leaving for work that morning, kissing his wife good-bye. Ten years of marriage and what did he have to show for it but four bratty kids and a big-butted wife. "Acres and acres of ass and she's all mine."

Again his attention was drawn behind him, not to the girl, but to the prissy young man seated beside her. The two presented a striking contrast. He muttered under his breath, "Goddamn little buck. Mixing races ain't no good. Whites oughta stay with whites, niggers with niggers, and Injuns belong on the reservation. What in the hell is the world coming to?"

The junction was near. He eased off on the throttle and downshifted. The bus pulled onto the wide shoulder like a fat duck plopping down on a desert pothole. The driver turned to the girl and asked, "Honey, sure you wanna get off here?"

She fixed her dark eyes on him and replied, "I'm sure." She woke the Indian beside her. "Creek, we're here."

Creek Pitsua sat straight up, looked around and shook his head to clear the cobwebs. He had atypical Klamath Indian features; instead of the wide-boned face, flat nose and square jaw that distinguished most members of his tribe, Creek was light-boned, with a thin face and a narrow, symmetrical nose. He was as perfect as a porcelain doll.

The driver watched as the girl reached high overhead to retrieve her coat and umbrella from the luggage rack. Her sweater rode up, exposing her willowy midriff. She tugged it down and pulled on a leather jacket.

Creek tapped the driver's shoulder. "We need to get our luggage." His voice was thin and high-pitched. It had never dropped the customary octave at puberty, and high school classmates had teased Creek, giving him the nickname Squeaky.

The driver, annoyed, climbed down from his seat and stepped through the splattering rain to the luggage compartment. He dug out a blue suitcase and an old duffel bag, set them on the wet gravel and slammed the door. Turning abruptly, he strode to the front of the bus, took the stairs two at a time and dropped back onto the seat. He stole one last lingering look at the girl and saw her pop open a brightly-colored lemon and green umbrella. Her jeans were tucked into knee-high boots and this sight stimulated his manhood. Boots on pretty girls always did that. What he wouldn't give to. . . . He flashed a wicked smile and kicked the bus in gear.

He would carry that mental picture of her for a good many miles, wondering over and over again why in hell such a sweet, young thing would voluntarily choose to get off at Chewaucan. So naive, so goddamn innocent. He doubted she had a clue of what terrible things could happen to her on the reservation. She would have fared better if she had stayed on the bus and taken her chances with him. If she had—the possibilities he contemplated were all indecent and he chuckled aloud.

Two

Shasta Edwards, a white girl with an Indian first name, used the thumb on her left hand to tuck loose strands of hair behind her ears. She studied the canopy protecting her from the raindrops. On campus at the University of Oregon the lemon and green umbrella had blended into hundreds of others, but now she vaguely wished she had never opened something so gay and cheerful. It seemed terribly out of place.

She took a deep breath, wrinkling her nose at the stench of the swirling diesel fumes, and scanned the oil road leading from the junction toward town, a half-mile away. The boundary of Chewaucan was loosely defined by pine-covered hills and the gentle sweep of the Chewaucan River. The most dominant feature of the landscape was the humpbacked skeleton of a wigwam burner. When the sawmill was in operation and the burner was fed a steady stream of scrap wood, it glowed like a yellow-orange beacon. Sparks and wood smoke muscled their way into the sky, and on days when the wind did not blow, smoke hung in a gray cloud over town. She had loved the smell, but that was long ago, and now the wigwam sat idle, a hulking mass of rusting metal. The air, scrubbed clean by the rain, smelled faintly of pine with a hint of sage.

Creek's shrill voice sliced into her thoughts, "Doesn't look like Dallas is here to meet us. Come on. We better start walking." He threw the strap of his duffel bag over his left shoulder and with his right hand picked up her blue suitcase.

"Here, I can take that." Shasta was taller than Creek. She reached one hand toward the suitcase.

"I got it," he said.

As they walked through the rain, the wind tugged at the umbrella and Shasta could feel anger and resentment beginning to fester. Her father, with a little prompting, had invited her to come and stay at the ranch. So how could he be so inconsiderate? No wonder her mother divorced him. This was supposed to be a special time, a homecoming of sorts. The bus had been on time. He had known the schedule. What possible excuse did he have? But when had that man ever been considerate? His idea of being a father had been to tuck a twenty-dollar bill in his Christmas card. Same thing every year. She had invited him to school plays, recitals, high school graduation, father's weekend her freshman year of college. He never had the decency to respond yes, no, or go jump in the lake. Christmas, a crisp twenty, nothing more.

On the bus ride south Shasta had braced herself for the possibility of a chilly reception but she had never entertained the notion her father might be a no-show. But what did she actually know about Dallas Edwards? He was a boyishly handsome face in a photograph, taken decades ago. Within a year or two after her mother left, he had remarried, and Shasta could not begin to conjure up an image of her stepmother. Her name was Dolly. Shasta had never known anyone named Dolly.

As they walked into town Shasta tried to make mental notes so later she could write down her impressions of Chewaucan—abject reservation poverty; shacks, primerless and paintless, brittle wood soaking up moisture; cast-aside cars and pickup trucks; chunks of broken beer bottles, pop bottles, discarded tires. Trash was being tugged and pushed around by the obstinate wind. The only sign of hope seemed to be the Roman Catholic Church glistening under a fresh coat of white paint. It stood aloof like a bright agate washed ashore on a beach of worthless stones.

Two Indian boys, oblivious to the rain, shot a basketball at a bent rim tacked onto the end of a dilapidated single-wide trailer house. An empty school bus backfired and the driver swung into a muddy circular drive leading to one of the shacks where, in a four-square-paned window, hung a Halloween leftover, a cardboard cutout of a black cat with his back humped and hair standing on end.

Shasta and Creek crossed the railroad tracks and reached the business district of Chewaucan, if it could be called that: a few buildings clustered around an intersection where a yellow caution light blinked in all four directions. On one corner was the Shell service station. The general store across from it appeared to have had a recent facelift. Pine boards had been tacked to the false front, giving it a decidedly western flair. There was even a hitching rail out front.

Kitty-cornered from the store was a vacant lot where the hotel once stood. The concrete foundation was still visible among the empty husks of wildflowers and weeds. It must have burned in the late '40s. Shasta was hit by the memory of being bundled in a blanket, held in her mother's arms, watching the fire. She remembered the heat on her face and the vivid flames dancing before her eyes. She had a child's perspective of the fire and no real notion of what was happening, that the destruction of the hotel marked the end of an era. It had been built for the railroad workers, who became dispensable after the steam engine gave way to diesel.

The other corner of downtown was dominated by city government. In front was the city-owned drinking establishment, The Tavern, the only government-run bar in the state. Behind it was City Hall, a cinder-block building painted green with orange trim. It housed a meeting room, the sheriff's office and a single-cell jail.

They trudged past the downtown core, and Creek, who was coming home for the first time in more than a year, nodded toward a house that seemed out of place with its neat yard defined by a chain-link fence. A sign tacked to the fence stated, "Worms for Sale," and beneath that was another sign advertising, "Saw Sharpening." Creek said, "Pattersons live there. Fred and Mildred. They're white. Fred was the janitor at school. Mildred cooked in the cafeteria. They retired when I was in high school. They get social security and a pension from the school district. Live good—anyway, good by reservation standards."

Across the road Shasta watched an old man with a battered prizefighter's face, a gimpy leg and a bum arm hanging loosely at his side, shuffling down a trail. His baggy jeans, held up with suspenders, rode low on his hips and were snagged above his work boots. He wore a ragtag flannel shirt and a knit cap pulled down on his head. In his good hand he clutched a paper sack. The screw cap of a cheap wine bottle peeked out the top.

Creek shook his head. "That's Lefty. He's one of the designated town drunks. Most towns only have one or two. We've got them by the dozens. Lefty's our official white drunk." Creek laughed.

They came to a fork in the road—one way led upriver to the ranch where Shasta had spent the first seven years of her life. She assumed Creek would walk her home and began to angle that way, but Creek stopped her. "Our place is closer. I'll borrow a rig from one of my brothers and drive you home."

Shasta recalled Creek's brothers—half-brothers actually. Rollin was the oldest. Big, mean and ugly, he was six or seven years older than she was. He used to throw rocks and dirt clods at her as she walked to and from school. He called her his "little white girl," making it sound shameful and lewd, even to a child.

The other brother was Pokey. The thought of him made her spirits brighten. The day she and her mom had pulled out for good, Pokey told her he was sorry she was leaving and gave her a pretty rock as a parting gift. She still had that rock, knew exactly where it was, tucked away in a box of personal treasures and keepsakes at her mother's house.

Where was her father? Why hadn't he come to meet her? She did not want to go to the Pitsua house, but what choice did she have?

Three

As they approached the bridge a brown and beige two-tone Chevy Biscayne turned down the lane and rattled and splashed through the chuckholes toward them. Creek and Shasta stepped to the side and waited as the car rolled forward a few more feet and then stopped. The window cranked down to reveal a man with a ruddy complexion and coils of red hair oozing from beneath the circle of a floppy-brimmed, dusty gray felt hat.

"So, how's it hanging, Creek?" The man's speech was laced with a liberal dose of Oklahoma twang.

Creek gave a vapid little laugh. "Long and loose."

"And who's this you brung home with you?" He jerked his head in Shasta's direction.

"Shasta Edwards. Dallas is her daddy. She used to live here, went through most of first grade here."

The driver leaned out the window and extended his right hand. As Shasta took it, her delicate piano-playing fingers were gobbled up and lost in his big mitt. Without taking his eyes from her, he said, "Name's Marion Durkee. Folks call me Red. We ain't none too formal around here. I'm the law, what there is of it." He held her hand longer than she found comfortable and flashed a grin. "Dallas is your father? Hard to believe that old cowboy could sire such a pretty thing. Sure there ain't been some mistake?"

Shasta held the umbrella with one hand and used her free hand to run stiff fingers through her hair, brushing back wayward strands. She could not think of a thing to say in her father's defense.

"This a social visit or strictly business?" Creek wanted to know. "Chief in some sort of trouble?"

Chief was a nickname bestowed on Rollin while he was in the Oregon State Penitentiary. Red grinned. "Tell me a time Chief wasn't in trouble." The grin faded, leaving him looking haggard, almost as if he were weary of fooling with this charade. Law and order on the reservation was a joke, though times were changing and Red knew that tomorrow there would be no more reservation. He was of the opinion that the wahoos should live like white men, see how they liked them apples. "We can jawbone in the car. I'll run you kids over to the house."

"Naw." Creek shook his head. "That's okay. If we come home with a police escort, I'll have to try and explain, and Grandma will figure I did something to get myself in hot water. Let's just save the aggravation. It's not far."

"Suit yourself." Red cranked up the window and the Chevy spurted toward the bridge. Then he stopped, unfolded his big frame, crawled out and walked to a half-sheet of plywood nailed to the bridge abutment. He squinted at letters crudely scrawled in white paint, pushed back his hat and scratched his head with two fingers while trying to make sense of it:

Must Dye
Chief
Tyler T.
Nathan

As a Klamath County sheriff's deputy, Red had investigated dozens of murders and sometimes referred to his territory as "Little Chicago." Like the mafia, the Indians had their own set of rules they lived by. It was generally accepted that if a young man hadn't killed someone by the time he was nineteen or twenty, then he wasn't much of a man at all. The prelude to a killing almost always involved a drinking party. At some point a fight would erupt. Someone would get killed and someone would do the killing. Red would make an arrest and the accused would stand trial. Manslaughter carried a penalty of three to seven in the state pen. After the prisoner was released he would make a beeline back to the reservation and the pecking order would have to be reestablished. There would be the ritual party, and by the time the booze ran out the top dog would have emerged. Red talked to himself, "Shoot 'em. Stick 'em with a knife or the jagged point of a broken bottle. A killing here, a killing there, no great shakes. All comes out in the wash."

As near as Red could recall, there never had been a death notice posted anywhere on the reservation. Usually the killings were a spur of the moment thing, with a revenge murder thrown in every now and then to even a score. Nobody went around making threats of violence. Violence was something that just happened. Like the sun coming up in the morning.

The Indians usually took care of their own business, but since Red was in a thinking mood he considered the possibility of a planned uprising. Was a vigilante group mounting a bid to take the law into its own hands? Red doubted it. Nothing but a bunch of bullshit. He had enough to worry about with termination looming on the horizon. But then he glanced at the plywood sign again and understood that the possibility of a vigilante skirmish was not something he could just put away and forget.

Creek walked up beside Red. "Dye Chief. What color do you suppose would suit him best? Forest Service green? Maybe a nice pastel blue?"

"You're taking things a bit too literal. Not everyone around here has been past fifth grade." Red shook loose a cigarette from a pack and wedged it between his lips. He took a wooden match from behind his ear, struck it with a thumbnail, protected the flame with cupped hands, lit the cigarette, drew in smoke and exhaled. "You don't have to be a college boy to figure out that whoever wrote it meant D-I-E."

"Think there is anything to it?" asked Creek.

"Might mean something, might not. Hard to tell unless people start dropping dead."

"You have to wait until someone dies before you do anything?"

Red studied the boy and saw that even though he had grown an inch or two, and put on a few pounds, he appeared like he always had, pint-sized and childlike. College hadn't changed him much, at least on the outside, so a person would notice. Red took a pull on his cigarette and blew away the smoke. "Son, all I can do is sit back and wait. Someone gets kilt I look for who kilt them. It don't work the other way around."

★ ★ ★

From his vantage on the knobby spine of the ridge, Pokey studied the flat that began at the bridge where redwood logs were strung from each bank to a piling in the middle of the river. Creosote-stained planking covered the stringers. On the near side of the river was a low-slung tin barn rusted orange. In the adjacent pasture a cow grazed. Opposite the pasture, in an open area, junked cars and pickup trucks were parked, like seeds waiting to sprout. The lane sliced between the pasture and the open field, jogged a time or two and ended at a tremendous ponderosa pine that stood like an exclamation point at the end of a rambling sentence. From a low limb hung a tire swing that had not been used in years.

Under the spreading branches of the big tree sat a wood-shed, and a hundred feet farther was a squat house. The house had once been painted white with shocking blue trim around the doors and windows, but the white had faded and was now stained with mud balls that someone had thrown at the siding. They resembled sad, black tears. The porches, front and back, were weathered dull gray. The front porch was open, the back encased in tattered plastic turned opaque by the sun.

Pokey saw Grandma emerge from the back door. She was wearing a gray dress, a shawl slung around her bony shoulders, high-topped Chuck Taylor Converse tennis shoes and a man's western-style hat. She set a galvanized milk pail on the steps and used two hands to pull shut the swollen door. A mongrel pup came to sniff at her. She kicked at him and he cowered, moved away, his tail tucked between his legs.

Grandma shuffled forward through chimney smoke that

dipped and swirled around her, and with the milk pail dangling at the end of one arm, she slowly made her way down the lane toward the barn. In the pasture the Holstein cow, milk dripping from her udder, gave an impassioned low and moved for the barn. As usual the cow's timing was impeccable, arriving at the instant Grandma pushed back the latch and threw open the barn door.

The cow lumbered in and Grandma circled around through a side door. The cow pawed at the stanchion boards and Grandma tossed a couple of pitchforks of loose hay into the manger and moved on to the chicken coop where she turned her attention to gathering eggs. Hens squawked and pecked at Grandma's dress and shoes but she paid them no mind as she went on robbing the nests, carefully placing the fragile eggs in her upturned hat. Then the old woman returned to the cow, squatted onto a low stool and began stripping milk from the teats. The rhythmic melody of milk, squirted against the bottom of the pail, masked all other sounds until the warm creamy froth built in the pail and the throaty growl of the river flowing around the bridge piling became audible again.

When Grandma emerged from the barn, the egg-filled hat in the crook of an arm, she was leaning to one side under the weight of the milk pail. On the way to the house she paused to change hands. Pokey had a notion to yell, tell her to leave the pail, that he would carry it the rest of the way. She was too far away and would never hear. And so he leaned back, melting against the gnarled bark of a juniper tree that had, somehow, three or four hundred years ago, gained a toehold in a rocky crevice.

Pokey shifted to one side to tuck the arrowhead into his pocket. He had once read about this land's long ago, when rhinoceroses, crocodiles, giant pigs, camels, and saber-toothed cats prowled in a jungle of giant sequoia and magnolia trees. According to this book version of how man came to populate the continent, the earth's atmosphere cooled, and far to the north the ocean froze and a courageous band of people crossed an ice bridge from Asia to North America. Slowly the earth warmed. The glaciers retreated and the melting water gave birth to rivers, lakes and marshes. Grandma held a different belief. She believed K'mukamtch, the Great Spirit, created earth for the native people and He populated it with fish, birds and animals so that His people would never go hungry. Whichever way it actually happened, Pokey knew it had been his ancestors, on his mother's side, who had jump-started civilization in this corner of the world. This thought, like the sight of Grandma, was unmistakably reassuring.

An Oregon junco, bobbing its black head, pecked for seeds under a tree. A dove bounced a clear note that was answered; a few seconds later a pair of doves, flying wingtip-to-wingtip, flashed across the mottled sky. A killdeer called from the pasture where a spring, choked by weeds and watercress, bubbled and bled off, meandering across the bench and trickling into the Chewaucan.

On the far side of the bridge Pokey saw a two-tone Chevy parked near the approach, exhaust coughing white puffs of smoke. He wondered what Red was up to. And then, recalling the plywood sign tacked to the abutment, Pokey grinned. Probably just somebody's idea of a joke, and yet, from the way Red was standing there in front of the sign and pondering, he must be taking it as a bona fide threat.

Pokey could make out two other figures as they walked toward the deputy sheriff. One was holding a yellow and green umbrella. He could not recall having ever seen an umbrella on the reservation and laughed at the absurdity of it. What harm could a little rain do? He slid off the rock, dropped to the ground and started for home.

★   ★   ★

Shasta watched Red kick at a chunk of neon cinders with the pointy toe of his cowboy boot and thought back to a conversation she had had with Creek on the bus ride south. Creek had described the deputy sheriff as "the nicest, and yet the meanest and toughest son-of-a-bitch on the reservation." When Shasta had pressed him on the matter, how Red could be both the nicest and the meanest, Creek had said, "He was always good to me. He never sees red or white. Treats everyone equal, until someone proves otherwise. Then, better watch out. Even Chief leaves him alone. He would have to be drunk out of his mind to fuck with Red. They say he could have been heavyweight champ but then the war came along."

Shasta became aware of the rhythm of cowboy music. Could it be Hank Williams singing a mournful tune or was it merely the song of the river as it strained against the bridge pilings? She was not sure.

Red lowered himself into his car. "See you later," he called and swung the Chevy in a circle, spinning the rear tires.

Creek picked up his duffel and Shasta's suitcase and led the way onto the bridge. He nodded ahead to the flat and said, "According to Grandma, way back when, the main Indian camp was scattered along over there. Filled up the whole area."

The wind puffed and tall grasses swayed. Shasta imagined the Indian village: earthen mounds used for winter quarters and wickiups, stick frames covered by tule mats, lived in during the warm weather months. She saw the campfires, saw the women cooking, the men talking among themselves, and the children playing.

The images were clear and defined, so real that it startled her. She had seen the old Indian village and the people who inhabited it. There was no rational explanation. The vision had been a gift from an unseen power, a quick and revealing glimpse into the past. And now it was gone. Shasta again became aware of her surroundings. Daylight was fading and the pine trees had lost their green luster. A raven gave a harsh, piercing cry and Shasta felt a strange sensation race the length of her spine. She shivered.

Creek was saying something. Shasta heard the words but did not comprehend them right away. ". . . and good fishing. Nice big trout. And the mullet run in the spring. Used to watch Pokey and Chief snag them. Mullet, they are sucker fish, bottom feeders, and they don't taste that good. Real fishy. Used to throw them up on the bank to rot. Get them out of the river. Pokey said it was to make more room for the trout."

The river came down from the high country, flowing cold and clear and always in a rush. It boiled through the canyon it had carved, flashed past the town of Chewaucan and the hay fields before emptying into tranquil Klamath Lake. Shasta paused to listen and she recognized the river's voice, a voice that had been with her for a long, long time.

"Come on," called Creek.

Shasta fell in step beside him. They passed the barn and Creek kept up his pitter-patter. "Pokey rode many a calf out there in the pasture. Climb on and they'd go one of two places—either along there by the spring or down below in the nettle patch. I tried it once, got bucked off into the nettles and almost itched my skin off. Never tried it again."

They walked farther and then Creek came to an abrupt stop. Shasta glanced at him and it appeared as though Creek were about to burst into tears. He blurted, "I hate it."

"What?"

"This." He made a sweeping gesture with his skinny arm and stopped with his fingers pointing toward the bridge and the sign on the far side. "Does Chief have to die? Is that what has to happen?"

"The sign? You hate the sign?" Shasta asked.

Creek shook his head. "No, the violence that everyone here accepts and lives with, the whole philosophy of friends sharing a bottle, until, at some point, they try to kill each other."

"You're getting all wet," Shasta said, offering him the protection of a corner of the umbrella.

Creek kept his distance. "I had to get away, for my own sanity. And now I have to take the money I have coming. Get away. Stay away."

They walked up the lane in silence until they reached the first of the many car bodies crowding the road. Creek patted the fender of a '49 Merc, chopped and channeled with a bullnose hood, frenched headlights and white tuck-and-rolled interior. The front was caved in. Chief had been drunk and ran the Merc into an elementary school teacher's car. The teacher died. Chief did three years in the state pen. Involuntary manslaughter.

Creek moved on to a '55 hardtop Chevy. Shasta surveyed the unraveled garter belt hanging from the interior mirror, the drooping lake pipes, the chrome wheel on the front end turned under, hood askew. "I remember this one. Chief dropped in 4:11 gears, three deuces. Could she ever scoot."

For a flickering moment he seemed almost proud and then once again he shook his head, "Look around. These cars were new and beautiful at one time, purchased with per capita checks from the government. Payment for the timber they were cutting and running through the sawmill. Every quarter another check. The cars got wrecked, some just quit running. The Indian doesn't have a background in the way things work, no mechanical aptitude to fix things. If the timing gear snaps—park it. Busted water pump— park it. Clogged fuel pump—park it. Wait for the government to give another handout, buy a new one."

Shasta wondered if Creek were trying to convince himself that he had escaped the reservation and had somehow replaced the blood in his veins. He was an anomaly, an Indian who was attending college and had goals of making something of himself in the white man's world.

★ ★ ★

If any Indian could make it on the outside it would be Creek. He was good with numbers. Math had always been his favorite subject in school because in an equation, if this number and that number were added or subtracted or divided, they always equaled the answer. Black and white. No gray. What was, definitely was, and could be proven. Creek wanted his world to be just as definitive and precise as a logarithm.

He did not subscribe to the Indian philosophy that no man could own land and, in fact, had been considering investing some of his termination money in commercial real estate. He could be a landlord and still go to school. And when he graduated he would go into the business of buying and managing property as if it were Monopoly. He liked to play Monopoly and was good at the game. That was his pragmatic side. But he also wanted to enjoy the money, spend at least some of it to buy nice clothes, a new stereo and records. But more than anything he wanted a bright red Corvette. A car like that, sleek and with power to burn, would help him stand out in a positive way. He would finally become the man he desperately wanted himself to be.

Simply put, Creek had come home for the money. Strictly for the money. He vowed he would not take so much as a sip of alcohol. Several times in the past he had been drunk. When he sobered up he detested the vague memories of his bizarre behavior and the pain of the hangover. When he drank he was aggressive and belligerent, or emotional and silly, and sometimes completely stupid and antisocial. Before he ever got on the bus he had promised himself he would not drink because once he tasted alcohol, he was powerless to stop, always wanting more, and more, and more.

Creek was imagining the termination money, bills stacked in front of him like the ultimate winning pot from a poker game, when a pack of snarling, snapping, growling dogs erupted from under the house and bounded toward him. Panic crackled like lightning through his brain. He flung the suitcase in one direction, his duffel bag in another. He was knocked to the ground by the lead dog, a thick-tailed, blue-eyed bitch with one droopy ear from a long-forgotten fight with a coyote. She caught Creek's scent and suddenly transformed into a squirming mass, pawing at him and trying to lick his face. The dogs shoved their noses into every unprotected part of Creek's body, leaping, nuzzling, licking. He writhed on the wet ground and began to giggle like a schoolgirl.

A gunshot, then another, and another. Shasta drew a quick breath and saw an Indian standing near the porch. He was as handsome as an Indian in a Frederic Remington painting, hair braided, the butt of a rifle held against his thigh, leg slightly bent, fire belching from the end of the barrel, empty casing flying away. Fire flashed. Again. Again. Again. Echoes cracked and rolled down the long spine of the ridge. Shasta's hands went to her mouth to smother a scream. Her yellow and green umbrella turned turtle and landed top down in the mud.

Grandma threw open the screen door and demanded, "Why you shoot so much?"

"Creek's come home," the young man with the rifle said.

As the echoes of gunfire rolled away Grandma hobbled across the porch, drying her hands on the soiled apron wrapped twice around her spindly hips and tied in front. She descended the two steps to the ground. The years had warped and wound her small frame into a question mark. Black netting, held in place with hairpins, confined her bun of silver hair. She came near and squinted at Shasta with eyes that were thin slits in a badland of wrinkled brown skin. She was toothless and her sunken jaw twitched as if someone were repeatedly jabbing needles into it.

Shasta's breath was coming fast and shallow and she told herself to draw a deep breath, hold it, let it out slowly. Creek had pulled himself off the ground and away from the dogs and was now making a beeline to Grandma. He threw his arms around her. The dogs whimpered and rubbed against his pants legs.

Shasta moved to retrieve her umbrella. She had it in her hands and was breaking it down when she found herself walking toward the Indian holding the rifle. She stood in front of him, staring up at him, searching the smallest details of his face as if she were studying a map. A breeze lifted a hank of her hair and let it back down. She pushed at it with the palm of one hand. In a voice too faint to be her own she scolded, "Why did you do that?"

"Give Creek a welcome home. That's all."

"You frightened me."

"Sorry about that."

Shasta recognized something about him. "You're Pokey, aren't you?"

He nodded.

She exhaled. "I'm Shasta Edwards. I used to live up the road. You were a couple years younger."

"Still am."

Shasta tried to smile as she extended her arm and opened her hand. It seemed to Shasta that most men sought to prove something with their grip, using a simple greeting as a way to establish their dominance, but Pokey merely touched her hand and released it. And then Creek was there with his arms around them both, ushering them toward the house.

He pulled open the screen door and held it. Shasta moved across the threshold and into the truculent light of the interior. It was not a journey of feet or inches, or any normal means of measurement, but a headlong plunge into another culture. She breathed in an overpowering accumulation of unfriendly smells: blood from deer steaks frying on the wood cook stove, stale beer and wine, wet dogs, and mice and pack rats that lived in the walls and attic. The front room floor was covered with cheap linoleum, nearly worn through in the places that saw the heaviest traffic. The kitchen floor was fitted with dark, narrow pine planking. Scattered about were empty bottles, bottle caps, cans, crumpled candy wrappers and empty potato chip bags.

Shasta's gaze went upward, to the ceiling, where a speckled length of flypaper dangled from a nail. And then she saw Chief. He was spread over an easy chair that leaked cotton stuffing onto the floor, his hair was wild, his face pockmarked, blunted, dumb. He opened his eyes. They were set far apart, and puffy. Looking into those eyes was like staring into the dead of night and seeing faint flickers of starlight that had taken a thousand years to reach earth. Chief began to stretch and half-heartedly tugged at his sweatshirt, trying to draw it over the exposed flab of his belly. One hand blindly felt for a quart of beer on the floor. He picked it up, wrapped his thick lips around the opening, tipped the bottle and guzzled the dusky liquid. When it was empty he carelessly dropped it on the floor beside him and issued a mighty belch.

He shifted his weight, groaned and pulled himself to a more traditional sitting position. With great effort and a loud grunt he stood. He was like a grizzly bear standing on two feet, swaying slightly from side to side, squinting and trying to bring the world around him into focus. In a lightning-quick burst of motion, his hands jumped out and thumped Creek on the chest, driving him back against the sofa, a ratty mate for the chair. Chief, in a pure Klamath Indian dialect, foreign to all but reservation dwellers, demanded, "What the what golly's goin' on 'round here? What ya got ta say fer yourself, Squeak?"

Chief stepped forward and threw a massive arm around Creek's neck, pulling him in, growling, "How's life treatin' ya, anyways?" And while he held Creek in a headlock he looked directly at Shasta, leered at her and grinned. He was missing all his front teeth. Without taking his eyes off her, he asked, "So, Squeak, been gettin' any?"

Creek pleaded, "Ease up. You're hurting me."

Chief squeezed harder, then lost interest. He trudged to the back porch, grabbed another quart bottle of beer from a case on the floor and returned to the living room. Perhaps to show off for Shasta, he pried loose the cap with his molars, spit the cap on the floor and offered her the first drink. She declined. He proceeded to Creek. "Have a drink." Creek nodded toward Pokey but Chief said, "He don't have ta. He's got a game tonight. Least you can do is 'ave a drink with me, ain't it."

Creek had told Shasta he never drank. At college, when he partied, Creek drank Pepsi and had almost as much fun as everyone else. Now he tried to appease Chief by wedging his tongue in the opening so it would appear he was drinking without having to swallow. But Chief grabbed the back of his neck with one hand and the bottle with the other. He pulled the bottle away so beer poured freely and Creek had no choice. He gulped and gulped again. Chief emptied the bottle and took a step back. Creek sputtered and spit and rubbed at the beer that ran down the front of his shirt. Chief's belly shook with a deathless laugh. He flopped back in his chair and turned his attention to Shasta. "What ya doin' here, little white girl?"

Shasta had hated him before and she hated him now— he was even bigger and more menacing. Was it too late to forget it all, forget her paper on termination, forget her father? Where was he? He obviously did not want to see her or he would have been at the junction. She should leave right now while the getting was still good.

★ ★ ★

Grandma shuffled to the wood cook stove, opened the damper and pried open the door. Smoke poured out, but she seemed in no particular hurry as she stirred the coals with an iron poker and laid a chunk of pitchy wood on top. The fire snapped to life, flames biting at the pitch pockets. She closed the door and turned down the damper. She used a knife to flip over the meat in the cast-iron skillet.

Grandma was the great-grandmother of Chief, Creek and Pokey. Her granddaughter, Puggy Pitsua, was responsible for bringing the boys, each fathered by a different man, into this world. None of these dalliances was ever blessed by the holy sacrament of matrimony. Chief's father was Klamath Indian, as was Creek's. Then Puggy got pregnant by a white man. Those were the chances you took when you drank with a man, went to bed with him, drank some more and moved on to the next.

Three boys—not bad, considering the odds and the fact Puggy saw her purpose in life, as near as she could figure, was to drink and party and die. Her sense of parental responsibility had been to bring the boys into the world and promptly dump them on Grandma. Grandma had tried to raise Puggy properly, tried to teach her right from wrong and to have respect for herself, other people and Mother Earth. But the river of whiskey, beer and cheap red wine swept her away. By now she might have succeeded in drowning herself. No one had heard from her in years.

Four

Dallas Edwards was a cowboy with a hard, well-traveled look. White hair capped his head and coarse stubble grew on his face like a dusting of snow on the craggy ravines and dry washes of the high desert. He was bowlegged and his frame was bent slightly in the middle. A mean scar gouged one cheek and ran down onto his neck, the result of attempting to tighten a strand of rusty fence wire. It broke, snapped back, and the sharp barbs carved a gully that had to be closed with 64 stitches. A little lower and it would have cut his jugular, a little higher could have cost him an eye. That scar had the power to make Dallas's past real, and each time he happened to catch his reflection he would be reminded of his careless mistake.

Dallas operated a small spread south of Chewaucan and pastured his cattle on reservation land. He had a sweet deal, paying the tribe a fraction of the going rate, and hated like hell to see the federal government terminate the reservation. Termination was changing the rules of the game. He would have to pay the government price or go out and rent private pasture. Either way, he figured, it was going to hit him hard in the pocket book.

Dallas sat in the Shell service station in Chewaucan and told Floyd Parsons, "It's a goddamn dirty shame. Government wants the timber an' after they get it they'll turn it inta a national forest an' log it off. Put up a goddamn fence around it. Keep my cattle out. The whole shitaree in a nutshell is, government steals the land, gives away all that money, an' them ungrateful redskins gonna go through it like grain through a goose."

Dallas and Floyd went way back. Floyd had owned the Shell station in Chewaucan for fifteen years. He was a small, wiry man who began each morning with a clean blue shirt that was always greasy by quitting time. He wore a black clip-on bow tie, the same one every day, and a stubby-billed welder's cap. An oily red rag hung limply from a hip pocket. Floyd had moved to Chewaucan right after the war, the big one, WWII, to avail himself of the abundant hunting and fishing opportunities that existed on the reservation. Within a year he was married to Tillie, an Indian girl, slender and pretty. She soon discovered soda pop and sugar and indulged herself until she resembled a birthday balloon.

Every Saturday night, small, diminutive Floyd was in the habit of pulling on a pair of pointy-toed boots, Levi's and a western shirt, wrapping a silk bandanna around his neck and stuffing a cowboy hat on his head. He would drive twenty miles to Klamath Falls, or forty miles to the Red Barn in Dorris, California, and twirl Tillie in circles around the square dance floor. He considered it an accomplishment that an introvert like himself had found such a wonderful, and public, way to express an outgoing facet of his personality.

Floyd's other passion was collecting the myths, legends and history of the Klamath tribe. Over the years he had interviewed most of the old-time Indians living on the reservation. Every so often he would close down the station and steal a week, traveling around the Northwest, visiting universities, museums and historical libraries. He read dusty field notes and reports that detailed the government's dealings with the Indians.

People around town never saw the dancing cowboy or the meticulous historian. Most folks saw Floyd only as that dull little man who pumped gas and did mechanic work down at the Shell station.

Dallas had never been quite sure what made Floyd tick, but all the same he liked Floyd and enjoyed stopping by the station to get his bitching and complaining out of his system before he went home to face his wife, Dolly.

"You've hit the nail on the head about the government wanting the timber," Floyd agreed. "This reservation contains twenty-two percent of all Indian-held timber in the United States. Sure, the government wants it. And what the government wants, the government gets. Fact of life. So what's new? Indian's been getting screwed ever since the days of John Smith and Pocahontas."

"They *screwed*?"

"Of course not. She was a little girl. Don't you know anything about history?"

"Not interested. What's in the past is done and gone."

"Maybe if you spent some time acquainting yourself with the facts, and saw how the Indian has been mistreated throughout history by the white invaders, you would—"

"Get off it, Floyd. Don't spout all this poor, pitiful Indian crap on me just 'cause you're married ta one."

"You made a generalization. You said every Indian is going to throw his money away, but I could name names, Indians who'll put it to good use."

"Name one."

"We're putting Tillie's government check, most of it anyway, into municipal, tax-free bonds. Down the road I'll retire and we can live off the interest. And there's Clarence Bean. He's buying a backhoe and setting himself up in the excavation business. Jimmy Jackson's getting a new skidder and the Wilson brothers are buying land and upgrading their ranch."

"Handful. Not many. The majority will drink it up an' have nothin' ta show fer it. How 'bout Chief and that bunch hangs 'round with 'im? Do the world a favor, drown 'em all like they was a gunny sack of barn cats. Who's gonna miss 'em? Floyd, you're gettin' me all wound up. Better step outside an' take me a quick peek at the moon."

"There's no moon, not yet, and with this here storm probably won't be," Floyd observed.

"You're missin' the point." Dallas got up and shuffled out the door. "I'm sober as a muley cow, can't be sober an' talk no sense ta ya, Floyd."

Floyd watched through the window, smudged with hand prints and fly tracks, as Dallas gimped to a sickly mustard-colored three-quarter-ton GMC flatbed. Dallas had bought the Jimmy new, twenty years before, as a regular pickup. When the bed wore out he had it converted to a flatbed. He always had a couple of bales of hay on back and a cow dog or two that slept on the hay. Another of Dallas's trademarks was the bottle of Old Crow he kept tucked under the seat. He opened the door and withdrew the bottle.

If he was going to keep bullshitting Floyd about the Indian situation, he needed fortification. He took a long drink, swished it around in his mouth, swallowed, smacked his lips. The alcohol hit his empty stomach and rushed to the nerve endings like forks of lightning seeking the ground. He breathed deeply, crunched his eyes closed, opened them. He capped the bottle and returned it under the seat, slammed the door shut and resumed his normal, stoop-shouldered posture as he shuffled back inside. His cowboy hat, a silver-belly Stetson stained around the crown with honest sweat and dust turned to gumbo, was pushed back on his head, revealing a line of white against the ruddy complexion of his face. He dug a knife out of his pocket, sat down on a folding chair, opened the blade and began working dirt from under his fingernails. And, as if he had been saving up words, he unleashed a flood.

"Government's gonna plumb run me outta business. They'll put in an allotment system, limit my grazin', jack up the fee. How in the goddamn hell am I suppose ta pay more? They make me pay property tax, state tax, federal tax, irrigation tax, gas tax, cigarette tax, tax my whiskey, tax when I sell a steer, even talkin' 'bout taxin' my goddamn dogs. What they're doin' is taxin' the workin' man ta death. Barely get by as is. Can't afford no more. Never make a go of it if they cut back my grazin' rights or jack up my per unit. Got me by the short hairs. Sure as hell do. Short hairs."

Dallas could have continued his one-sided tirade indefinitely, but, luckily for Floyd the worn tires of Red's Chevy Biscayne crossed over the sensor hose, making the bell ding. He parked beside the outside pump. Dallas put away his pocketknife and removed a rolling paper and a pouch of Bull Durham from his shirt pocket, shook out a paperful, started building a smoke. "What the 'ell's he want?"

Red walked in and plopped himself on one of the folding chairs, leaned back and stole most of the heat from the electric wall heater. "I got a question for you two yahoos. Heard anything about a vigilante outfit?"

Floyd shook his head. Dallas lit his cigarette, casually blew out a cloud of smoke and asked, "What's the deal?"

"A death list. Someone tacked it to the river bridge. Don't figure it means a whole hell of a lot. But you just never know." It was quiet except for the hum of the electric heater and a moth bashing itself against the fluorescent light. The compressor engine kicked on, ran for a few seconds and shuddered to a stop.

"Looks like we're in for a big storm. Be good in the long run. Add to the snow pack. Farmers in the lower basin sure as hell can use the moisture. Floyd, you best pull on your raincoat and rubber boots." Red turned his attention to Dallas. "Say, didn't know you was such a stud horse."

Dallas frowned.

"The girl."

"What girl?"

"Shasta."

"Huh. What the 'ell . . . ?"

The two turned to confront each other like banty roosters trying to protect a manure pile. Red grinned. "Happened to have a real nice visit with her. She said you was her daddy. Don't remember you mentioning you had a daughter."

"That happened a long, long time ago." Past failures

were not something Dallas was in the habit of mentioning. "Where'd ya see 'er?"

"Down by the bridge. Headed for the river place. Was running with Creek."

"Shit." Dallas removed his hat and slapped it hard across his leg. "Christ on a crutch. Son-of-a-bitch. I was supposed ta pick her up. She come down on the bus. Slipped my mind big as hell."

"Best not waste time. Never know what them wahoos across the river are up to but you know it ain't gonna be no good." Almost as an afterthought Red added, "Thought I ought to let you know."

★　★　★

Dallas marched out to his truck. His dog barked and he told it to shut up. He climbed in the cab and slammed the door. The latch did not catch and he rolled down the window, jimmied the outside handle, and slammed it again. He cranked over the tired engine and while it idled he wiped at a layer of condensation on the interior of the windshield with the palm of his hand, clearing a hole so he could see. The defroster blew cold air up at him. He flipped a toggle switch he had wired himself, and when the vacuum pump built up enough suction the wipers began to slap at the rain pelting the windshield. The truck jerked into forward motion and the dog whined.

★　★　★

Dolly was cooking in a cafe when she met Dallas. She was a damn fine cook. From the very start that seemed to be the thread that bound the two of them, her cooking ability and his hungry stomach. Other than that, they had very little in common. She liked television, movie magazines, romance novels and fantasy love. He liked dirt on his hands, cow shit on his boots and open range with no barbed wire in sight.

During their married life they talked when they had to exchange information, never to swap ideas, discuss a current event, an opinion, or even to share a sentiment. Once a month or so they had sex. Usually Dolly was the instigator. On those nights she would have a whiskey and water waiting for Dallas, a candle burning gaily on the table, and dinner that was appropriate for a meat and potatoes man. Dessert would be something special: strawberry shortcake, banana cream pie, German chocolate cake. It was not a perfect marriage; it was just what it was.

Dolly, wearing pink rubber gloves to protect her delicate skin from the harsh detergent, stood at the sink washing tight circles on a plate. She projected herself into the drama of *The Secret Storm* on the twelve-inch portable black and white television staring down from atop the refrigerator. She stole a quick glance out the window at the road. Dallas should already be here. The bus was probably late. Nothing was ever on time.

The thought of the girl, Dallas's daughter, coming to visit made Dolly break out in hives. She rubbed at her belly with the back of a wrist. She promised herself that at the next commercial she would check her face in the bathroom mirror, maybe splash on a dab of perfume and take off the red plastic hoop earrings. The dangly silver and turquoise ones Dallas had given her on their tenth wedding anniversary would be more appropriate. They gave her self-confidence, symbolizing the fact she had been able to hold on to her man for a decade. He was so sweet that time, coming in from chores, giving her the jewelry box, watching her reaction. Dolly had opened the box with trembling fingers and slipped on the earrings, feeling so deliriously happy she had cried. Then she kissed him and put aside the tuna casserole she had been planning to serve and fixed him a T-bone steak and mashed potatoes with thick white gravy, just how he liked it.

The television gently tugged Dolly back to the program and she found herself identifying with the woman on the screen who was kissing the man who had murdered her husband. And now the lovers could be together. Dolly was in that man's arms and she could feel the heat of his skin against her. She licked her lips, ruby red lipstick glistened. Tears streamed freely down her powdered cheeks and popped tiny soap bubbles in the sink. Dolly suffered for herself, and for every discontented woman who married for love and afterwards realized marriage was not, and never would be, exciting, passionate or fulfilling.

★　★　★

Shasta watched Grandma slide along the wall like some night creature, stopping at a window and appearing to become engrossed in the sight of rainwater cascading off the overhang of the roof, then turned to Creek. "I need to go. Would you run me over to the ranch?"

Creek tipped the bottle of beer and drank. Chief slapped him on the back. "Squeak, you're a real man. Chug it." Creek checked with a knuckle to see if the bottle had cut his lip. There was no blood.

"Let's go ta the Knife and Gun Club, aye," Chief said. "Drink a few beers."

"Hold on," Creek said, noticing that Shasta had picked up her suitcase and started for the door. He said, "We can drop you off on the way. Unless—wanna go have a drink at The Tavern?"

"I just want to get to the ranch," Shasta replied, stepping onto the porch. Chief elbowed past her. The flimsy screen door slammed in his wake. Creek pushed it open again and made a stab for the handle of Shasta's suitcase. She pulled away. He shrugged, grinned and went ahead of her.

Shasta saw a pair of yellow headlights, weakened either from age or from not getting enough juice, drifting down the lane. The bouncing lights revealed themselves to be pulling a flatbed truck through the darkness. The porch light illuminated a yellow-colored cab that Shasta recognized, recalling a bitterly cold morning in the meadow pasture, trying to see over the dash to steer while her father stood in back breaking bales, flaking hay and feeding the cattle scattered behind in a long, moving line. The memory was jarred by the screech of brake shoe rivets scraping metal drums. Dallas brought his rig to a stop a few feet shy of the front bumper of Chief's black Impala. The Impala had been wrecked several times, nothing big, just the usual reservation assortment of dinged fenders and creased side panels. Chief turned the key. The ignition caught and the engine sprang to life, pistons screaming as Chief stomped the gas pedal.

The cold rain slid down Shasta's cheeks and burned gases stung her nostrils; the haggard old cowboy staring through a hole in the foggy windshield was her father, and the sounds of engine noise and dogs barking made the sight of him all the more preposterous and rowdy. One by one the male dogs made their way over to the truck to lift a hind leg on the back tire while Dallas's dog paced the edge of the flatbed and growled his defiance.

Chief cranked down his window and bellowed, "Get yer ass in gear," at Shasta or Dallas or both of them.

Dallas reached to open the passenger door. Shasta placed her suitcase on the floor and climbed in. Chief impatiently goosed his engine. Dallas kicked his rig into reverse and crept back a few feet. Chief went around him with a roar and sent mud splattering against the flatbed.

"Ya son of a bitch," Dallas barked, and then he remembered his daughter seated next to him. "Sorry fer my language, an' sorry I wasn't there ta pick ya up. Got ta workin' an' time just slipped away."

Five

Red completed a slow loop through town, pulled over and parked near the bridge. He unscrewed the lid of his Stanley thermos, poured a cup of coffee, lit a cigarette, cranked the window down a couple of turns for ventilation and heard the snarl of an engine as it reverberated over the river. The roar of straining rpms was punctuated by a heavy-handed speed shift, followed seconds later by a shadowy streak of Chief's black car shooting off the bridge and fishtailing down the dirt road. Tires screeched as they bit in at the edge of the pavement.

"Chief, you're gonna kill yourself before you ever get to spend a dime of the money. Turn on your goddamn headlights." Red took a contemplative puff, blew smoke out the opening and thought about the Blackfoot reservation in Montana. He was there once and saw that along the highways they put up white crosses and fake flowers at the site of every fatal wreck. At some of the most dangerous curves the white crosses and cheap plastic flowers piled up like tumbleweeds along a fence line. At one time the Blackfoot had been some of the best horsemen in North America, but they proved to be among the very worst drivers. Red laughed at the absurd thought that an artificial shrine would serve as a symbolic reminder to slow Chief down. He took a sip of coffee. The windows began to fog. Red started the engine and turned on the defroster. He mulled over what might happen in the upcoming hours. After the game the party would kick into high gear. Tomorrow—termination. Money. Booze. Guns. Drunks. Hot rods. And then there was the prospect of a vigilante uprising. Hell's Bells, maybe he should call in the National Guard, get it over with.

Red watched Dallas's truck cross the bridge and turn right. He knew that Dallas had rescued his daughter and was thankful for that. It was one less thing for him to be concerned about.

Red Durkee was a product of the dust bowl; his family was the quintessential Okie clan who pulled out of Oklahoma with all their belongings piled on the back of a Model-A pickup truck. They arrived in southern California, where Red worked in the fields alongside his parents and his brothers and sisters. Like a character in *The Grapes of Wrath*, he suffered all the indignities of being another damn Okie. He fought the bigotry by becoming a thug and a boozehound.

And then one night a police sergeant happened to witness four hoodlums jump a rawboned, redheaded boy. The boy whipped three of them and the fourth turned tail and ran. The sergeant, who spent his off-duty hours as a trainer at a local boxing club, recognized God-given talent, even if it was rough and unrefined. He approached Red and complimented him.

"Say Buster, you handle yourself pretty well." He followed that with a threat, saying he would be compelled to arrest Red for disorderly conduct unless he promised to show up at the Thirty-first Street gym the following day. Red kept his promise and the sergeant was able to channel the boy's anger and aggressiveness into an unbeaten record as an amateur boxer.

Red fought under the moniker Irish Red and compiled a record of 97 straight wins, 81 by knockout. He had the potential to turn pro, but the Japs interceded, bombing Pearl Harbor. Red took it personally and joined the army. He was with the landing force at Guadalcanal, fought in the Philippines and helped take Okinawa. After the war he thought about making a career of the military. He did a tour in the Korean War and that was enough. When it came time he refused to re-up. With his muster-out pay he bought a case of bourbon and a new car, drove north until, two miles shy of Chewaucan, he ran off the road and plowed into a tree. He hiked into town and his first, and only, stop that night was The Tavern.

Before the week was out Red was falling timber for an outfit logging on the reservation. He sweated out the booze and got on with his life. His final social visit to The Tavern was the night a burly Indian from Warm Springs, a reservation two hundred miles to the north, came to Chewaucan, walked up behind Red and hit him over the head with the barrel of a .22 caliber six-shooter. Red turned to face his antagonist. He smiled—just smiled—and that unnerved the Indian so much that he pointed the pistol at the center of Red's chest.

Red calmly advised, "Better hope to hell that thing don't accidentally discharge, 'cause if it does, it's liable to sting and really piss me off." And then he backhanded the pistol away. It skittered across the floor and under the pool table. The Indian swung wildly, missed, and Red hit him so many times, so fast and with such force, that the poor bastard fell back and busted down the door to the men's john.

The story of the fight quickly made the rounds. The next day the Klamath County sheriff paid a visit to Red and offered him the job as deputy. "Most reservations are controlled by the BIA, that's the Bureau of Indian Affairs," the sheriff told him. "The Klamath reservation is a little different. After the vote on termination this here became a no-man's-land. The BIA keeps at arm's length. So does the state. As a deputy sheriff you won't have any official legal authority. The way it works is this—I leave you alone and the feds and state leave you alone—you'll be the arresting officer, judge and jury. Take care of the little things. Something big comes up, we step in and the legal system takes over. Otherwise you run the show."

"What makes you think I can handle the job?"

The sheriff grinned, handed Red the badge and that was that. Red became a popular lawman because he treated everyone, white and Indian, equally. He could be tough as a railroad spike or softhearted as a Sunday school teacher—like the time he came across a dog dragging its hindquarters off the road after being hit by a truck. Another man might have shot the mongrel to put it out of its misery. Not Red. He wrapped his coat around the mutt and drove all the way to Klamath Falls where, out of his own pocket, he paid a vet to put the dog to sleep.

When a crime was committed, Red would simply drop by the offender's house, go over the charge, listen to the other side of the story and, if it was warranted, would suggest,

"Maybe you oughta come in for a few days an' give me a hand." Such a suggestion seemed to take the sting out of being arrested and confined to jail. As a result, the town of Chewaucan got potholes filled with free inmate labor and prided itself on having the best-kept jail in the state. The shining star was the small, manicured lawn and the flowerbeds planted in red and white snapdragons, Red's favorites.

The Chewaucan jail was considered easy time. Red's wife, Marg, provided meals and prisoners ate whatever Red was having. He got meatloaf and a big #1 Klamath Basin potato, they got meatloaf and a big #1 Klamath Basin potato. He got spaghetti with garlic bread and they got spaghetti with garlic bread. On holidays they enjoyed ham or turkey and all the trimmings, including a generous helping of dessert.

★ ★ ★

The city of Chewaucan and Cap Andrews were partners in The Tavern. The city furnished the building and the liquor license, Cap did all the work and split profits down the middle, except for the cream he was able to skim off the top. He was proud of the fact that more beer was sold in The Tavern, on a per capita basis, than at any other bar in the solar system.

Cap had invested twenty years in the Marine Corps and did not drink because he did not want to get fat and be less of a man. He was not tall but he had a massive chest, bull neck and the look of a one-time athlete in a contact sport. He wore sleeveless T-shirts that seemed ironed to his skin and kept a pair of fifty-pound barbells at the ready. Between customers he did curls. He could do twenty a minute. His goal each day was to do at least a thousand curls. He kept track on a pad of paper; each four lines got a diagonal line, making one hundred curls. As a result of his exercise regime Cap's biceps were as big as a rhino's leg. He prided himself on his physique, and on the fact that he had never, ever, had to call for help. Any disturbance, no matter if fists, broken bottles, knives or guns came into play, Cap had always managed to handle the situation.

He shaved his head every couple of days because he thought it gave him a disconcerting, mean look. He ran one hand over his square jaw and felt the little ripples of muscles that ran along the jaw line. He did not try to suppress a smirk because he felt powerful and looked so great. Termination money was going to flow and it promised to be one nonstop party. This was the big pop. The one he had been waiting for all his life. He was going to grab that tit of Indian money and not let go until every last dollar had been squeezed from it. Then he would retire, maybe open a gym, but for certain he was going on an African hunting safari. That was something he had been promising himself forever. To kill a lion—what fun, what terrific sport, what a noble and heroic measure of a man.

Cap was oblivious to the notion that the only reason he had not been shot in the back some dark night was because he provided an indispensable service. With him at the helm, The Tavern was a relatively safe place to drink. It always pissed Cap off when someone slipped up and called him by the nickname Chief had laid on him, Popeye. In Cap's mind he epitomized everything that Popeye was not, except for maybe the forearms. Popeye was a cartoon character with a sunken chest, biceps the size of swizzle sticks and besides that, he was ugly.

Cap poured a beer for one of his customers and strutted to the jukebox, dropped fifty cents through the points and pushed buttons from memory. Colored lights whirled. On the way back to the bar he passed the mirror and flexed one of his biceps as he sang along with Elvis, "I'm stuck, stuck, stuck on you."

Headlights played across the front windows. A few seconds later the door was thrown open and there stood Chief. Cap smiled and muttered under his breath, "Start the party. Here's the biggest dipshit of them all." He began pouring a pitcher of beer.

★ ★ ★

Raindrops pinged against the windows of the blue and white house, drew back and struck again. Grandma rested on her cot, feeling the wind and rain. The silver moon showed through the moisture-laden clouds and illuminated a spider in the window walking its webbed tightrope.

Grandma closed her eyes; darkness rushed in. She contemplated the flow of years. Dreams. The river ran emerald green, bringing the fresh, delicate fragrance of blooming camas and wild strawberries. Campfire smoke stung her eyes. She could smell fish drying on the racks and saw her mother's strong fingers pull and cajole the tule reeds, weaving them into a basket.

When Grandma was a girl the tribe had lived in earthen lodges and wickiups. The women gathered wocus and tules, dug camas, harvested berries. The men hunted in the mountains and fished the lake and the rivers and streams. Grandma, who was born the same year the treaty was signed, 1864, had lived long enough to become the oldest member of the Klamath tribe. Her time was passing. She knew that. And the old ways were dying, too. What did it matter? The young people did not care about history. Someday, maybe fifty or a hundred years from now, there would come a time when the children would want to know about the past, want to know where they came from. But there would be no answers. The history of the Klamath nation would be buried in the graves of those who had passed to the far side.

Grandma awakened. She lay still on her cot, hoping the storm would lull her back into a peaceful sleep once again, where dreams would not be invaded by lingering concerns of death and loss. Sleep did not come easily, and after a while Grandma groaned like an old horse going downhill and sat upright. She leaned forward and turned on the black and white television. It flickered atop a wooden ammunition box and Grandma lay back, mesmerized by the glare of white snow and the movement of ghostlike figures. Pokey had tried wrapping aluminum foil around the rabbit ears but it had not improved the picture very much.

★　★　★

After the others departed, Pokey turned on the feeble light in the woodshed, which doubled as his bunkhouse, and began splitting firewood rounds with a wedge and an eight-pound mall. He hoped it would take his mind off the upcoming basketball game and help loosen his muscles.

He held out his misshapen left hand. The incident that had cost him part of two fingers happened right here in the woodshed. It was not an accident. Chief was holding the axe and had dared Pokey to put his hand on the chopping block.

Chief taunted his younger brother, saying Pokey did not have the guts to leave his hand on the block. In the end it had boiled down to who would chicken out first. Would Chief swing the axe? Would Pokey jerk his hand away? Turned out neither of them gave an inch. As a result the tips of two of Pokey's fingers were severed. That happened long, long ago.

Between the rhythmic clank of metal against metal, quiet punctuated the heavy air. The rain came again. With heavy drops drumming on the tin roof, Pokey swung the long-handled mall and knew the rain would bring the river up. Come morning, the rainbow trout would stick their snouts in the cool water brought down from the mountains and charge upstream to spawn. Pokey thought about the sections of the river that might hold fish—channels, pockets, undercut banks. Tomorrow he should go fishing.

★ ★ ★

The truck bumped and pitched like a mechanical horse, windows rattling. Wayward smoke and noise, coming from a crack in the exhaust manifold, drifted inside the cab. The heater blasted hot air and pushed around the smells from Dallas's day. He had branded, earmarked, castrated, de-horned and inoculated calves.

Shasta stole a peek at her father and was disillusioned by what she saw. This old buckaroo wearing the battered hat and soiled Levi jacket was not the man she wanted him to be. She pictured him more like the photograph her mother had, Dallas mounted on a white gelding, sitting as dignified as a king on a throne, confident and proud. That was who her mother fell in love with and married, not this shell of a man whose scarred face glowed in the dash light.

"We're gonna have ta eat quick," Dallas shouted to her over the noise. "Thought we'd go to the basketball game. Finals of the All-Indian tournament. Chewaucan Hunters are goin' fer all the marbles. Oughta be a good on'. Pokey'll be playin'. He's 'bout the best we got."

The last thing Shasta wanted to do was attend a basketball game. What she really would enjoy would be lowering herself into a hot bubble bath and, after a long soak, lying in bed between clean sheets. But she quickly resigned herself. Maybe she could somehow tie the game in to her paper on termination. If nothing else, it would give her some perspective and insight into the Klamath people and why the white man's game had become one of the Indian's favorite pastimes.

Shasta had put a great deal of preparation into gaining department approval from her adviser for the paper she wanted to write on termination. She had applied for, and received, permission to submit an honors thesis that would give her upper-division credit, and if she did a concise and compelling job of putting it into words, there was a possibility of more. This might prove to be the first rung on the ladder of her journalistic career. Her sights were set on working for a newspaper like *The Oregonian*. Her long-range goal was to become the editor of *Life* magazine.

Shasta and Creek had met by chance at college. They had happened to sit together in the student union one day. Shasta was eating a tossed salad and Creek was killing time drinking a Pepsi. They exchanged a few words and Shasta recognized something about him, the way he touched things with only his fingertips, his shy smile, his demure mannerisms, his meekness, something in his voice, the way he spoke certain words.

"I remember you," Shasta said. "You're from Chewaucan—Creek Pitsua."

They talked for fifteen minutes. A week later, when they ran into each other in the library, they visited again. Creek mentioned the upcoming termination and said that as far as he was concerned, "The government can have the reservation. It doesn't matter to me. All I want is the money."

Shasta was astute enough to realize there was much more at stake in termination than simply exchanging money for land. Termination also meant the loss of the reservation, a culture, a tribe of people. She thought about it for a few days and then found the courage to get in touch with her father, who said he would have to check with Dolly, but he thought it would be just fine if Shasta stayed at the ranch while she conducted her research.

When the details were in place, Shasta called Creek and told him about her paper and that her father had invited her to stay at the ranch. Creek said, "Why don't you go with me? I'm riding the bus on the way down but I'll be driving a new Corvette back to Eugene."

Six

Dolly recognized the rattle of the Jimmy and dashed into the bathroom to check her face. In her mind she was still that pretty majorette of thirty years ago, with dreamy skin tone and a body the boys had lusted over. She allowed herself the luxury of a single, vivid reminiscence. A magical night: the gloating moon overhead, frost crystals suspended in the air, banks of light bathing the football field in a surreal glow, the anxious crowd buzzing like a hive of bees. Strike up the band! Dolly, dressed in a skimpy white outfit with silver spangles and pushed by the music, pranced onto the field like an expensive thoroughbred going to the gate. Her white-tipped baton, seventeen perfectly balanced ounces, thirty inches of gleaming chrome, spun in tight circles in the air over her head.

The routine was still fresh in Dolly's mind; wrist twirls, four-finger twirls, figure eights, two-handed spins. She gazed into the mirror and her reflection ruined the perfect moment. She had to bite her lip to keep from crying out and she told herself the change of life was making her crazy. She dabbed at her teeth with a Kleenex, applied a layer of fresh red gloss on her lips and turned away from the unflattering image. Never again would she lead a parade. Never again would boys try to engage her in a backseat rumba. And that realization devastated Dolly. She stepped to the door to greet her husband and his daughter, struggling to maintain the fake smile she had so resolutely painted on her face.

★ ★ ★

Shasta had trouble opening the pickup door and Dallas came around to help. When the door let go it gave a loud metallic pop.

"Here we are. Look familiar?" Dallas asked.

A bat swooped low, caught a bug near the night light and flashed away to fly erratically between charcoal treetops. The river rumbled. A calf bawled from the barn. Nostalgia jolted Shasta and she flashed on a marvelous afternoon spent in the hayloft, cuddled by the aromatic loose hay, playing with one of the barn kittens.

"I remember some," she admitted to her father.

Dallas strolled up the walkway to the house. He set down the blue suitcase, opened the door and stepped to the side. As Shasta moved forward she saw a woman standing there. From behind her Dallas's voice said, "Dolly, this here's Shasta. Shasta, Dolly."

Dolly had bright red hair and was wearing enough makeup to have decorated a billboard. She extended her hand. Her fingers were bony, the palm wet, and she looked as though she might cry with the least provocation. Shasta realized she could never, not in her wildest dreams, call this woman Mother. "Nice to meet you, Dolly," Shasta found herself saying. They shook hands with their arms extended.

"Here's your suitcase," Dallas said, setting it on the floor near the door. "Gotta do chores."

"Dinner will be ready in twenty minutes," Dolly called. "We still going to the game?"

"O' course. Wouldn't miss it."

Dolly closed the door firmly but stood for a moment with her hand on the knob as if she might suddenly jerk it open and flee. Shasta crossed the room and the springy floor caused china to tinkle in the glass cabinet. She went to the wood heater and stood there, shivering in the warmth it gave off. The room had been swept so recently and violently that it smelled of dust. Tiny particles glistened in the bars of light radiating from the reading lamp.

Dolly watched the way the comely girl moved and it reminded her of herself—but she was fooling herself and knew it. She gushed, "Terrible the buses can't run on time. Suppose you would like to freshen up. You have time for a quick shower if you like. I put a clean towel out. The blue one. You'll be upstairs, first room to your left. Dallas said that was your old room. I use it for sewing. Hope you don't mind the clutter."

Shasta knew it must be hard to have your husband's daughter walk into your life after so many years. She thanked Dolly, flashed her a smile, and started up the stairs with her suitcase in hand.

Flipping on the light, Shasta surveyed her old room and noticed all the rude differences. Only the bed, with the tall wooden headboard, was familiar. The stuffed animals, the little writing desk, the doll house—all gone—replaced by a garish chair made of cow horns, a sewing machine and cardboard boxes of patterns and material that lined the walls.

Dolly called from the kitchen, "I cleaned out the top two drawers of the dresser special for you. Put your things in there."

Shasta opened her suitcase on the bed and wondered what she should wear. She would be most comfortable in pants and a sweater, but Dolly had on a dress and intuition told Shasta she should wear a dress. She had packed one because she thought Dallas might want to take her out for dinner. Fat chance. All the same she was glad she brought the dress. It was blue and feminine. She gathered her clothes and her makeup bag and walked into the bathroom. She undressed and stood in front of the mirror. She was comfortable with her body, although maybe her waist could be an inch or two thinner. She ignored any other imperfections, imagined or real, and before stepping into the tub-shower she reached through the curtain to test the temperature of the water and adjust the tap.

★   ★   ★

Dallas poured an extra measure of grain into the trough for the cow with the new calf. He was aware of the light when it came on in the upstairs bathroom and stood in the dark night, wind kicking up dry barn dirt around him, watching the vague female form behind the frosted glass. The figure appeared to take off her clothes and stand for a moment in front of the mirror.

Dallas felt uncomfortable. This image was no longer his

little girl. He was not expecting her to be a kid, but he was not anticipating a full-blown woman either. He had missed all those important years. Cheated himself, but that was what he had chosen. He had been the one who had wanted to keep his ex-wife and their daughter on the opposite side of the fence.

What unnerved him were the recollections that flashed behind his eyes like an avalanche. They began small but quickly threatened to bury him. Dallas had met Kay in biology class at Oregon State College, where he had gone because his father sent him there, saying it would do him good to get away from the ranch. He was a bit older than the other students, but when he met Kay and they started dating, the age difference did not seem like much.

One day Dallas received a phone call. His father had dropped dead of a heart attack and Dallas had no choice but to quit school, go home and run the ranch. He was afraid that having to live in Chewaucan, he would never get a chance at marriage, unless he were willing to settle for an Indian bride. On the spur of the moment he asked Kay to marry him.

For Kay it was hardly head-over-heels love, no banging cymbals and fireworks. She grabbed Dallas because he drove his own car, had a ranch, a future, and she had always wanted to live in the country. She had not been that serious about gaining an academic education, was at school husband-hunting, and Dallas seemed the best prospect. She could have it all without having to wait.

After the Benton County Justice of the Peace, in a quick civil ceremony, pronounced them man and wife, they enjoyed a honeymoon night on the Oregon coast. Then they drove to Chewaucan. Entering the city limits, Kay was stunned by this dirty little reservation town stuck out in the middle of nowhere. Dallas had bragged about the home place, but instead of the idyllic rambling ranch house tucked back into the timber, with a thin line of smoke curling from a rock chimney, Dallas parked beside a tarpaper shack that they would have to share with his mother, Lois.

Lois was an unhealthy woman who soon became an invalid. Kay nursed her, in addition to cooking, washing, cleaning house and milking the cow. When Lois finally died it was a tremendous relief.

Kay got pregnant simply because she wanted someone to love and someone to love her. Dallas had loved Kay as much as he could any woman. Loved her looks, the way she talked, the way she walked, the way she sometimes smiled. He loved her as he would love a good, steady, hard-working, dependable saddle horse. In Dallas's book, that was as high a compliment as he was capable of articulating. But Kay never did adapt to ranch life, and after Shasta came along, she spent all her time with the girl and Dallas felt as though he were the odd man out.

It took Kay seven years after Shasta was born to come to the realization that if she stayed in the relationship with Dallas, she would be throwing her life away on a man who would never know the meaning of the words love, affection, appreciation, sharing or passion. She wrote him a note. It read, "Dallas, I'm leaving you. I've taken my girl with me. Don't try to follow." She left the note on the kitchen table, propped against the sugar bowl.

Dallas glanced in the direction of the bathroom window and once again saw Shasta's silhouette behind the frosted glass. He turned away and went to slop the hogs.

★ ★ ★

The annual Klamath Reservation Jaycee All-Indian Basketball Tournament was a regional event. The teams, with players ranging from high school athletes to middle-aged men, featured the best Indian athletes in the Northwest. Reservation teams came from Warm Springs, Toppenish, Lodge Grass, Browning and Chewaucan, and all-star teams came from Portland, Salem and Seattle. Preliminary rounds had been played and the Chewaucan Hunters and the Portland Hawks were squaring off tonight for the championship.

On the Chewaucan end of the court Pokey broke from the line and in mid-stride caught the ball and put it on the floor. He dribbled once, twice, and was about to go for a layup when his attention was diverted by a white girl wearing a dress, glacial blue and clingy; sleek knees flashed and long black hair shimmered under the bright lights. Pokey clanked the ball off the underside of the rim, and as he trotted to the back of the line he was appalled at his lack of concentration and cursed under his breath. He needed to get his head in the game.

★ ★ ★

Shasta followed Dallas and Dolly along the far sidelines and up the bleacher stairs. They took a seat and Dallas pointed out Billy Walker. He was the starting guard and a perennial All-Indian tournament player, but he was nearly thirty years old and his considerable talents had eroded. Pokey threw a pass that hit Billy in the chest and bounced away. Billy made a silly, slapstick grab for it but missed. Dallas said he was going to get some treats and departed, crawling over Shasta's knees and obstructing her view as he went.

The PA system played "Itsy Bitsy Teeny Weeny Yellow Polka Dot Bikini." On the sidelines, spunky brown-skinned girls in pleated skirts and bulky sweaters jumped, kicked and clapped, trying to encourage the crowd, who mostly ignored them.

The Hunters and the Hawks continued to warm up and Shasta watched Pokey. He caught passes, dribbled and glided across the hardwood floor with an effortless familiarity. When he shot from the perimeter he cocked his shooting hand behind his right ear, launching rainbow shots that arced high and almost touched the ceiling before dropping so cleanly through the net they barely tickled the twine. When he moved, his braids bounced up and down.

By game time the small gymnasium was overflowing. The crowd was almost exclusively Indian. It was clear to Shasta that basketball was a big draw in Chewaucan, and she wondered if it carried more meaning on this night because the Klamath reservation team was playing for its last hurrah.

Dallas returned from the concession stand with a bag of popcorn and a large Coke. He said they could share. Seated together, Dallas, Dolly and Shasta looked like three marshmallows bobbing in a cup of hot chocolate. Most of those around Shasta were heavyset adults: men clad in colored T-shirts and blue jeans and women wearing flowered print blouses or sweatshirts that made them look even larger. Both sexes wore tennis shoes and sunglasses. It seemed funny to Shasta that so many people wore sunglasses indoors. She wondered if Indians' eyes were particularly sensitive to artificial light.

Shasta attended most home basketball games at the University of Oregon. She liked the excitement, the way it ebbed and flowed through the crowd. But this crowd had a much different feel than the student section to which she was accustomed. This was more unsettling, more like a lynch mob. The smell of alcohol ripened the air. Shasta turned her attention to the conversation of two men seated in front of her.

"What kind of car ya gonna get?"

"Impala."

"Super Sport?"

"Yeah."

"Gonna go with the three forty-eight block? Probably get that four-barrel instead of the three-two. Suppose ta give like three-fifteen horsepower, somethin' like that. That what ya' gettin'?"

"Naw. Want some real muscle. Gonna hold out for the four-oh-nine."

"Hard ta get that four-oh-nine. Might have ta wait 'til the end of the year."

"Cost me a little more but they're gettin' me one early. How 'bout you?"

"Old lady wants a silver and black Continental. Have ta go with it. Probably get me a pickup. Kinda wonderin' 'bout droppin' a big block in a short box Apache."

"Be a squirrelly son of a bitch." Both men laughed.

Shasta looked back to the court. At the university she viewed basketball in terms of geometry, the elusive possibilities of angles, rotations and teammates working together to form a cohesive unit stronger than the sum of the individuals. But she wondered, down on the floor, if these players saw it some other way. Rather than elevating the game to a level of theory and equations, of x's and o's, was their basic philosophy to simply put the ball through the hoop more times than their opponent? At both ends of the gym, players bounced balls against the hardwood floor. It sounded like the beating of drums.

Shasta watched the cute and bubbly brown-skinned cheerleaders, wondering if, in a few short years, they would be as overweight and spiritless as their mothers. At the far end of the gym Shasta noticed Red slide through the door, lean against the brick wall and push his floppy hat back on his head. He seemed to take in the entire gymnasium in one long, lingering look.

★   ★   ★

The horn sounded and both teams rushed to their respective coaches. The coach of the Chewaucan Hunters, Gavin Wright, was an aggressive young man who had been a small-college hoop star in Idaho. Gavin claimed to have Cherokee blood, but if he did, it did not show. He was looking to make a name for himself, hoping to parlay his success as an All-Indian tournament champion into an assistant coaching position at the college level.

The starting players stripped off their warmups and stuck their heads in a huddle. Pokey got a strong whiff of alcohol but convinced himself it was nothing more than wandering vapor from the crowd. A lot of heavy drinkers showed up for basketball games at Chewaucan. Billy Walker drifted to the outside of the huddle.

"All right, boys. Listen up," Gavin told his team. "This is the game we've been aiming for all season. You worked your butts off to reach this point. This is our home. Our reservation. Play with pride. Fight for it. Shoot these bastards back to the city!"

Hands touched. The Hunters yelled in unison, "Offense!" Again Pokey got a strong whiff of alcohol. He patted Billy on the butt, told him, "Have a good one," trotted to the center circle and shook hands with the opposing center.

Pokey played forward, but because he was the best leaper on the team, he was called on to jump center. The white referee bounced the ball on the floor, held it for a split second in front of his face and then launched the ball straight up. As the ball reached its zenith Pokey leaped and tipped the ball to Billy Walker, who was straddling the center line. Billy caught the ball and unleashed an impossible hook shot, a catapult that missed the backboard and ricocheted off the brick wall. Then Billy stood there laughing, as if this was the funniest thing ever.

Shit. Why would a player of Billy's caliber get drunk before the biggest game of the year? Gavin stood staring in disbelief. His only signs of life were the arteries on either side of his neck bulging and swelling like mercury in a thermometer dipped in boiling water. When the liquid hit the top he exploded, jamming five stubby fingers of one hand into the palm of his other, signaling for a time-out. Billy trotted to the sidelines, the silly grin still plastered across his face. Gavin grabbed him by the jersey and jerked him close. "What the hell is wrong with you?"

Gavin had, on several occasions, persuaded Red to temporarily release a team member from jail, where he might have been serving time for an accumulation of traffic citations, public drunkenness, assault, or some other misdemeanor charge. As soon as the game was over, the prisoners were promptly returned to the jail to finish out their time. Gavin was not above bending a few rules when the outcome of a game was on the line, but Billy Walker showing up smashed for a game was inexcusable.

"Must've got 'old of some bad pineapple juice," Billy blurted. He broke into a giggling fit he could not seem to control.

"Get the hell outta here!" Gavin barked. He pushed Billy away and with a theatrical wave sent him to the showers.

Seven

Quivering red and yellow collided behind Creek's eyes. He was sweating. When he tried to talk he slurred his words. "What say, maybe we should head up to the game."

"Keep your goddamn pants on. We'll get there when we get there, aye." Chief grabbed the handle of the nearly empty beer pitcher as if it were a big mug, gulped and then raised the pitcher over his head and hollered, "Hey, Popeye, get off your dead ass. More beer, ain't it."

Creek did not protest. For the moment, he was content to merely exist in Chief's shadow, and drink with him and his hangers-on. Chief was the barroom star; bigger, badder and more depraved than any other drunk. In a strange way Creek felt safe with Chief, recognizing that he would protect those people in the circle around him, but then again, who was crazy enough to fuck with Chief?

A little of the respect that Chief commanded began to

rub off on Creek. The alcohol he consumed gave him courage. He pointed at his brother and said, "You and me, challenge the pool game. We run the table. Kick ass!"

He started to get up but Chief used the fingers on one beefy hand to push him down. Creek fell awkwardly onto the floor and the chair toppled over.

"Fuck that," Chief said, "let's just drink."

As Creek struggled to his feet all of his cockiness dissipated like windblown fog. He righted his chair, sat down, took a drink of beer and wished he were away from this place and sitting in the stands in the gymnasium. If he were in the gym he could watch Pokey score baskets and cheer. That was what appealed to Creek the most about the game of basketball, the way accomplishments were greeted with instantaneous rewards.

Pokey was such a gifted natural athlete. He possessed the perfect blend of agility, speed and power. But what set him further apart, and what made Creek even more proud, was the size of Pokey's heart. He hated to lose at anything. Pokey had always run faster and jumped higher than other kids. Creek recalled one specific time during football practice. Creek was the team manager, Pokey the star halfback. The team was practicing the kicking game and Pokey took the kickoff on the fifteen-yard line and ran it back for a touchdown, then shouted, "Now, everyone!" and started up the field, running left, dodging right, faking, feigning, juking his way through twenty-one tacklers, as well as a handful of substitutes who charged onto the field. After he scored, he tossed the ball on the ground and stood facing the field with his arms held triumphantly over his head as if this were the climactic scene in a movie. Roll the credits.

Creek took a gulp of beer and was unaware he had missed his mouth until he felt the cold liquid spilling down his chin, chest and belly. He swiped at it but only succeeded in spreading the wetness. He noticed his shirt was ripped. The room around him was a warm hive, with tribal members working overtime on their unending shifts of drunkenness. Voices buzzed—Elvis, Jerry Lee, Connie Francis and the Everly Brothers. Colored lights flashed from the jukebox. The quiet madness Creek normally kept confined deep inside himself began to ooze into his conscious mind. If only he had been born white, he could grab the world by the balls and squeeze until it screamed—cream rises and shit floats—termination was the best damn thing ever happened—get off the reservation and into the real world—never come back—everyone is running away from something . . .

In the far corner of the room, cards were shuffled and dealt; red, white and blue chips were tossed into the center of the table without any sound and nobody seemed to win the pot. The game went on and on. Chief sat scowling. He looked very much like the guy his classmates once voted most likely to be murdered. Beer had made his face darken and his hands had formed into fists. His shirt was taut across his shoulders and did not begin to cover his protruding stomach. His thick neck bulged like a buck in the rut. He had a burning desire to punch someone in the face. No reason needed. Break his nose. Right now the sight of red blood would soothe him, make him feel better.

"Goddamn! More beer. More beer!"

Cap ignored him and announced to the customer at the bar, "Nothing wild, one flop." He shook the leather cup and slammed it mouth down on the bar. He removed the cup to reveal five sixes. Natural winner. He grinned. "Play

B-seven." The loser toppled off his stool clutching a fifty-cent piece.

Cap poured a pitcher of beer, crossed the floor pock-marked by decades of hobnails, mute testimony to the days when logging was a way of life on the reservation, and set the pitcher on the table in front of Chief.

"Put it on my tab. I'll pay when I get my money, aye." Chief's words were cut with hatred. Hatred that the white man wanted his money. Hatred that he had to drink to feel good. Hatred of everything and anything.

"Fine. Make sure you do." Cap looked at him with eyes hard as gray slate. He walked away.

Chief said to his back, "Eat shit and die, Popeye."

Cap moved behind the bar, knowing that before the night was over there would be at least one, maybe a dozen fights— women pulling hair and scratching, men wrestling and gouging, together with a bit of white man–style slugging thrown in. He would move the fight outside, and when one side got the worst of it they would leave, vowing to return with a weapon. Sometimes they did.

Cap was not much interested in the outcome of the fights, one way or the other. You run a reservation drinking establishment and you endure the fights and the killings like a short-order cook tolerates the heat of the grill. "Do what you gotta do," he muttered to no one in particular and smiled as he padded the tab and charged Chief for two pitchers instead of one.

★　★　★

The house groaned under the weight of the storm. Grandma repacked the stove with wood and returned to her room, where she settled into her rocking chair. She pulled her shawl around her bony shoulders and began rocking with no definite destination in mind.

What was the white girl doing here? Why had she come with Creek? Where had everyone gone? It had all been so much easier to understand years ago. When Grandma was a small girl, the Klamath Basin was known as the Land of Many Waters. It belonged to no one and everyone. The Klamaths were confined to the reservation, but the reservation was young and they were still allowed to hunt and fish and gather in all their traditional places. Once a year they traveled north to the Columbia River to fish for salmon and trade and gamble with the Indians who gathered there. Some tribes came from the far side of the Rocky Mountains.

In the old days the various tribes in the region had engaged in feuds and wars—conducting raids, killing each other, stealing horses, and young girls who were used as slaves. But the hostilities the Indians harbored in their intertribal relationships paled when compared to the annihilation caused by the coming of the white man. New diseases were introduced to which the Indians had no immunity. Thousands died. Those who remained were frequently shot down like animals, and squaws were hunted down and violated for the sport of it. White men were rarely punished for these outrages. The Klamaths, once a proud and self-sufficient people, were forced to live within the confines of the reservation. They were reduced to wearing white people's castoffs and begging for blankets and food. The white man attempted to make the nomadic Indians into farmers. He took away their children and sent them to boarding schools, where they were educated, indoctrinated, and civilized. Bit by bit the Indian spirit was broken.

Grandma had seen it, lived it. She rocked back and forth, back and forth. The wood floor creaked. The fire crackled in the stove. Memories flowed easily. It rained and cleared off some. The moon played peek-a-boo with the clouds. Time passed.

★ ★ ★

Chief advanced up the flight of steps leading into the school gymnasium. In his wake, Creek was able to squeeze through before the door slammed shut. They crossed the narrow lobby and stood bleary-eyed and drunk in the archway where the air was close and the noise of the crowd seemed to fill and round the corners of the gym.

The Hawks were leading the Hunters by a skinny point, 110 to 109. Only seconds remained in the game. Pokey had the ball and was headed up the court. He kept his dribble low and squeezed between an aggressive double-team, crossed the center stripe and stole a glance at the clock. He slapped the ball against the floor one last time and launched himself into the air. With the ball cocked behind his ear he seemed to hang up there like the harvest moon in the night sky. Even the scoreboard quit counting. When time resumed the ball was already on its long arc that would carry it over the outstretched hands of a defender. Spectators drew a collective gasp. The red light came on at the scorer's table. The final buzzer sounded. The ball dropped through the mouth of the rim so fast it made the net pop like a skirt at the end of a swift twirl.

Absolute silence, and then the stands erupted into a panorama of sound, and movement, and commotion. The crowd collectively rose to its feet and a spontaneous cheer erupted, so loud it threatened to shake loose the mortar from between the bricks and bring the gym walls down. Cheerleaders embraced and danced in a tight circle. Several players leaped into the air and others simply raised their fists in the universal sign of victory. People spilled from the bleachers and were threatening to overrun the court when, one by one, they gradually became aware of the referee under the basket. He was running forward, tenaciously blowing his whistle while crossing and uncrossing his arms in a frantic gesture that could only signal one thing. He was disallowing the final basket. The last two points would not count. The game was over. The Chewaucan Hunters had lost.

The second official, standing near mid-court, never moved, but his eyes widened and his lower jaw dropped open in disbelief at what he was witnessing. He was an old pro who would have rather swallowed his whistle than blow it at such a time. Fear for his personal safety, hell, for his life, propelled him into a sprint for the locker room. He wanted nothing to do with whatever was going to transpire next. He only wanted to get as far away from this place as he possibly could.

Later, when the whistle-blowing ref was safely home and his wife was dabbing at the dried blood on his cut lip, he described the scene at the end of the game. "The shot came late. It was close. But I think I made a good call. Game over. All of a sudden the crowd charges onto the court and this buck grabs me from behind, spins me around. What I remember most of all, besides the fact he had no front teeth and was about the biggest, meanest buck I ever did see, were his eyes. They were beady, like poison berries or something. He grabs the front of my shirt, pulls me off my feet, backhands me across the face and throws me halfway across the gym.

"Let me tell you, that big son of a bitch and the rest of them would've killed me for sure, but the deputy sheriff came to my rescue. He was something. You should have seen him. He was like a rodeo bullfighter protecting a cowboy when he's down. I was sprawled out on the floor and he steps over the top of me, tells those damn Indians, 'Boys, you don't want any part of me. Step away!' And by God if they didn't. He sure enough had the bluff in on them. He pulls me to my feet, keeps hold of my arm and escorts me to the car. Earl had grabbed our street clothes and had the motor running. The sheriff followed us clear to Algoma. If he hadn't of, we never would have made it home. Never made it home."

His wife got up and went to the kitchen. He called after her, "Those Indian tournaments pay good but I tell you, no amount of money is gonna get me back to call another game. They were like a bunch of blood-thirsty savages."

His wife returned. "Here, honey," and handed him a beer.

He rolled the cold bottle across his forehead to cool his sweat, finally took a sip and let out an exaggerated sigh. "Hell, I'm just thankful to be alive."

★　★　★

At home, after the game, Dolly dished up apple pie. Dallas had vanilla ice cream on his. They sat with Shasta around the kitchen table and talked about how Pokey and the Hunters had been robbed, that Chief should have been arrested for slugging the ref, and then Dolly asked, "What are you taking in school?"

"Journalism."

"What kind of a job do you want when you graduate?"

"I'd like to work for a newspaper, or a magazine, maybe someday write a book."

"Do you have a boyfriend?"

Shasta shook her head and gazed at the blue lace curtains and the towels neatly folded over the oven handle. She examined every cupboard and drawer without touching them. Dallas watched her over the rim of his coffee mug. Then he put the mug down on the table, moved to the closet, shrugged on his Levi coat and announced, "Better check the calf."

Dolly picked up the plates and took them to the sink. She put in the plug, squeezed out a gob of green Palmolive liquid detergent and added hot water. As she dug out her rubber gloves from the rack under the sink, Shasta offered, "Let me do those."

"No, no, you must be tired. Why don't you just go on up to bed."

★   ★   ★

Dallas pulled off his boots with a bootjack and left them by the door. The wet weather made his feet swell. He slipped on his old pair of sheepskin slippers and padded across the hardwood floor that was partially covered with braided throw rugs. He took a seat in the leather easy chair that was molded to the reverse image of his backside, propped his feet on a cowhide-covered footstool and shook open the *Herald and News*. In a pool of light cast by the three-way floor lamp, he glanced through the obituary section looking for familiar names. Soon he was dozing. Dolly sat on the couch, at the edge of the good light, knitting a purple and white afghan. Her fingers deftly maneuvered the needles and yarn through the intricate pattern.

Dallas woke himself with a snort, shuffled into the kitchen and poured a nightcap of Old Crow into a shot glass. Water back in a separate glass. He studied the multitude of colored lights in the facets of the shot glass, swished the rust-colored liquid around a time or two and gulped it down. Alcohol flushed his face before he lifted the water glass.

"Damn it," he thought to himself. "What kind of bullshit is this? Termination. My achin' ass. Pretty soon the government's gonna have all the rights an' the average man ain't gonna have shit."

He set the empty shot glass and the companion water glass on the drain board, unconcerned that Dolly would feel compelled to wash them before she went to bed. He returned to his chair.

"What ya think of 'er?" he asked.

"Seems pleasant enough. You can be proud." It hurt Dolly to say that because she had never been able to have children of her own. The doctors said her fallopian tubes were horned or hooked or something like that. It was so long ago it no longer mattered.

★   ★   ★

Lying in her childhood bed, covers pulled to her chin, Shasta was shielded from the cool air and the light rain denting the roof. As she drifted toward sleep she became that little girl again, remembering the smells of her mother cooking breakfast on a school morning, the feel of pulling on warm mittens and proceeding out into the cold, walking to school hearing the songs of blackbirds in the willows and quail on the ridge. One day she watched a lanky coyote skulk from tree to tree and felt like Little Red Riding Hood.

Weariness seeped through her. She squirmed in the void beneath the blankets and yawned. As she closed her eyes she could hear her father's voice, "We're facing a goddamn dilemma." That could mean anything from Dolly's forgetting the yeast and her biscuits not rising, to a decline in the quotation on beef prices, trouble with the bank, or the loss of cheap pasture for his cattle.

Sheltered, safe, secure. What did any of it matter? A man's muffled footsteps padded down the hall, paused at her door, went on.

Eight

Steve and Debbie Atwood, Southern California born and raised, met at Orange County Junior College, fell madly in love, ran off to Las Vegas and got married at the Tranquility Wedding Chapel. Steve transferred to UCLA and switched his major from business to secondary education/biology. Teaching seemed an honorable and stable career for a married man. Debbie dropped out of school and went to work hustling burgers and fries at a drive-in. They decided to wait to start a family until they were financially stable. They wanted to be able to have the money to spoil their kids rotten.

But then Debbie got pregnant and Steve got mugged. Three days later their house was burglarized. Their television, stereo, record collection and irreplaceable personal items were stolen. Debbie felt violated. Steve concurred. "I don't want to raise our child in this type of environment. There are too many people in California. Let's go where we can have some elbow room, find a little place in the woods, live off the land, raise our kids. Let's move. I hear Oregon is nice. I can always finish my degree once we get settled."

They sold the small house they were buying, making seventeen hundred dollars profit, and escaped, traveling north in their Olds Golden Rocket 88, towing a small U-Haul trailer. North of Klamath Falls Debbie felt some abdominal discomfort and, even though she was barely five months pregnant, Steve felt it was imperative they not waste time finding a place to settle. The destination they had in mind was Bend, a nice little logging community a few hours north. They swung off Highway 97 at the Chewaucan junction, drove into town and stopped for gas at Floyd's Shell station. Floyd struck up a conversation, one thing led to another, and before nightfall the Atwoods had spent most of their meager savings on a down payment in the Chewaucan Grocery and the attached two-bedroom apartment. All the pieces fell into place so smoothly that Steve told Debbie it had to be destiny. In reality, they gave up their fantasy of the cottage in the woods and their dream of living off the land and traded it for a job and a place to live.

The living quarters were nothing to shout about, but Debbie immediately went to work covering the horrible magenta walls with a fresh coat of paint, a soothing sky blue. While she worked to convert the apartment into a comfortable home, Steve gave the front of the store a facelift, nailing up rough-cut pine lumber in a board-and-batten style. Debbie said, "It looks real cute in sort of a Wild West way." Steve, expanding on that theme, put up a hitching rail out front, joking it would be an ideal spot for customers to tie their vehicle reins when they came to shop.

A routine was quickly established. Steve opened the

store and worked until Debbie spelled him at lunch. That gave him afternoons free to watch television, go hiking or bike riding, or run to Klamath Falls for supplies. He took over again while she fixed dinner and ate; then she left his dinner in the oven and returned to work. Steve locked up. The one thing that maintained their enthusiasm was the anticipation of the birth of their first child. Steve, with all his heart and soul, wanted it to be a boy. Debbie said she did not care as long as the baby was born healthy.

★ ★ ★

Creek was bent over, heaving into a mud puddle. The wave of nausea swept past and he straightened and staggered over to lean against a car. He backhanded the corners of his mouth and tried to focus on the ripples of sounds and quivering neon that throbbed from The Tavern. Elvis asked, *Are You Lonesome Tonight?* Moments later Brenda Lee answered, *I Want to be Wanted.* Creek dropped a shoulder into a gusty wind and felt the rain soaking him. It sobered him enough that he thought he needed another beer, and wobbled inside.

★ ★ ★

After making his rounds Red returned to his office. He slid onto his leather swivel chair and watched through the open venetian blinds as water poured from the drain spout. The floor vent surrounded him in a cocoon of warmth and the real world seemed far away. He was drowsy and his eyelids slowly began to close.

Red fought sleep, telling himself something big was

about to happen. He felt a burning in the pit of his stomach, the same way Marg's spicy chili affected him, and knew whatever was going to happen might occur in five minutes, five hours, five days. Would it be the vigilantes? Something to do with termination? Another killing? He told himself he would grab a few winks now, while he could. His chin dropped to his breastbone. He slept.

In a dream Red saw Steve Atwood as a chicken, a chicken with an open sore on its head. All the other chickens kept pecking at him, drawing more blood, pecking, pecking, pecking until they finally pecked him to death.

★   ★   ★

Lefty lived in a one-room shack downriver from Pitsua bridge. The place was surrounded by years of discarded junk. Scrap metal, grinding wheels, hand forges and other unwanted items had been tossed in the yard where they gradually sank into the soil, weeds grew around them and they became a part of the landscape, inert and timeless.

Lefty faced the kitchen sink, squinting into a broken chunk of mirror propped on the exposed hot water pipe. A single bare bulb threw off a harsh, sterile light. He noticed his black eye had nearly healed; the swelling had subsided and there was only a bit of yellow-gray in the corner by his nose. Lefty fingered the cut on his cheek. It had scabbed over but he probably should have had stitches. He vowed that the next time a doctor saw him it would be to pronounce him dead. He tried to grin but his lips fell at odd angles. The left side of his face was slightly paralyzed. His ruddy skin was giving off the shine of an alcohol sweat.

The face in the mirror belonged to a bygone era, when

the big logging outfits were hacking their way through the virgin pine forests east of the Cascades. Back then Lefty moved from one logging camp to the next whenever the mood struck, felling towering trees with an axe and a cross-cut saw. Now he rubbed a hand across the dry, silver stubble on his face. It made a hollow parchment sound. He needed a shave. Instead he took a gulp of wine from a green jug. He used booze like a bulldozer, to skim off the high peaks and fill in the low spots.

"Much better," he growled and told himself that, by God, he was still a man. Hadn't he put in thirty-some-odd ball-busting years in the woods? And in turn the woods had left indelible marks on him, arthritis bowing his shoulders, bending his back and deforming his fingers. Sometimes he got cramps so damn bad the only thing that cut the pain to a tolerable level was getting drunk and passing out. He told himself that a man who only felt pain had to settle for that; if he didn't, he was as good as dead. And in spite of it all, Lefty wasn't quite ready to die, not just yet; so he drank to mollify the pain and he drank to commemorate the past.

Lefty knew it would improve his looks if he put in his dentures. And he would have—if only they fit, if only they did not hurt him. His reflection called him a broken-down tramp logger with a liver shot through with booze. He could not argue, the honesty haunted him, and before he turned away he told the face, "Old man, you ain't long for this world."

If he were to pull on his boots and hike uptown at least he would not have to drink by himself. But he did not want to open the door to trouble from that band of renegade Indians again and so he drank alone, in the dark.

Nine

The game burned in Pokey's mind as he pushed through the hard right corner and raced over the bridge. He was disgusted with Billy Walker for showing up drunk, and furious at the referee. One full second had remained on the scoreboard clock when the ball left his hands. He was sure of that, had looked up, saw it clearly. The ref had been out of position and never should have made that call.

When Pokey reached the big pine tree at the end of the lane he slammed on the brakes and the Jeep slid to a stop. He shut off the engine and sat in the quiet with a light rain pinging the taunt canvas top. Grandma was probably waiting up to find out the score but Pokey could not bring himself to go talk to her. He got out of the Jeep and headed to his bunk in the lean-to off the back of the woodshed.

He opened the door, latched it behind him and groped in the dark until his fingers located the pull string. A light bulb, hanging by a wire from one of the rafters, winked on and illuminated a bed and thin mattress, a heat-blistered dresser rescued from a house that burned, a stool and a few wooden ammunition boxes filled with fishing waders, hunting gear and other stuff. Tacked to exposed two-by-four studs were pencil drawings. Pokey had sketched them all. Finely detailed, they were good, very good: a likeness of an Indian girl with a pretty smile, a four-point buck standing broadside in a thicket of lodge pole pine and several self-portraits of Pokey riding a bronc, holding a nice stringer of fish, shooting a jump shot. Pokey ripped that one from the nail and tossed the paper face down on the dresser.

He unrolled his sleeping bag—he rolled it tightly every morning so insects and mice would not be able to crawl inside—and flung it open on the bunk. He peeled off his boots and pants and reached to pull the string dangling from the light bulb. In the dark, the bedsprings gave a rusty chirp as he lay down. From somewhere in the woodpile came the dry scratching of a mouse. The river gurgled deep and low. Fatigue tugged at him. It was almost too much trouble to draw another breath.

★   ★   ★

After the game, a surge of customers invaded The Tavern. Indians tumbled together and apart like seaweed tangling in a churning surf. Cap hustled to make the rounds, filling mugs and pitchers in danger of running dry. With so many party-minded Indians together under one roof there was bound to be trouble, and Cap kept constant vigil. Wherever a skirmish broke out he was there in a flash, pulling the combatants apart, pointing to the sign on the back of the door, "Want To Drink In Another Bar—Just Start A Fight Here." Of course there was no other bar within twenty miles. Sometimes Cap would snap at a customer, "Knock it off," or, "Take it outside," or, "One more ounce of trouble and you're eighty-sixed."

At a quarter to one Cap flipped the light switch on and off and thundered, "Last call for alcohol." As the mugs and pitchers emptied he took them. The crowd drifted away. Car engines roared. Tires squealed.

"Drink up. Drink up or I'll take it," Cap admonished as he passed the pool table, hands full of empties. Apparently one of the players resented having his game interrupted. He swung his 21-ounce cue, catching Cap across the back.

Cap set the mugs and pitchers on the nearest table. He hooked thumbs on hip bones and flexed his trapezius and latissimus dorsi, spreading the muscles to their widest, showing off their enormity under his clinging T-shirt. He grabbed the offending Indian, one hand on the belt and the other on the collar, jerked him off his feet and charged across the room, using the Indian as a battering ram to shove aside chairs and tables. He banged the man's head into the swinging door and flung him a good ten feet. The drunk landed face down in the muck and Cap dusted his hands like the hero in a western movie. A few revelers stood around and Cap barked, "Rest of you clowns, clear the hell outta here."

★　★　★

The baritone rumble of lake pipes trumpeting across the river awakened Pokey. A moment later headlights flickered between cracks in the boards. The engine howled and then died. The lights went out. Pokey held his breath and listened as one door slammed and then another, so close in time it could have been a nimble echo. He heard someone approach, shoes sucked against the muddy ground, and then a fist pounded the side of the woodshed.

"Goddamn, get your ass up, 'ave a drink. Poke, you son of a bitch."

Silence. Pokey stared at black.

Again Chief's voice bellowed, "Hey, I know you're in there. Poke, come on. Drink 'ith us. We get the money tomorrow, eh. Let's party it up, ain't it."

More silence.

Creek's voice sounded like a fingernail dragged across a chalkboard. "Maybe he's got a girl."

Chief beat against the boards. "Pop 'er fer me." His laugh receded. A moment later music erupted in the house and spilled out into the night. The door to the back porch opened. Glass bottles rattled together. The door slammed shut.

★   ★   ★

Grandma awoke. She opened her bedroom door and called out, wanting to know, "Pokey, you win game?"

"Go back to bed," Chief barked. Grandma pulled the door closed and returned to stand near her bed. The frame was wrought iron and had been purchased from the Klamath Agency as surplus when it closed after the vote on termination. She eased herself onto the sagging mattress, moved around until her body was comfortable and lay still.

Grandma's room was more orderly than the other rooms in the house. Her domain included her rocking chair, the bed and a shelf Pokey had built for her. All it amounted to was a couple of boards held up by concrete blocks, where she stacked faded cotton dresses, rolled-up socks, wool shirts and sweaters. Knickknacks were scattered around, including ceramic owls and horse figurines. A plastic Jesus, nailed to a crucifix, hung on one wall. A St. Christopher medal dangled on a chain looped over a nail. A drawing Pokey had sketched of Grandma sitting on a three-legged stool milking the Holstein was thumbtacked to the Sheetrock. The local television channel was off the air and the flat screen of the portable TV spit snow and flickered, casting an eerie combination of blanched light and gray shadows. An agile mouse scurried across one corner of the room and plunged into a hole in the wall.

★ ★ ★

The party ebbed and flowed through the night. Car engines raced. Voices and laughter and shouts rose and fell over the driving beat of one song after another: *Hound Dog, Party Doll, All Shook Up, Wake Up Little Susie, You Send Me, Hard-Headed Woman, Poor Little Fool, Lonely Boy, Alley-Oop.* The words, the twang of guitars, the drums all mixed in a boiling cauldron of noise, mayhem and blaring confusion. Several times during the night there were the unmistakable sounds of fighting: blows landing, grunts, howls, moans, cries of pain. At one point the men took turns with high-powered rifles, trying to shoot empty bottles thrown into the air. But the porch light provided insufficient illumination and they soon tired of the sport.

Lefty was awakened by gunfire. After it ended he lay on his ratty sofa listening to the wind whistle in the willows and strum the power lines that drooped from his house, over the Chewaucan, to the Pitsua place. Lying there, a quarter mile away, he could make out the unmistakable sounds of a party, a big one.

Lefty had never viewed the Indian as a noble savage. He knew all too well what they became when they were drunk. He had endured the shouting, whooping, screaming, and the gunfire that could suddenly erupt anytime, day or night. As far as he was concerned the Indians were always only a beer or two away from going on the warpath. As he pushed himself into a sitting position he felt around on the floor for the wine jug, found it, unscrewed the lid, took a long drink. The warm burgundy covered the rough exterior of Lefty's world with a fresh coat of paint. He hauled the jug outside, stood in the wind catching flickering glimpses of lights through the willows. The music and the voices made noises that yakked like crows and laughed like loons.

"Goddamn. All that money. What makes them think they're entitled to it? Goddamn them to hell." More shots were fired and he contemplated lobbing a few of his own. He stood there in his long johns, a cloud spit on him, he guzzled more wine and meditated on how his life's only true love, logging, had let him down.

"Hell, man used to could take a breath of piney air and feel it all the ways to his toes," he told the night. "Hear the sh-sh-sh of a misery whip bite into the wood, the birds sing, until that old tree starts to shimmy and shake. Fly away little bird, fly away. Just before that tree comes down, the woods she gets mighty still, be so still you could hear a porcupine fart a mile away. Then over she comes. Kerwomp!

"It was nice in the woods until they brung in them damn power saws. Heavier than a goddamn anchor they was.

Pack them around up and down hills. They bark, occasionally bite, and foul the air with stink. About that same time in come them educated boys, wanna work eight hours, have overtime pay, holidays, vacation, sick leave, insurance. Bullshit. Done ruined it. Done ruined it for sure. Glad I ain't in the woods no more."

Lefty would have given anything if he were young, tight-bellied and hard-muscled again. But he hurt all over and was so frail he could barely chop his own firewood. He took another drink. If he went to sleep and never woke up it would be just fine. He was nothing but a worn-out husk of a man, all used up, and he ought to be throwed away like yesterday's trash.

Ten

On the morning of April 12, 1961, a twenty-seven-year-old Russian, Major Yuri Gagarin, was strapped into a five-ton spacecraft. Fifteen minutes after blasting off, the cosmonaut radioed back that the flight was going well. "The visibility is good," he said. "I see the ball-shape form of the earth. I must say the view of the horizon is unusual and very beautiful. Up here the sun is tens of times brighter and the stars are even more brilliant. I find weightlessness to be quite natural. Objects float in the cabin. I hang in midair. I eat and drink and everything occurs just as it does on earth."

It took eighty-nine minutes for Gagarin to circle Earth. Soviet Premier Nikita Khrushchev and his fellow communists gloated. International news proclaimed this first step into space as the single most important event in the history of mankind. But half a world away, in the Klamath Basin, hardly anyone took notice. It was termination day!

★ ★ ★

Dallas was an early riser. He came out of the house stretching his shoulders and trying to work a kink out of his back. He flexed his knees and rotated his hips. The parts of his body that had been cracked, crushed or broken took a little longer to wake up. He squinted watery gray eyes at the eastern sky that, having taken on the color of crayon orange, was hinting at the promise of a break between storms. He loosened his belt, unbuttoned his fly and tucked the tails of his shirt into his blue jeans. His stiff fingers wrestled with the chore of slipping the metal buttons back into the holes and then he cinched the buckle into the leather belt. For a moment his square hands framed the silver buckle, a gold inlay of a bucking bronc and rider on sterling silver over the inscription, "All-Around Cowboy, Myrtle Point, 1933."

That had been some day. Dallas won the rough stock events as well as the bulldogging title. Took home the buckle and $73.50. A handsome amount back then but a pittance to what a current rodeo performer could pull down. Dallas told himself if he were a young man like Ross Dollarhide, Chuck Shepard, or Casey Tibbs, he could hit the circuit and pocket some real money, have a hell of a lot of fun, too. But he was not a young man. And yet it seemed as if Myrtle Point had happened only yesterday, or maybe the day before. He could feel himself stepping over the chute railing and easing down onto the bay bronc, taking a deep seat into the contours of the saddle. He could feel that jolt of electricity course through his body in anticipation, just itching for the gate to swing open and that broomtail to detonate. He nodded his head as he had done that day and pictured himself sitting there, rein in hand, cool and calm and in command like God Almighty.

One of the dogs barked and the image Dallas had of himself crashed to the ground like a bronc rider who had lost his stirrup. He swore under his breath and then cleared each nostril by holding its mate closed with a thumb and blowing fiercely. After that he walked to the barn rubbing his hands together. He fed the cattle and the horses, doctored the sick calf, threw some cracked corn to the chickens and slopped the hogs. When he returned to the house he eased inside just in case Dolly and Shasta were still asleep. His Levi jacket went on the wall peg, hat over it. He removed his boots and wandered down the hall in his stockinged feet. The door to the bathroom was ajar and he stood for a moment watching the reflection of his wife in the mirror. He felt a welling of depression. Maybe it was caused by his wife working so hard to be glamorous, or was it his reminiscing about his rodeo days? Was it having the girl in the house that had brought back the memories? Something was wrong.

Dallas guessed he loved Dolly, although he never had felt for her what he had felt for Kay. Kay had been special. It was possible the passing of time had made her more special than she was when the two of them lived under the same roof. Kay walked out on him, walked out and never looked back. A thing like that stings a man, puts a damning scar on his ego. Dallas had never gotten over it.

★ ★ ★

Dolly finally took notice of Dallas standing framed in the sliver of the open doorway. She wondered how long he had been there, hoped he had not caught her plucking that wild hair she found growing on her chin. Her hand subconsciously went to the counter and hid the tweezers. She roused a diluted smile. "Morning."

"You check the girl?"

"I peeked."

"Sleeping?"

"No." Dolly could have volunteered more but she had a habit of wanting to play out her hand any time she felt she had the better cards. When Dallas pressed her she would give a dab of information here, a dab there, making him work for every little dab he got.

"Where the hell is she?"

"Gone." Dolly slipped the tweezers in the drawer and slid it shut, patted her hair and turned to face him.

"Gone where?"

"She left a note. It's on the kitchen table."

"What's it say?"

"Said she was going out for a walk."

"Oh," he said. "Well, how 'bout some breakfast? Hot cakes. Venison steak. Coffee made?"

"Of course it's made. It's always made when you come in."

"Not always. Ya slept in one day last week. Had ta fix it myself."

"Your arm ain't broke. You can do something like that for me every once in a great while."

"Jesus. What's got you on the peck? All I said was ya slept in last week."

"You might have fixed coffee, but I noticed you waited for me to cook your breakfast."

"You're a good cook. Ya know that's why I married ya."

"I'm supposed to be flattered?"

He dropped one eyebrow slightly.

"Cook your meals, clean up after you, be at your beck and call. Right?"

Dallas grinned, "Pretty much it." Occasionally he took pleasure in ruffling her feathers. The fact was, when she got feisty she reminded him of a pet turkey they used to have, back when he and Kay were married. Kay named that turkey Elwood, after a cousin of hers. She refused to allow Dallas to kill the bird, even though, as Elwood got a little age on him, when something upset him he puffed his feathers and charged. One morning Elwood took after Shasta, she must have been three or four at the time, and knocked her to the ground. That was it for Elwood. Dallas popped him in the head with a .22 and they ate him. Damn tough bird, he was.

Dolly started to cry. She grabbed a towel and used it to dab at her leaky eyes. Dallas hated it when she cried. Crying was the weakest thing a human being could do. Having that power over her made him despise her even more. Dolly fled past him and Dallas cursed under his breath, knowing she was not going to be fixing his breakfast this morning.

"Hell's bells, too nice a day ta spoil it. Guess I'll run uptown," he mumbled to the empty room. "Swing by an' bullshit ol' Floyd." He shook his head. "Women."

★ ★ ★

A shrill whoop split the morning air followed by someone hollering, "We're rich. Yahoo!" The shout still hung in the air as a beer bottle hit the tin roof of the woodshed, bounced a time or two without breaking, and rolled off with an alarming clatter.

Pokey forced his eyes open. Sunlight was visible in long slanting shafts where it squeezed through cracks in the wall, turning suspended dust particles into lively sparks. He drew in a long breath and began working himself free of the mummy bag like a wet moth shedding the tight confines of a cocoon. He emerged wearing only plaid boxer shorts, crossed the dirt floor, threw back the latch and moved outside. He stood in the sunlight, feeling it warm his skin. But the air was still cool, he could see his breath, and shivered. Pokey stepped to a scrub pine and took a leak.

This was termination day. The day tribal members would drive twenty miles to Klamath Falls to cash their checks. Pokey was not sure he wanted to be a party to the foolhardy parade. The money would still be there tomorrow. It was not going anywhere. Not until he claimed it. If he did not get around to it right away, what then? He was not sure. He decided to go for a ride. It seemed important to him to be out in the hills, to be a part of the reservation one last time before it was gone.

He ducked inside and, moving with conviction, pulled on a pair of Levis, cowboy boots, flannel shirt and a down vest. He buckled on a pair of silver spurs and grabbed his black, flat-brimmed reservation hat with a beaded headband. He set it on his head and worked it down tight.

Pokey cut across the pasture, his trail clearly visible in the dew-laden grass. He made sure to keep the woodshed between himself and the house just in case Chief, or one of his henchmen who had kept the party alive, happened to be looking. They would give him hell for slipping away.

As he passed the cow she rippled her hide to fend off the cloud of mosquitoes hovering around her. When Pokey reached the corral he put one hand on the rail and vaulted it cleanly. His spurs, flying freely, jangled a lively tune. In the distance a few morning birds sang. The sun hung low in an orange sky and Pokey noticed, off to the southeast, a sun dog glistening like an overripe peach. He entered the barn, grabbed a bucket, ladled in a can of rolled oats, went to the corral and shook the oats in the bucket. From the willow thicket bordering the river, a horse whinnied. A moment later a sleek paint gelding appeared on the dead run, head held high, his light-colored mane and tail flowing in the wind he created. Pokey set the pail on the ground and went to the tack room. A few weeks before, he had come in from a ride and found Grandma standing in the dark room humming to herself. When she noticed Pokey she abruptly stopped, pointed an accusing finger in his direction and told him he should be a strong hunter, a fearless warrior, and chastised him for not fasting and going in search of his weyekin, his Indian spirit. He had laughed and told her, "You're a crazy old woman."

There was a hollow pounding of hooves on pumice. Shadow, Pokey's horse, rattled the metal bucket in his haste to eat the oats but pulled his head up when Pokey appeared. "How you doin', buddy," Pokey called and patted Shadow's well-muscled shoulder as he snapped a lead on the halter and tied off to a corral post. He used a curry comb to brush away the dirt and burrs. The rich aroma of dust and horse sweat was replaced by the fresh smell of manure as the paint lifted his tail. But even horse shit smelled good.

Shadow demanded more oats by nuzzling his head against Pokey. "Knock it off. Stand still." He laid the saddle blanket in place, worked out a few wrinkles and tossed the saddle over Shadow's back. He reached under the horse's belly, grabbed the cinch, brought it up and looped it through the rings. He slipped the bit between the horse's teeth and stretched the bridle over his ears. Shadow rolled the bit in his mouth as he continued to work on oat slobbers.

Shadow had a smart horse's trick of bloating himself with air whenever he was saddled. Pokey was wise, led the horse in a tight circle, pulled him up short, took the slack out of the cinch and tied it off. Moving quickly he took the reins, grabbed the saddle horn and swung up and onto the saddle. The big paint wheeled and side-stepped a time or two before lining out into a trot. Pokey encouraged him with a light touch of the silver rowels and Shadow broke into a ground-eating gallop. A cool wind chewed at Pokey's ears like needle teeth and he grinned because it felt so good to be alive.

At the lower end of the pasture Pokey reined in, stepped off, opened the gate, led the horse through and closed the gate behind him. He did not mount right away but paused to drink in the wonders of the day. Last night's downpour had left water everywhere; water whispering, murmuring, grumbling, running off to fill the low spots. The river was pushed over its banks and the current made the willows whistle. White petals, rain-stripped from daisies, littered the ground. Lupine lay on its side like ripe grain. Overhead the jet stream was blowing away the last remnants of the storm; tattered clouds scuttled across the mottled blue sky. The air was rich with smells of humus, wet grass and earthworms.

Shadow, impatient to be on the move, pawed at the ground and snorted. Pokey swung onto the horse and reined him down a well-worn trail that followed the river. The moisture that had matted the grasses and made the lupine bow began to evaporate and ever so slowly the plants found the strength to stand.

★ ★ ★

The sun was edging over the hill and soft tentacles of light stretched to touch Shasta as she hurried away from the house. She followed a stock trail that wound down along the river and felt a stirring, like tiny bursts of static electricity, sweep across her soul. How many times in the past had she traveled this trail? Sometimes she had pretended to be a pioneer child sent to fetch water—a homesteader's wife on the way to pick berries—an explorer like John C. Fremont or the famous scout, Kit Carson.

Shasta's secret place was located on a small bench, a short distance above and overlooking the river. When she was a child her mother allowed her to go for walks and play by herself, as long as she promised never to go near the river. Now, as she approached her miniature Garden of Eden, she began to comprehend her mother's fear. She crossed the fence where the constant coming and going of deer had loosened the top wire from the posts. The posts had turned light gray, and fuzzy moss was growing on the shady side. From the fence line the trail descended and Shasta leaned against a boulder already beginning to store a little of the sun's heat. She had not realized how much pleasure she took from the spacious country east of the Cascades. On the west side, the woods were crowded with fir, spruce, hemlock, cedar and leafy deciduous trees that grew out of an uninviting tangle of underbrush; blackberries, vine maples, thorny roses. Here the country was free of underbrush. It was accessible and rich with the earthy fragrances of rain on volcanic rock and the sweet smells of the cinnamon-barked ponderosa pine.

Perhaps it was only human nature to embrace one's birth land, but she felt more than that; this land tugged at her heart the way she supposed it had for Indians in the past, those who had lived here and taken the bounty of this land. But after a moment of reflection she realized her musings were more than a little presumptuous. How could she, a modern interloper, ever begin to know, or feel, what the land had meant to the ancient people?

★   ★   ★

As he rode along the trail Pokey viewed the artificial boundaries of the reservation, established by treaty between his forefathers and the federal government, as a pair of hands that surrounded him, protected him, cradled him. But he also recognized that those same hands imposed limitations. There was not a chance in hell that NASA would come to the reservation to choose an astronaut. No major corporation was going to recruit a CEO from Chewaucan. And it was a damn absolute guarantee that the next President of the United States was not going to be a Klamath Indian. But Pokey had always known that if he stayed within the confines of the reservation he could hunt, fish and rely on government handouts to provide a subsistence income. He had plenty of company. Nearly everyone he knew was a welfare Indian. That social order had existed for nearly a hundred years.

His brother Creek might be the only one to make it on the outside. Creek had always been unlike everyone else. He never played mock war with sticks and stones like the other boys, rarely hunted or fished. He took pleasure in finding a place of solitude so he could be alone and read books. In school Creek had a teacher who recognized his potential and taught him the art of debate. In his senior year Creek won a silver medal at a statewide competition. That achievement opened his eyes and he began to view himself as not just the brightest kid on the reservation, but on equal footing with white kids from Medford, Salem and Portland. His greatest accomplishment was in possessing the personal courage it took to escape the reservation and attend college.

Pokey knew the reason Creek had come home. Once he had the cash he was as good as gone. Even Chief could not bully Creek into staying and becoming another reservation alcoholic. In the end, if any of them were going to make something of themselves, it would be Creek. But Pokey also recognized Creek as a self-absorbed man who would never return to help his own people. But maybe, for him to survive and maintain his individuality, that was the way it had to be.

As for Chief, there was no changing the course of his life. He was running wide open down a dead-end street. At some point there was going to be a violent collision that would end it all. It might happen today, tomorrow, next week, or next year but it was going to happen. Chief, nothing but a mean-spirited alcoholic who was cruel to anyone, or anything, he perceived as weak, would crash and burn. Bet the farm on it.

Grandma was never going to change, nor would she allow the world around her to change her. She would forever be simply Grandma. For Pokey, she was the single most stabilizing influence on his life. He did not know, did not even want to consider, what would become of him when he lost her.

Otherwise, whether Pokey liked it or not, the future was here. The future was change. Nothing of the past would ever again be the same. With the rising of the sun this day, the reservation and the Klamath tribe had ceased to exist. Under the articles of termination, the land had become the new Winema National Forest, and the Klamath Indians were a part of the whole, merely citizens of the United States, and nothing more. For the sake of a few thousand dollars he was being forced to give up his birthright. Money was never going to buy what he wanted. He was not even sure what he did want. He supposed it was for his life to continue as it had: playing ball, rodeoing, hunting, fishing, riding horseback, drawing.

Shadow rounded a bend and Pokey looked up. Ahead was a tall rock, formed when lava poured like hot fudge over a layer of sandstone. The softer rock had been clawed by erosion, and twin caves were formed. At some point long ago the site had been inhabited by a clan of Klamath cave dwellers. In more recent times looters had sifted the caves' floors with tight mesh screens and had unearthed arrowheads, spear points and scrapers. They stole the history of the people who once dwelled here. The cave openings gave the illusion of dark brooding eyes. Eyes that watched Pokey as he passed.

★   ★   ★

The secret spot where Shasta had played as a child was exactly as she remembered. A trickle of water, nurtured by a seep in the rock wall, tumbled in a tiny waterfall into a pond inhabited by the descendants of water skippers, tadpoles and strange bugs that Shasta had known as a child. A bluebird flitted away as she drew near. Shasta went to the crooked aspen tree where she had carved her initials. The letters were there but sap, like brown scabs, had covered over the wound.

★　★　★

Shadow worked his way down the hill toward the river, kicking loose small rocks that skittered and clattered down the slope. Pokey was absorbed in his thoughts, that the Indian had possessed what the white man had wanted most—the land. The first wave of white invaders had figured the best way to resolve the problem was simply to eliminate the Indian population from North America. Native people were given blankets infected with smallpox; their food source, the buffalo, was removed; and finally Indians were shot. But the native people had endured. And now, the white man had finally gotten smart and was giving the Indians money. With money the Indians would buy fast cars and die on the road. They would get drunk and shoot and stab each other. They would drink themselves to death. Money was the perfect weapon. With money the Indians would simply kill themselves.

When Shadow came to the river Pokey saw it was running high but still safe to cross. He turned his heels in and nudged Shadow forward. He glanced up toward the little bench that overlooked the river and wondered if Shasta were there. Those many years ago, when he had been out riding and happened to find her, she had told him this was her secret spot. Whenever he rode this way he remembered the girl and how sad she had been, how she had cried and said she was never coming back.

At midstream he sensed Shasta watching him. For an instant he wished he were something more than what he was. It was a sensation like stepping into a muddy bog and not being able to feel the bottom. He wondered how a half-breed would measure up in her eyes. And then Shadow was coming out of the water and lunging up the bank. Pokey wrapped one hand around the saddle horn and lifted the reins with the other. When he reached the bench Shasta was sitting on a boulder. Her head was turned toward him and she was smiling, as if genuinely pleased to see him.

"Howdy."

"Howdy yourself," she called. He reined in. Shadow shook his head and snorted. Shasta patted the boulder beside her. "Want to join me?"

After dismounting, Pokey ground-tied Shadow by simply dropping the reins. Since the day had warmed considerably he pulled off his vest and tied it on behind the saddle. He unsnapped the cuffs of his shirt and rolled them up as he moved to join Shasta.

"When we were kids," Shasta said, "we sat right here and you gave me a rock. Do you remember?"

Pokey flipped back one of his braids, "Yeah, I remember."

"I've still got it."

Eleven

Soviet Premier Nikita Khrushchev telephoned Yuri Gagarin after his return to earth. The Premier offered his congratulations and told the young cosmonaut, "You have made yourself immortal. I will meet you in Moscow. You and I and all our people will solemnly celebrate this great feat in the conquering of space. Let the whole world see what our country is capable of."

Gagarin responded, "Now let the other countries try to catch us."

"That's right. Let the capitalist countries try to follow the trail we have blazed into space."

★ ★ ★

Red was up early, making his rounds. As he approached Pitsua bridge he watched a narrow layer of fog spill over the highest point on the humped-back ridge and engulf the pine trees as it flowed sluggishly downhill. Red knew the fog would burn off long before it reached the valley floor. He checked the bridge abutment—the vigilante sign was still there. He lit a cigarette, slowly read the names, and said to himself, "Sooner or later, and probably sooner, the shit is really gonna hit the fan."

On the way back into town he flipped on the radio and heard a news flash that the Soviet Union had launched a man into orbit. Red remembered watching Sputnik flash across the sky back in October of 1957. It had appeared like a firefly running a tightrope from the northwest to the southeast. A month later the Russians launched Sputnik II with a dog, Laika, aboard. But it caught fire on reentry and Laika perished. They sent more dogs and then rabbits, mice, flies and plant life into space. They even launched a spacecraft around the sun and another that circled the moon, taking photographs from the dark side. But all of this paled in comparison to the news they had blasted a manned spaceship into orbit around earth. It angered Red. After all, he had fought two wars to assure that the United States would be the most powerful nation in the world, and now the country was having to play second fiddle to the Russians. He cranked off the radio. "Commie bastards."

★　★　★

When the telephone rang, Marg was dusting the end table where Red kept his *Outdoor Life* and *Field & Stream* magazines. She set aside the dust rag and answered, "Durkee residence."

"Is Red there?"

"He's on patrol. If it's an emergency I can radio him."

"Better do it. Nathan wrecked. He done hit a tree."

"Where did this happen?" Marg picked up a pencil and shifted the phone to her shoulder so she could write.

"A mile north of town, on the S-curve. He run off the road. Don't bother calling no ambulance. He's deader than a doornail."

There was a click and the line hissed in Marg's ear. She hung up and keyed the mike. "Base to car one."

There was a pause and then Red answered, "Car one."

"Honey, I just got a call. I think it was Tony Abrams. He says there's been a bad wreck on the S-curve north of town. I guess Nathan hit a tree. He's dead."

"Jesus H. Christ. Okay. I'm headed that way. Thanks, Marg. Car one clear."

"Base clear."

Red opened the jockey box, removed the mechanical strobe, shook out the cord, plugged the end into the cigarette lighter and placed the magnetic light on the dash. Red light whirled.

When he arrived at the scene Red found the twisted hunk of sheet metal that had been Nathan's '32 Ford hot rod a hundred yards down the hill, wrapped around a lone pine tree. Red made a clicking sound with his tongue.

★   ★   ★

Tony Abrams had come to town to call about the accident. As long as he was there he thought to replenish his supply of beer and was coming out of the store with a case of Oly when Red shot past with red light flashing. Tony tossed the case on the front seat and drove to the scene of the accident. He opened a beer and drank, watching Red climb the hill after confirming that Nathan was dead. When Red was within hearing distance Tony offered, "Not a whole hell of a lot left. But it don't look like them chrome rims got hurt none at all. I been lookin' 'round for some deep-dish chromies just like that. Think his old lady'd sell them to me? I'll give her forty bucks for the rims and tires. That's fair. Ain't gonna do her no good anyhow."

Red said nothing. He went to his Chevy, reached through the open window, snatched up the hand mike and keyed it. "Car one to base."

Marg rushed across the trailer. "Base."

"Marg, you better contact the coroner, have him come out. And the funeral home. Call the sheriff, too. Guess you better mention Nathan was on the vigilante . . . Naw, skip that part. I'll worry about that later. Better just get this mess cleaned up."

"Should I get a tow truck?"

"Suppose so."

"Okay. Base clear."

"Car one clear."

Red leaned against a fender, withdrew a wooden match from a breast pocket, cleaned one ear and then the other, checking to see how much wax had accumulated and absent-mindedly rolled it between his thumb and forefinger before flicking it onto the ground. He tapped a cigarette loose from his pack, lit it and took several meditative puffs.

"Ain't no skid marks," Tony said. He belched. "Either he passed out and run off the road, or he didn't have no brakes."

Red tossed down his cigarette and violently ground it out with his boot heel while drawling a single word, "Shit." Having to deal with the aftermath of the wreck was one thing, but what pissed Red off even more was standing there thinking about that Russian space capsule circling overhead. A man in orbit—if that didn't beat all. It was bad enough when they were sending up dogs.

★ ★ ★

Pokey and Shasta sat together on the boulder. "You played a fantastic game last night," Shasta said.

"Not quite good enough."

"It seemed like you were the only one out there who followed the game plan. You drove and passed off. But it seemed as though your teammates were reluctant to return the favor."

Pokey grinned. "As soon as the ball goes up on the tip-off, the game plan pretty much goes out the window. It gets down to the basics—dribble and shoot. Defense? What's that? Dribble and shoot."

"How many points did you score?"

He shrugged. "Two less than I should have."

"I try to go to all the home games at Oregon," Shasta said. "Have you ever thought about playing college ball?"

"Never been that interested."

"In playing basketball, or going to college?"

"You spend four years, get a degree and then what are you supposed to do? Teach school? Be an accountant? Own a business? Work for the government? Can't see myself being any one thing."

Pokey was sitting so close to Shasta that he could feel the tiny hairs on her arm brush against him and could smell the soap she used to wash her face that morning. It had been a while since Pokey had been with a girl. Not since Rhonda.

Life would have been a lot different if she had lived. She had been a full-blood. Their children would have been more Indian than he was. She was killed when her car slammed into a rock wall. She was driving drunk. She had been three months pregnant, with a son. His son. She never even told him she was pregnant.

Shasta said, "Do you mind if I ask sort of a personal question?"

"What about?"

"Termination."

Pokey tightened his jaw. "Shoot."

"How do you feel about it?"

"What's there to feel?"

"Give me your thoughts."

"Why?"

"I'm writing a paper on termination," she said, and added, "for school."

"Came back for that, huh?"

"Mostly."

"Things changed a lot since we were kids."

"Creek says that as long as Indians are kept on reservations they'll remain second-class citizens. What do you think?"

Pokey flipped the troublesome braid over his shoulder and stared hard at the river.

Shasta tried again. "Creek says we should do away with all reservations. He says wardship is outdated and never has worked."

Pokey said nothing.

"Maybe money is the answer. I guess if the offer is good enough, anything and everything is for sale. Creek says— "

"Bull. Creek takes what the government hands out. He

milks the system for books, tuition, living expenses. And when he graduates, the BIA will snap him up to show off how good a job they're doing educating the savage. They'll pat him on the back and give him fifteen grand a year. His success will be measured on how well he fits into the white man's world."

"What about you?"

"Me?"

"Yeah, what are you going to do with your life? What do you want to be when you grow up?" She smiled as she said it.

What could he say? That his life was in limbo and he was unclear as to what direction he might be headed? "Well, up until the mill closed I worked there, pulling green chain. It was a job. Decent pay. But they shut down. I haven't worked full-time since. I ride for some of the ranchers around here, your dad included—roundup, turnout, working calves."

"Why did the mill close?"

"Government locked up the timber."

"Do you have goals, something you want to accomplish?"

Pokey snorted. "One little, two little, three little Indians. We're supposed to be wind-up toys, this one like the next, like the next. Goals? Ambition? Why? Anytime I see an Indian try to make money from the white man I hear our ancestors laughing in the trees. I don't know if they're laughing at the Indians or the whites, but they're laughing."

"And you probably think that Tonto should be boss."

"Yeah, let the Lone Ranger be his sidekick." A kingfisher flew upriver scolding with its caustic tongue. Pokey knew that if Rhonda and his son had lived they would certainly have continued to live at Chewaucan, but now, with them gone and the reservation sold, there were fewer strings holding him. He was in a quandary and did not know what he would do.

Finally he said, "Here's the way I see it. The Indian has lived here for fourteen thousand years. Do you have any concept of fourteen thousand years? I'll put it in perspective. The last ice age was still going on fourteen thousand years ago. Our people were here then, hunting mastodons with spears. They saw Mount Mazama blow her top and create Crater Lake seven thousand years ago. They survived the ash cloud, and floods, and fires, and famines. For what? So this generation could betray their ancestors?"

"You're opposed to termination?"

"I can't stop it from happening no more than I can stop a cloud from raining."

"Is the problem the amount? You don't think you're getting a fair price for the land?"

"It's like if Russia came over and said they wanted to buy Oregon from the United States. Would you sell?"

"Of course not."

"Well, there you go. I'm saying I don't want to sell, either." A muskrat surfaced in the middle of the river and went gliding with the current.

"But forty-three thousand dollars is a lot. You could start a business. You could make a down payment on a ranch. It would give you a start on owning a place."

"Yes and no. Maybe for a while, but in the end it won't make any difference. Listen to this story I'm going to tell you. It'll explain what I mean. There was this fisherman who lived on the coast and one day he came in and set two baskets on the dock. A fellow asked why one basket had a lid on it and the other did not. The fisherman told him, 'I've got white crabs in the covered basket and red crabs in the other.' The fellow wanted to know, 'Why don't you cover the red crabs?' The fisherman said, 'The red crabs are like Indians—every time one tries to crawl out, the others will pull him back down.' "

"You're suggesting Indians don't want each other to succeed?"

"Does it make any difference? In the long run all the crabs are gonna get cooked. I don't know. Maybe it's best we stick together, look out for each other. In a tribe nobody has it better or worse than anybody else. Equals. The white man is geared different. He only cares about himself. He goes to school to get an education, works a job, busy making money, buying on time, planning for today, planning for tomorrow. He buys fire insurance, car insurance, life insurance, health insurance. All safety'd up and secure. Protected. Indian lives today for today."

"You're half white, is that what allows you to see the Indian side so well?"

He thumped his chest and told her, "Indian. Nothing but."

"And you think termination is a—"

"Mistake. The worst kind of mistake. Government gets the land. And in a month, three months, six months, a year, the white man will have all his money back. What will we have? Not a goddamn thing."

"I assumed everyone was for it, for termination. I'm a little surprised."

Pokey pushed himself off the rock, picked up a twig, found no spring in it, broke it, threw it away and reached for the reins of his patient horse.

"Don't run off," Shasta said.

But he was already swinging up onto the saddle. "We'll get together again." He laid the reins against Shadow's neck and forced the big paint off the bench and into the river. Water splashed and sparkled in tiny rainbows. Pokey never looked back but rode straight across the gravel bar and disappeared into the willows on the far side. Shasta watched and several times he reappeared, as a galloping apparition of a paint horse and rider weaving in and out of breaks in the willows, flashing through sunlight and plunging into shadows.

Twelve

C hief had a beer shoved between his legs and his foot jammed all the way to the carburetor. He hit the junction, slid across both lanes of Highway 97, and fishtailed back onto the pavement, throwing gravel and kicking up dust. If traffic had been coming he surely would have killed someone. That thought never crossed Chief's mind. His sole objective was to get to Klamath Falls—the bank, the money—as fast as he could.

"Time me," he barked at Creek.

Chief was shooting for the record, twenty miles to town in less than twelve minutes and seventeen seconds. The Impala's three-quarter cam screamed, the scavenger headers howled, the needle on the tachometer raced toward red line, pegged out. He slammed the linkage into second gear. Tires squealed. Rubber burned. And Chief began pounding on the steering wheel with his fists, shouting, "Faster. Faster. Faster."

He gulped beer. His face did not seem to know who or what or why, or even care very much. He felt around on the seat until he located his sunglasses, put them on, cranked down the window and tossed his empty at a road sign, missing.

"Squeak, make yourself useful, get me a beer, aye."

Creek leaned over the seat, grabbed the necks of two beers and opened them. Chief took one and let the pale liquid flow down his gullet. The Impala veered into the oncoming lane. An air horn shrieked, Chief jerked the wheel, and a tractor-trailer loaded with lumber flashed past. Chief thought that was hilarious.

There was nothing but engine noise and the whistling wind as they sped through shadows cast by pine trees, curling around corners and thundering down straight-aways. White lines flickered like tiny dots. Wet tires hissed. Chief drank great gulps of beer while seconds ticked dangerously away. On a blind corner they passed three trucks in a row and then roared up to the back bumper of a pea green Biscayne. They pulled alongside. A lanky boy, wearing thick glasses held together with athletic tape, was driving and his girlfriend was snuggled beside him, her head leaned against his knobby shoulder. Chief cranked down his window, played like he was pulling the pin of a grenade, and lobbed an empty over the car. It would be a hoot if the bottle had broken the windshield, causing the kid to run off the road and kill himself and his girlfriend. But the grenade sailed harmlessly over its intended target. All the while, happy-go-lucky Chief was wearing a crooked grin like a man about to lay down a full boat to beat an ace high flush. In just a little while he would be rich. The party would never end. He gunned the Impala and screamed ahead of the Biscayne as if it had suddenly been thrown into reverse.

★ ★ ★

In Klamath Falls, a round-shouldered, tattooed hunk of a truck driver sat on a stool in the Pastime Tavern. He was drinking a beer and taking his mandatory layover before he could get back on the road. The bartender came over and said, "How about them Ruskies sending a man into orbit?"

"Bunch of Cold War propaganda. Don't believe it."

"Even if they did, it's not gonna change my life," the bartender said. "We've got bigger fish to fry. Word of warning—soon as the bank opens, the Klamath Injuns gonna get their hands on forty-three thousand dollars, cash money. That's each and every last one—forty-three grand. You ever seen Injuns on the warpath?"

The truck driver shook his head, "I'm from Tennessee. We ain't got none. We killed them all. Every last one." He chuckled and took another swig of beer.

The bartender leaned across the bar and lowered his voice. "Another hour or two an it's gonna be completely uncivilized around here. I imported me some Portland gals. I'm not shittin'. There's gonna be high-heeled, red-sweatered gals parading around, hiking up their skirts for Ben Franklin. Squealers and squawkers every last one. Before the night's out one of them is likely to be humping some buck and get caught by his squaw. Gonna be hell to pay. Drinkin'. Fuckin'. Fightin'. Knifin'. Shootin'. Killin'. Hell, we're likely to see it all. Be something to tell the grand-kids about—if you live. I gotta stick it out—money's gonna be too goddamn good not to. But now, if I was you, I'd throw my log book away, hop in my rig and drive like hell. Get outta here before some crazy-assed Injun lifts my scalp."

"Thanks," the driver said. He ran his fingers through what little bit of hair he had and pushed himself off the stool. "Give me a short-case to go."

★ ★ ★

Creek woke from an alcoholic daze. The Impala was stopped at an empty intersection and an overhead traffic light throbbed colors. Green. Yellow. Red. Green. Yellow. The red was too intense and penetrating and when Creek sensed it coming he closed his eyes. Suddenly the engine roared and the Impala leaped forward. "Grab me a beer," commanded Chief. "Next time ya pass out like that I'm gonna shove a dog turd down yer throat."

"I was resting my eyes."

"My ass. Gimme da beer."

Coming down Klamath Avenue Chief alternately goosed and let off on the gas, making the tires shriek and the Chevy leap forward and dip low. He pulled into an open parking spot in front of the U.S. West Bank, hit the curb, bounced up on the sidewalk and sat there revving the engine. Finally he turned off the ignition. The engine backfired once in protest and then stopped with a shudder.

Creek squinted at his watch, "Bank doesn't open for a half hour."

"Wanna be first in line, aye." Chief got out and plopped himself down on the hood. The engine made tinkling sounds as the metal cooled. Johnny High stumbled toward them, a fifth of Black Velvet in either hand. He tripped and fell, breaking one of the whiskey bottles and driving a jagged piece of glass into the fleshy part of his palm. He got to his feet and stood bleeding onto the pavement. He took a swig from the unbroken bottle and handed it to Chief, "'Ave one on me."

"Sure 'nough need it."

Creek made his way around the car and waited his turn. By then a group of Klamaths had assembled like a small war party. More bottles made the rounds. This group of Indians drank and talked about what they were going to buy; new cars, pickups, Jeeps, motorcycles, horses, saddles, rifles, shotguns, pistols, ammunition, knives, record players, radios, stoves, refrigerators. One woman wanted aluminum siding to spruce up the shack where she lived and the others were amused and told her not to throw her money away.

A city police cruiser slid past like a hungry shark eyeing plump sunbathers on a beach. One of the women hissed, "Cops. Hide the booze."

But Chief held up a bottle to salute the officers. "Ain't no dip-shit cop dumb 'nough to arrest us 'fore we get our money, ain't it." He shouted, "Let's get drunk an' be somebody." He drank from a half-gallon jug and his Adam's apple bobbed up and down. He lost his balance and fell back against the windshield of his Impala. It was the car's fault. He flailed out, bashing the windshield with a meaty fist. The glass shattered into a spider web. His fury not satisfied, Chief kicked in the rear quarter panel and enjoyed that so much he marched to the front and slammed a heel into each headlight. He threw back his head, laughed that terrible, heartless laugh of his and went over and started beating on the bank doors, calling out in his rage, "Open up! Open up these motherfuckin' doors!"

★ ★ ★

U.S. West Bank employees were required to report for work an hour early on termination day. They spent the time around the conference table, munching on maple bars, sipping hot coffee and listening to the radio about the Russians' astounding space achievement.

Everything was in place for the business of termination; files on each withdrawing member had been alphabetized and the termination checks were paper-clipped to the front of each file folder. The smallest amount was for $33,000. Some members had elected to take a $10,000 draw against the money they had coming. Other members were entitled to receive compensation from heirs who had died in the seven years between the vote on termination, in 1954, and when the government finally got around to paying its debt. A check made out to Ambrose George for a total of $172,000 was his share and, as the sole surviving heir, full shares from a sister who was dumped onto the highway from a speeding car, a younger brother who was shot to death at a party, and an older brother who finally succeeded in drinking himself to death at the ripe old age of thirty-two.

A gray slug of an armored truck appeared at the back door of the bank. Two security men, pistols drawn, stood guard while two others wheeled canvas bags of cash into the bank's walk-in vault. The action inside seemed to attract the attention of the crowd of Indians who had gathered in front of the building and were openly drinking from bottles. Several of them banged on the door. One man left bloody hand prints smeared on the glass.

Arny Osborne, the branch manager, called his employees to man their battle stations. His keys jangled as he walked toward the double doors. The grandfather clock in the lobby chimed ten o'clock. Arny could see the distorted faces pressed against the glass and as he drew near, sounds oozed through, a low murmur, like the surging excitement of a race track crowd as the horses are led into the starting gate. The key slid into the lock. Points and tumblers tripped. The lock opened. A great cheer welled up and the glass doors were flung inward, momentarily pinning Arny as a wave of brown-skinned humanity surged past him and into the lobby of the bank.

Chief was in the lead. He stumbled and fell onto the polished floor but was able to somersault and pop back onto his feet. It was a slick maneuver for a big, drunk man. He was scrambling, pushing, shoving and running all at once. He arrived at the nearest teller's cage and gripped the sides of the window to secure his position. Instinct caused the teller, a pert young woman in a pretty green dress, to retreat. She took a step back, but even at a distance she could smell Chief's foul, boozy breath. It seemed to the teller that her first customer, whether from his state of inebriation or his obsession to have the money, belonged in an insane asylum. His face was puffy and distorted, his hair was standing on end, and his dark eyes blinked neon madness. She looked around for someone to call, for someone to come to her assistance, but no one else was available.

★　★　★

Those not directly involved in the termination payoff moved like independent pieces in a leisurely game of chess. Red sat in his office, feet propped on the desk, chewing scenarios of "what ifs" as if they were pieces of gristle and he was unsure whether to swallow or spit. Floyd walked around the station bay collecting oily rags. He would take Tillie to the bank in the afternoon, after the crowd thinned out some. Debbie Atwood called the distributor and doubled the store's beer order. Dallas sicced his dog on a cow that refused to be driven through the open gate. Shasta picked a bouquet of wildflowers. Dolly stood in front of the television watching the news. Grandma rocked. The spider spun. Lefty passed out. Pokey sat easy in the saddle, watching clouds from a fresh Pacific storm brewing along the long line of the Cascades, creating a glowing citadel of cumulus clouds, translucent on top, their bellies opaque with moisture. Soon it would rain.

★　★　★

The teller made a stab at normal conversation. "Boy, wasn't that something about the Russians sending a man into orbit? We listened to it on the radio."

Chief's face was compressed to a snarl. "I don't give a fuck! Get my money!"

The young woman in the green dress was shocked and yet she was able to mount some semblance of composure. "Your name, please."

Chief told her his given name, Rollin Pitsua. She moved to a series of tables holding boxes marked with letters of the alphabet and pawed through the P section, selected Chief's folder and, returning to her window, nervously fumbled the papers.

Chief was intently watching her and noticed that the material on her dress was pulled tight between freckled breasts. The top button was tilted at an odd angle, so that even the slightest pressure would cause it to slip through the buttonhole. Desire, despair or plain orneriness made him lean over and flick the button. The material spread apart, exposing more freckled skin and the top of a pure white Cross-Your-Heart bra. The woman dropped the papers on the floor and her hands came up to hide and protect herself. She blushed with anger and embarrassment, refastened the button and hissed a single word, "Don't." Again she glanced left and right.

"Quit fiddly-fartin' 'round. Just give me my goddamn money."

The teller picked up the file from the floor and moved a safe distance away. She made the necessary entries, had Chief show identification, and pushed a paper across the counter and directed him to sign his name. When he finished she took back the paper and slid his termination check toward him.

He squinted at the number, $33,000. "Where's the rest?"

"Mr. Pitsua, as allowed by the termination act, you took a $10,000 draw against the proceeds of the final payoff. That money was deducted from the total."

Chief grabbed a pen that was fastened to the counter and jerked it free, breaking the light chain. He scribbled his name on the back of the check and then reached in his shirt and yanked out a paper sack. He thrust the sack and the endorsed check at the teller. "Fill 'er up."

"You mean you want cash?"

"What I say?"

Again she could smell him in front of her, all flyblown and rank and for an instant she stood frozen, and then the words, "Large bills?" tumbled from her mouth.

"Regular size be fine," Chief said, and then broke into a toothless grin.

The teller counted hundreds into stacks of tens, and when she had thirty-three piles Chief grabbed them up and stuffed them all in the paper sack. He turned and headed for the door.

Arny Osborne had been watching the exchange between his teller and Chief. As branch manager, it was Arny's responsibility to speak with customers and attempt to convince them to leave a substantial portion of their termination payoff with the bank. He approached on a course that would intercept Chief. His purpose was to advise his customer that it would be a prudent fiscal move to invest a portion of the money in a savings account, or perhaps in a certificate of deposit. He positioned himself between Chief and the door, politely said, "Sir, there are several options you might want to consider in regards to sound financial planning and investment oppor—"

One of Chief's hands firmly gripped the scrunched up neck of the paper sack. The other hand shot out and hit Arny squarely on the chest, driving the small man back and off his feet. He landed on the seat of his pants and slid, while his pocket change fell out and clattered across the marble floor.

Chief never missed a stride and when he reached the front door, a Klamath Falls police officer advanced from the shadows and brought a night stick down hard on the back of his head. Chief sank to his knees, but his big body kept its forward momentum. He fell face first onto the sidewalk and was promptly handcuffed. Four officers were required to drag him to the paddy wagon and lift him inside.

When Chief came awake his mouth was as dry as a cotton ball and his head ached something fierce. He felt the back of his head. There was a big knot there. He did not know how he had gotten it. He desperately needed a drink and shouted, "Gimme a beer," before he realized he was sitting on a dank concrete floor and was surrounded by metal bars. He got to his feet and took hold of the bars to steady himself. He tried to shake his way to freedom but the iron refused to yield. His tongue flicked in and out, licking dry lips.

"Hey, guard," he clamored. "I'll give ya a hundred bucks if ya bring me a beer."

★ ★ ★

Creek had witnessed the four cops drag Chief across the sidewalk and unceremoniously deposit him in the back of the paddy wagon. He thought that since Chief had gotten himself into this mess, he could get himself out. Sure, the cops might have busted him but what were they going to do, really? Fine him, take away some of his money? He'd be out in a couple of hours. Might do him good to cool his heels, sober up a little, not be quite so crazy. Wasn't Chief the one who was always saying, "I don't fuckin' need nobody"?

Still, Creek felt a twinge of compassion and promised himself before he left town he would check to see if Chief had been able to spring himself. But Chief was not his number one priority. Creek had his money, eight grand in cash in his wallet and the remainder in a savings account, and he told himself he needed a drink, just one to dull the raw edges of the running drunk he had been on since he hit home and Chief had forced the first beer on him. As soon as he had that one drink he was going to buy the car he had wanted forever—the red Corvette. The adjective that came to Creek's mind most often to describe his dream car was cute. And this was the day he was going to be the proud owner of a bright red, cute Corvette.

He ducked into the bar around the corner from the bank and ordered a whiskey and water, and then, magnanimously, he did something he had never done before, buy a round for the house. He paid for it with a hundred-dollar bill. He drank. Someone bought him another. Creek started to protest. He had promised himself he was going to have only one drink and then buy the Corvette. But the drink was right there. He wavered. What was the harm in one more? He drank and before he finished, a third drink appeared. And, as each suddenly wealthy Indian came through the door, they bought another round, paying with hundred-dollar bills, never getting change. The drinks were stacking up in front of Creek. He could not drink them fast enough and arranged them like little soldiers waiting to go into battle. He felt numb and tired but he was too excited to sleep or pass out.

A mill worker, wearing a plaid shirt and sporting a tattoo of a naked girl on his right forearm, saddled up on the stool next to Creek. He stole one of Creek's drinks and offered, "Gettin' pretty loosey-goosey, huh?"

"Yep," Creek said. "Let the good times roll."

The mill worker stole another drink and swivelled around on his stool to face the room, a glass in either hand. "Now I know how Custer felt."

Creek sort of laughed. The mill worker seemed like an all right guy and the alcohol was putting him in a talkative mood. "You think this is wild. If my brother were here, this place would be going nuts. You never seen anyone crazier than Chief."

"Oh yeah?"

"This one time the per capita check came and Chief buys a fifty-seven Chevy hardtop, two eighty-three, bored out to twenty over, stick shift. Red and silver. Real pretty. Coming across Algoma Flat he tried to pass a line of cars, drifted left, caught a front wheel in the gravel, overcorrected and ended up going back and forth across the highway twice before he rolled it into the borrow pit. He crawled up to the road but not a single car stopped."

"You can't blame them. I sure as hell wouldn't," the mill worker said.

"But this truck driver stopped. He had to, either stop or run over Chief because he was standing in the middle of the road waving his arms over his head. Chief climbed up into the cab and told the driver to take him to town. The driver started through the gears. Chief opened the door, stepped onto the running board, climbed the ladder to the top of the trailer. The driver slowed and was passed by a dump truck. When it came alongside, Chief jumped into the back of the dump truck, landing spread eagle on a load of sand."

"Did the driver know he had taken on a passenger?"

"Not until Chief reached through the window and shoved a knife to his throat. He made him drive to Klamath Avenue, where he got out and went in the closest bar. That was where they arrested him. Got three months."

"Sounds like a swell fellow." The mill worker glanced around the room. "Where is he?"

"In jail. He hit a man in the bank. But I expect he'll make bail and come walking through those doors any minute."

The mill worker glanced toward the door. He finished

one drink, stole another, and moved to the far side of the room. Creek started to lift his glass, but it hit him that he was already feeling no pain and pushed it away. He called to the bartender, asking him to please call a taxi.

"Call one yourself. I'm busy."

Some white guy shook his head, said to no one in particular, "Busy stealing money."

A table of high rollers was engaged in a game of cutting high card for hundred-dollar bills. Two Indians were quarreling about who got into a girl first, ten years back. Creek felt like vomiting and wandered outside, lost his balance and grabbed a parking meter to steady himself, ended up sliding down into a sitting position on the curb. A cattle truck, jam-packed with Hereford yearlings bawling and shitting green slime through the sideboards, stopped for a red light. After it was gone the smell lingered until dissipating on a breeze out of the west. A tumbleweed skittered across the pavement and a bus ran over it. Creek got to his feet and, with hands jammed in his pockets, allowed the wind to blow him down the street. He thought that if he were in the country, stumbling along like this through the sage, the turkey vultures would line up on the fence posts to watch, and wait, for him to die. At least then his dying would have an audience. That thought amused him.

Overhead, a crow, flying so high that the sun reflected off its breast, was chased down the sky by a single blackbird. Creek chewed on a stick of beef jerky he found in his pocket. He could not recall when or where he bought it but welcomed the taste. An orange tomcat materialized and coaxed him into an alley. Creek eyed the cat with calm indifference. Suddenly he lost his balance and stumbled into a pair of garbage cans, falling between them. He was wedged there and it did not seem worthwhile for him to expend the effort to free himself.

Later Creek regained enough of his senses to be sick and, after laboring to his feet and tottering out of the alley, he wandered aimlessly until his attention was drawn to the fluttering flags and blinking lights at Link Brothers Pontiac/Chevrolet dealership. Light bounced off the ripe, polished skins of new cars. Whether from the walk or the sight of the automobiles, Creek sensed a sobering enthusiasm beginning to well up within his slight frame.

The car he had wanted for so long, the car of his dreams, graced center stage of the showroom. Creek advanced up the steps and through the door, his eyes gorging on a cherry red Corvette convertible roadster with a white inlay shooting like a flame along the side panel. He was drawn to it like a moth to fire. Maroon interior, fuel injection, 315 horses coupled to a stump-pulling 4.11:1 rear axle ratio. Zero to sixty in five-point-five; the quarter in 14.2 at an even 100 miles per hour. His car. He had to have it.

The closest salesman was telling a white customer, who was complaining about the price of a Brookwood station wagon, "You don't have to pay that price. That's the Indian price."

Creek whistled through his thumbs to get the salesman's attention, "Hey, I want this car."

And the salesman hollered, "In a second. Just hang onto your horses."

He told the couple, "Your cost is nine hundred under sticker."

Creek noticed the Corvette's keys in the ignition. He read the list price, fifty-four hundred and some change. He opened his wallet and counted fifty-five hundred dollar bills and placed them in a pile on the hood of a baby blue

Tempest Le Mans. As an afterthought he peeled off three more bills and added them to the pile.

He shouted to the salesman. "Money for the car . . ." he pointed towards the Tempest, "right there."

Creek hopped over the door and slid onto the Corvette's leather seat. Again he shouted to the salesman. "And extra for the window."

Lightning flashed, gas vapors exploded inside cylinders, tailpipes belched and bellowed. The salesman, mouth agape, stood frozen. The likeness of Pontiac, chief of the Ottawa nation, stared sullenly from the wall. Tires shrieked. Wax incinerated. The red Corvette left the launching pad, hit the plate glass window, which graciously yielded, and, as bits of glass rained down, the cute little red car hurdled into space, touching down a full thirty feet out on the apron of asphalt.

Thirteen

D olly sat at the kitchen table, the portable radio in front of her, fascinated by the information she was learning about the Russian cosmonaut: he had grown up on a collective farm west of Moscow, joined a local aviation club and learned to fly, was a married man, father of two daughters, currently held the rank of major in the Soviet Air Force and the communists had simplified his name to "Gaga."

The radio station cut away from its coverage to air an advertisement for Pacific Empire Credit. "Don't be a debt slave, get out of debt without borrowing. If installment payments or past-due bills are troubling you, let us consolidate and arrange to pay all your outstanding bills with one simple payment you can afford. Bring your debt problems to us today. No security, no co-signers, no credit references required. . . ."

In the middle of the radio spot Shasta walked in and handed Dolly a bouquet of wildflowers. "They were so pretty I knew you would enjoy them, too."

"Thank you, dearie, but you shouldn't have," Dolly said. She poured tap water into a Mason jar, plunged the stems into the water and set the jar on the table, pausing to arrange some of the flowers while adding, "Big news, better sit and listen. The Russians sent a man into orbit."

Shasta said, "Wow, that really is something."

"When the news comes back on, they're cutting away to a live nationwide poll to find out what the average Joe thinks of the Russian space achievement. They're going to be calling men named Joe Smith, from all around the country, asking for their reaction."

Shasta took a seat and listened with Dolly while Joe Smiths were interviewed on the radio. Joe Smith, a seventy-two-year-old retired tool and die maker in Detroit, said, "They can put all the Russians into space as far as I'm concerned. We can still take care of ourselves, don't worry."

Joe Smith, a WWI veteran from Charlotte, North Carolina, said, "I think it's nothing but a bunch of damn Russian lies to try and break us down. But we aren't going to be broken down. We're going to stand up and fight. If it takes more money to get into space, then we have to be willing to spend it."

Joseph B. Smith, a Seattle attorney, said, "We will have a man in space when it is safe to send one there. We're not like the Russians. We have to be more careful. Putting a man up there is a lot different than sending a dog into orbit. We're talking about a human life here."

The news reporter concluded the poll and recapped the details of the historic event. After he promised updates as they became available, the station returned to its regular programming. Dolly turned the radio off and said, "Dallas was concerned about you."

"I left a note."

"Yes. I told him."

"And?"

"I think he wanted to do something with you this morning. Maybe show you the calves."

"I wish he would have said so last night."

"Not your fault, Honey."

"Maybe this afternoon we can."

"I don't expect him back before dinner."

The room was silent, except for the plastic cat clock. It was pink and had glass jewels denoting the hours and a twitching tail that counted each prolonged second. Tick-tock, tick-tock, tick-tock. Dolly looked from the clock to the blank television screen. Five minutes before *As the World Turns* came on the air. She wished the girl were not here, that she were alone, and felt a stab of guilt for thinking such a thing. She offered, "If you have something to do, you know, for your research, some place to go, whatever, you can take my station wagon."

"Thanks. If you really don't mind, I'll take you up on it."

"Of course, but I'll need to run uptown a little later, to the store for a few little odds and ends." Dolly dug the keys from her purse and slid them across the table.

The keys were in a miniature leather boot. "Dolly" was stamped on one side and a rose was stamped on the other. Both were worn, the leather shiny and pressed flat.

"Your father gave me that when we were first going together."

"Oh." Shasta nodded.

"He was so sweet. He really was. One time he even brought me a handful of bachelor buttons. Picked them special. Brought them into the café where I was cooking.

So romantic. Oh my, that day he could of had his choice of any gal in the joint, but he wanted me."

Tick-tock. Tick-tock.

"Sorry we never got to know each other before this. But your daddy, he didn't want to fight with your mommy. Mind you, nothing against her, just that sometimes people—oh, you know, they don't want to deal with unpleasantness. But he's thought of you—often—over the years."

Shasta had nothing to offer.

Tick-tock.

"I'll run upstairs," Shasta said, "and grab my notebook."

When she returned, Dolly was reaching toward the television. Shasta stopped her with a question, "What do you think of termination?"

Dolly dropped her arm and wrung her hands. "Dallas thinks the Indians are crazy."

"Why?"

"For taking the money."

"What do you think?"

"Me? Oh, I don't rightly know. Dallas says when the money is gone they're going to have nothing to show for it."

"Do you agree?"

"To be perfectly honest, I kind of resent them getting the money. After all, they never had to work for it or anything like that. They get it just because they were born Indian." She glanced at the clock. One minute before the hour.

"Should we just forget about the treaty? Take their land away without any compensation?"

"Don't guess that would be fair. Maybe the government should have left things the way they was. It wasn't hurting nobody."

Shasta moved toward the door, then turned back to

Dolly. "I was just wondering if you know—the Indian children—what happens to their money?"

"Those born before 1954 have the money held for them in trust until they turn twenty-one. Those born after '54 are out of luck. They don't get nothing."

"They don't? Nothing at all? That seems absurd."

Dolly shrugged. "Had to be some cutoff date."

"I suppose," Shasta said. She turned away and as she closed the door shut behind her she heard the television come on and the voice of a young woman pleading for respect.

★   ★   ★

Shasta drove through town, and near the schoolyard she pulled over and watched kids, mostly Indians, at recess. A few played on the swings. Two boys were squared off, bashing a dirty yellow ball around a tether pole. Others shot a rubber ball into a rusty hoop, devoid of a net and bent at an odd angle. Most stood around in small, sullen groups.

After first grade at Chewaucan, she had attended a suburban school and played and learned beside white children, all meticulously groomed, hair cutely curled and faces sparkling. These boys and girls were nothing at all like that and Shasta quietly wondered how much of a chance for success did these Indian kids have?

★   ★   ★

A long train of log cars rumbled through town. The tracks took the path of least resistance, the same route that Peter Skene Ogden and his motley band of trappers, the first recorded white men into the basin country, had followed. Ogden wrote in his diary on May 28, 1829: "*3 of the trappers came in with word of more traps stolen. They pursued the Indian thieves and punished them but could not recover the traps.*

"*A man who had gone to explore the lake at this moment dashed in and gave the alarm of the enemy. He had a most narrow escape, only the fleetness of his horse saved his life. When rounding a point within sight of the lake, 20 Indians on horseback gave the war cry. He fled. An Indian would have overtaken him, but he discharged his gun. He says the hills are covered with Indians.*

"*I gave orders to secure the horses, 10 men then started in advance to ascertain what the Indians were doing but not to risk a battle as we were too weak. They reported upwards of 200 Indians marching on our camp. They came on. Having signaled a spot for them about 500 yards from our camp, I desired them to be seated. This order was obeyed. From their dress and arms and the fact only one elderly man was with them, I concluded it was a war party. If they had not been discovered, they had intended to attack us, weak as we were in guns—only 12— they would have been successful. It was a narrow escape.*"

There was another side to the story, quite different from what Ogden had recorded in his diary. According to the Indian version, a small hunting party, without provocation, was attacked by a band of trappers with thunder sticks. The Indians were massacred and their bodies left where they fell. Grandma was recalling the details of that story as the sun winked at her through scattered clouds. She was the only one still alive who had heard eyewitnesses speak of the events. Her television hissed static. Nobody was in the house, no voices, no kids squealing and playing, no music, no drunken orgies, no fighting—nothing.

Loneliness washed over Grandma, sharpening the lines etched on her face. If anyone had been watching her, she would have appeared lifeless, except for the tremble of her jaw.

★　★　★

The dogs ran as a pack. They roamed the long ridge line behind the house chasing down jackrabbits and the occasional crippled or sick deer. They were constantly bringing in bones and hides as proof of their hunting prowess, dragging them under the porch to gnaw on at their leisure.

Shasta never considered having to get past the dogs until she crossed over the bridge and started up the lane. The dog pack came out from under the porch as she rolled to a stop. They howled, barked, whined and paused to smell the wheels of the station wagon. Shasta looked toward the house for help and saw Grandma at a window. Her face was ghostlike behind the corner of a tattered plastic curtain. One shaky hand was above her squinting eyes, trying to block out the glare. She went to the door, opened it, stood behind the torn screen and snapped at the dogs. "Shut up." They scurried under the porch.

Shasta quickly got out of the car. She could smell the wet dogs and the stench of their accumulated treasures. One growled menacingly. Shasta came up the steps and hurried onto the porch. From behind the screen door Grandma demanded, "What you want?"

"May I talk to you?"

"Why?"

Shasta bent at the waist so she would not be as tall and said, "Creek said you could tell me about the way things used to be, back in the early days."

"You girl come with Creek?"

"Yes."

"He went town."

"That's okay. I came to talk to you. May I come in?"

Grandma shrugged, moved back. Shasta opened the screen door and slid inside. Grandma trudged toward her bedroom. Shasta followed, stepping around the accumulated clutter of the party, wondering privately if Indians had a junk drawer like she did growing up, where things like letters, snapshots, checkbook stubs, flashlight batteries and rubber bands tended to collect. She figured not, the whole damn house was a junk drawer.

Shasta had researched the Klamath Indians at the college library. She had read about Ogden and the next white visitors, John C. Fremont and his expedition, who had passed through the basin in 1843. A band of Indians to the south had mounted a raid against the Fremont expedition and three Delaware scouts were killed. In retaliation, and many miles away from the killings, Fremont's men charged a peaceful village of Klamath Indians camped along the Chewaucan and killed every man, woman and child.

Shasta sat on the cot beside Grandma and asked about the coming of the white man.

"No talk." Grandma sat in the half light, jaw twitching, looking frail and very old.

The history books related that white men continued to come to the Klamath Basin and hinted that both sides had committed injustices. Indians attacked a wagon train at Bloody Point and massacred the pioneers. A group of miners from Yreka, led by Ben Wright, invited all the Indians in the lower Klamath Basin to a feast and then poisoned the food. In a loud voice, clearly annunciating each word, Shasta asked, "Can you tell me anything about Bloody Point?" Grandma shook her head. "Have you ever heard the name Ben Wright?" Again Grandma shook her head.

"Creek thought you were born the same year the treaty was signed? That was in 1864." Shasta had seen a copy of the treaty; saw where twenty-seven of the most important tribal leaders had made an X beside their name. "Can you tell me anything about the treaty?"

Feeling acutely aware of Grandma's flat stare and her silence, she asked, "Could you tell me about the early days of the reservation?"

"No want think 'bout that."

"Could you tell me about any of the legends?"

"No."

"I'm very interested." Silence. "Could you tell me about the changes you have seen on the reservation in your lifetime?"

"Nothing tell."

"When you were a girl you must have traveled by horseback. Is that how you traveled?"

"Men ride. Squaw walk."

"Do you remember seeing your first automobile?"

Grandma feebly shook her head.

"Airplane? Do you remember what you thought when you saw your first airplane? What about that Russian shot into space this morning?"

Grandma started to speak, her voice was slow and throaty, like a Cat engine trying to crank over on a cold morning. "White man take land. Say go reservation, take care us." Her old voice changed and began to screech, "Lies! Lies!" Then all was quiet for a moment, until she began again, this time very softly, whispering, "We should have made white man kill us. Kill us, all. No more talk. You go away."

★ ★ ★

Shadow dropped over the edge of the hill and started down the sharp pitch of the side hill. Pokey wedged his hat on tight, mashed the balls of his feet against the stirrups and extended them out in front, ready to absorb some of the shock and yet prepared to kick loose in case of a wreck. He leaned way back, one arm extended over his head for balance and the other held close to his body, clutching a fistful of reins. The loose pumice soil gave way beneath the hard charging paint and they slid, picking up speed as they went downhill. Bull pine and rocky outcroppings flashed in his peripheral vision. A cloud of fine pumice dust rolled and seethed around him. For this moment of near free-fall he was unchained from natural laws. Gravity did not exist. The normal cadence of breathing and heartbeats was lost. His body tingled with the stimulation of living in the moment, for the moment. A wayward thought occurred to Pokey, that it was possible to live an entire lifetime in the span of seconds it took to get from the top of the ridge to the bottom, and the person living that life would not feel shortchanged in the least.

Just when it seemed this descent might go on forever, it was over. They were at the bottom of the incline and shooting from the miasma like a rocket hurtling through the smoke and fire of the launch pad.

Pokey allowed Shadow to run across the flat for a distance but finally reined him in to an easy lope. As the narcotic of speed and danger seeped away, Pokey was left acutely aware of a single and overwhelming fact—nothing of this land belonged to him. Not anymore.

Fourteen

The Klamath reservation varied from the verdant green of the heavily timbered ridges, ideal for late summer and early fall grazing, to open hillsides cut by bald-faced canyons. The canyons spilled out onto sage-brush flats where the predominant colors were soft pastels and the grass grew early and burned off fast.

Dallas had worked this range since he was a boy. He knew it by heart. He herded his truck down the rutted road. A line of dust slithered behind like a long yellow snake. As each passing mile put distance between himself and the rest of the world, the hard lines at the corners of his eyes seemed to ease a little.

He thought back to the telephone call, when Shasta had said she wanted to come to Chewaucan. It had caught him off guard and he had felt like she backed him into a corner. And yet she was not to blame. He had made the offer, inviting her to stay at the ranch. But really, what else could he have done? How was he supposed to know his daughter was all grown up and had become a carbon copy of her mother, and that the pain he felt when she was around was almost too much to bear?

She had come home to write a paper on termination. But she could never see things like they were, really were. See how the damn government was taking it all away and hamstringing his cattle operation. The Forest Service would be lord of the manor. They would stretch fences where no fences were needed, establish grazing allotments and put them up for public bid. Operators with pockets a whole lot deeper than Dallas's would simply outbid him. They would overgraze the range, would have to in order to make it pay, and the grass would turn to crap. Dallas had purposely kept the grazing down and tried to preserve the delicate balance of nature. Some newcomer wouldn't care a good goddamn about that. Oh, the range might survive a year or two but along would come a drought and the grass would die. Try feeding a cow sagebrush and sand.

He parked on a high point and got out, sat on the crooked front bumper of his truck and allowed his gaze to follow a barbed wire fence that chased infinity. He saw clusters of cows circling an isolated salt and mineral lick and drinking from a rusty water tank. The sun slid behind a bank of clouds, touching their feathery edges with brilliant shades of gold and red and orange that seemed to catch fire and burn with the same powerful intensity as the sun. The wind began to blow from out of the west, carrying with it a strong suggestion of rain.

Another time Dallas might have broken out his jug, watched evening draw a curtain over the land and the Milky Way pour starlight across the sky, but he felt a desire to go home. He owed it to his daughter to spend time with her. He stalled for a minute more, drew in a deep breath and tasted the pungency of the sage on his tongue. He walked back to the pickup door and paused to pet his dog. The dog was a willing listener. "Can you believe the government gave 'em the huntin' and fishin' rights. Ain't nothin' but a foot in the door. Hell, once those rights are exercised, the Indians control every damn drop of water that flows across what used to be the reservation. Dry year comes along, push comes to shove, an' some city judge who doesn't know diddly-squat about the real world is gonna rule in favor of the Indians. He'll suspend grazin' an' shut off irrigation water ta all the farmers downstream. Do that an' those thousands of acres of homestead ground in the lower basin, all lake bottom an' some of the finest farm ground in the world, is gonna dry up and blow away. Sure as shit, that's exactly what's gonna happen. When it does, there's likely ta be an uprisin'. You can't take away a farmer's right ta make a living an' expect him not ta put up a mighty stiff fight.

"We'd be better off ta stand up and fight the Indians right now. Kick their butts once an' for all like we should've done a hundred years ago. Get it over with. Otherwise, it's gonna come back ta haunt us all. Sure as hell, it will."

The dog whimpered. Dallas scratched him behind his ears. "Cougar always come out right 'fore a storm. Gets 'em movin'. If you was a hound dog, we'd go chase ourselves a cat an' run him up a tree."

★　★　★

Lefty cradled his wine jug and advanced onto the porch where he could see the river best. He took a drink and looked over the top of the hill where spiteful clouds threatened the afternoon sun. A raven traversed the sky laughing its hard and jaded laugh. Lefty thought that if the old woman heard the raven she would believe it was K'mukamtch, the creating spirit of the Klamaths and all living things. It would be K'mukamtch merely assuming the form of a raven. Now that termination had ended the existence of the Klamath Indians, what would become of K'mukamtch? Lefty told himself he would ask the old woman next time he saw her. Maybe he should walk over the bridge and visit her. He used to be friends with her husband, Sam. "Hell, that was a long time ago."

The sun slid down a long slot in the clouds and tucked itself in behind the Cascade Range. Clouds wheeled and clashed and before long a gentle shower began, soon maturing to an intense rain that collided against the shingled roof of Lefty's shack. Back in the hills the deluge would soon claw at the timbered ridges and run off into the gullies and draws. Lefty knew that before morning the Chewaucan would be on the rise, the current swirling with the brown clods of soil it had ripped loose and the surface of the river flecked with yellow foam like sweat on a horse after a good, long run.

Lefty was feeling depressed and sorry for himself. He despised his feeble, infirm body. It was nothing more than a pile of brittle bones and rickety joints that hurt all the time. He told himself he drank to control the pain but that was only part of it; he also drank to tame the ghosts. He took another drink and concentrated on the beating of his heart and the quiet rustle of blood coursing through his arteries. The arteries were deteriorating—the pump was wearing out. He knew it. Knew that the little episode the week before last, when blue-white electricity flashed behind his eyes, was a small stroke. A stroke that left him mostly the same, except that he could no longer read.

Inside on the table was an overflowing ashtray, a pencil that had been sharpened with a pocketknife and a book lying open. One of Lefty's lasting true pleasures had been reading two-bit westerns. The kind where there was a bad guy, a pretty girl and the hero always won. But those days were over, the print no longer held still, letters squirmed and wiggled without respect to words and lines and paragraphs. This upset Lefty more than anything, except maybe power saws. He muttered to himself, "Ain't it hell gettin' old," and managed to massage some feeling back into his left arm, the one he hurt when the widow-maker shattered it his last year in the woods. That was the accident that gave him his nickname. Before that he was Lloyd. Hell's bells, if he wanted to, he could have been the best damn one-armed faller there ever was. He tested the bum arm by opening and closing his fist, muttering, "It ain't like it's completely useless."

He rolled himself a smoke. Sure, he could go to the doctor and the doctor would tell him all the things he did not want to hear: quit drinking, give up cigarettes, eat well-balanced meals, get more sleep, exercise. Follow the doctor's advice and what—live another year, five years, ten? Who the hell cared? For all it mattered he could have been killed in WWI, like most of the rest of 'em in his company. What did it matter that he was allowed to live, that he was granted a pardon, while so many others had died. And what did he do with his gift of time? After the war he squandered the remainder of his youth and his middle-aged years cutting a wide swath through the pine forests of the

Northwest. All he got was old and crippled and used up. He knew time was to blame. Time had reduced him to a tinker toy body controlled by a scrambled-egg brain. It took him several tries before he could keep the match burning long enough to light his cigarette.

A wet wind blew the length of the porch and Lefty blamed it on the devil, blamed it on the booze and resigned himself to suffer in his personal hell, groping with ghosts, knowing in his heart the sad reality that man no longer logged the forest, machinery did, and the real loggers had all but died off. He was a senseless, bewildered, crippled-up old man. Piss on it all.

"Hey," he suddenly called out.

He hollered to hear the echo, the sound of another human voice. He had been shouting for so many years that this time he forgot the echo was his own and it surprised him. He went inside, leaving wet footprints across the worn linoleum, and flopped down on the couch. Dust rose up and drifted in pale light.

So, just when was the big jolt going to come? He thought about that a lot lately. He waited for it. Anticipated it. Would it kill him outright or only make him suffer more? Warm, salty tears began slithering down his weathered face.

He found himself crying often these days and was not sure if it was alcohol, or unhappiness, or a combination of the two. Christ on a crutch. If there were a merciful God he would take him right now. He did not want to wait around and die like his father had. The old man had lived way too long. There near the end, Lefty's mother had had to put diapers on him and dab drool from his mouth like he was a goddamn baby. All the old man could do was sit, stare and make whiny noises like a puppy needing to be let out or fed. Lefty went to see him once when he was like that. Never went back.

Since his stroke Lefty had seriously contemplated cashing in. He thought the right way to do it would be to go up in the mountains and take a long walk on a cold night. He would go to sleep and never feel a thing. A time or two in his life he had been almost that cold and sleep became a seducer. Not that unpleasant a way to go. But spring had come and the weather had turned warm. There was not a snowball's chance in hell he was going to freeze.

He could kill himself if he got his old pickup running—it had not been started for more than a year, ever since the state failed to renew his driver's license. The '37 Chevrolet had been a reliable rig. He planned to drive it to the top of the hill, come off the grade and run into the cliff, or steer head-on into a log truck. He went as far as buying a new battery, but even then the tired old pickup would not fire. Forget that.

Lefty had actually tried to do himself in. It was the night he was jumped and robbed on the way home from The Tavern. Three men had taken what was left of his measly social security check. He knew who they were, and instead of settling the score, as he vowed to do, he used the sharp point of his pocketknife to prick a vein on his forearm. He took a small vial of cyanide, bought to kill a family of pack rats that had taken up residence in his woodshed, and it would have been easy to pour the cyanide into the open wound and wait the few seconds it required for the powerful poison to reach his heart. Easy. But he passed out before he finished the job.

"You're born, live, get old, die. That's all there is to it. Don't matter what them preacher types tell you about how swell heaven is or how horrible roasting in the fires of damnation might be. Don't believe none of that bullshit. You die and it ends, just like unplugging a light. Stop the juice and the light quits shining. Simple."

Lefty tipped the bottle to drink but the bottle was empty. He stood, went out into the night and in disgust heaved the bottle toward the river. He heard it hit the bank and bounce, splashing into the roily water. He never saw the whirlpool suck it down, leaving a trail of bubbles behind, bubbles that popped and left no trace they were ever there.

He went to the woodshed, gathered an armload of wood and built a fire in the stove. The only light in the room was wavering yellow firelight coming from the open door. Flames leaped up the chimney and pushed sparks out the top to twinkle like tiny stars before being gobbled up by the big, black, wet night.

There was no conscious thought that went into it, no planning, no preparation. The pistol was simply in his hands, a little .22 caliber Colt Woodsman with a four-and-a-half-inch barrel. He had used it for several years when he was running a trap line. One quick shot between the eyes, or behind the ear, and there was no fight from the raccoon, coyote, or the occasional bobcat. The unyielding barrel touched his lips. The metal was cold and smelled of Hoppe's number 9 powder solvent. To an outdoorsman like Lefty, it was one of the most sentimental fragrances in the land and yet he did not falter. Hallucinations. Luminous trees and screaming nocturnal shapes came rushing at him. Very clearly the lifeline connecting him to the world rup-tured. There would be no more loneliness, depression, pain. The point had been reached where it was too late to avoid the finality as scorching heat sent twisted metal on a clean path through his brain. He jerked the trigger. But the firing pin dropped on an empty chamber.

Realizing what he had done, how close he had come to ending his life and failing at even this final act of salvation, caused Lefty to start shaking and wheezing and that led to a coughing jag that ran away, as his coughing sometimes did, and he could not draw a breath. He got sick to his stomach and finally had to stumble over to the sink and get a drink of water. That helped. And then he went back, sat there in the vomit-scented room, rolled a cigarette, smoked it and stared hard at the flames in the stove.

When the fire had been reduced to nothing more than a pile of glowing embers Lefty shrugged on his coat, shoved the pistol in his pocket, walked uptown to the Chewaucan Grocery and traded it to Steve Atwood for a bottle of Red Mountain wine.

★   ★   ★

The red Corvette blasted through the long shadows of evening, and despite spitting rain and a nip to the air, the top remained down. Mark Dinning was singing *Teen Angel* on the radio, and Creek sang along: "Are you somewhere up above and am I still your own true love." Despite the tragedy of the lyrics Creek thought this moment, right now, was the happiest of his life. He told himself that.

"You lucky bastard," he squawked to the wind and the wind whisked the words away as though it were embarrassed he had uttered them. Creek had everything he wanted: the car, money in his pocket, and more money in the bank. He jerked the wheel back and forth, playing like the yellow stripes on the black road were gates on a slalom course. He gulped down the last of his beer, veered toward a sign warning "curve" and pitched it, turning to watch the graceful arc of the reflective brown bottle until it disappeared in the night. A fraction of a second later came the sharp crack of glass exploding against metal.

"Chalk it up," Creek laughed, "a new international record, five in a row." He told himself he was having fun. He reached to the open case on the passenger's seat, grabbed another beer, and when he looked up, the road swung left but he was going way too fast to make the corner and he jabbed for the brake, stopping the reflex to mash it, do that, he thought, and they clean you up with a spoon. Pump the pedal. Dump the speed. Tires whined in protest. Creek searched to find that delicate groove of control in the flatness of the unforgiving pavement. G-force tugged at him. The rear end of the Corvette shimmied and threatened to break loose. Creek's brain told him the only chance was to pour the coal to her and hope she could pull herself out. Creek was grinning and he knew this was the only way to fly—guts, muscle, and roaring rpms.

The Corvette shot around the corner and onto the straightaway. Creek was laughing in his high-pitched cackle and felt ten feet tall, as powerful as Superman; but a mile down the road the hot sweat cooled, leaving him weak and feeling puny. He stopped, got out and walked around to the front of his car. He stood in the light of a single headlight, the other had broken going through the showroom window, and for a moment Creek was swept away in remorse. This was the car of his dreams and he had damaged it. It also occurred to him that he did not hold title to the Corvette. He would have to go back to the dealership, and when he did they might want more money, or they could press charges, have him arrested and take away his car. He unzipped his pants and pissed on the center line.

Coming into Chewaucan, Creek missed a throw at the "Green River Ordinance Strictly Enforced" sign, erected to limit home solicitation from any traveling salesmen dumb enough to venture onto the reservation. He raced across the cattle guard, white stripes painted on black asphalt, and took his right foot off the gas pedal. The damned reservation never seemed to change—same shacks, same piles of garbage and wrecked cars that he remembered. And then the thought hit him: "Hey, hold it. Everything's different. This is just a town, like Monroe or Mapleton, or Elmira. Just another goddamn town." A quick shudder raced up his spine and he might have been a tad distraught, but it passed quickly when he remembered Chief. Had he gotten out of jail? Creek decided to forgo The Tavern and shoot straight home. He could either grab his duffel and go, or stay for a while and party. The river place was where the big celebration would be going on. Everyone getting together. Be wild and woolly tonight. A quick beer or two and he would be on his way.

Fifteen

After dinner Dallas, Dolly and Shasta sat in the front room and watched President Kennedy's live press conference on the console television. The President occasionally fingered papers on the lectern and spoke with a somber tone like a losing coach speaking to a group of disgruntled fans. His speech was brief and to the point. He called the Russian triumph of space a most impressive scientific achievement, "one that all humans can admire."

As soon as the press conference concluded, Dallas flipped off the television, returned to his chair and began thumbing through the Klamath Falls *Herald and News* classified section. He was trying to get a handle on the worth of some of his haying implements, just in case the government forced him out of business. Dolly and Shasta went to the kitchen to finish up the dishes. Dallas could hear them out there talking but could make out only a few words. Goddamn, he probably needed a hearing aid. He went back to reading.

After the dishes were washed Dolly pulled the plug and began to peel off her pink latex gloves. She said, "Too bad she wouldn't talk to you."

Shasta reached for a plate. It was still warm through the thin towel. She began drying the plate. "I really wanted to get her perspective. Find out what she thought about termination."

"Don't take it personal. Most Indians won't talk, especially the older ones. Guess they don't trust white people. If one of her grandsons was around, maybe." Dolly was interrupted by lights coming up the drive and called to Dallas, "You expectin' anyone?" She moved to the doorway and repeated herself.

"Floyd said he and Tillie might stop if they got home from town early enough."

Dolly, hands on her hips, directed an icy glare at Dallas. "Wish you'd said something. I could have fixed up a special dessert."

"No big deal."

★   ★   ★

Floyd and Tillie sat on the sofa drinking Pepsi-Cola. Floyd said to Shasta, "Been a while. Last time I saw you, you were about so tall." He held his hand about three and a half feet off the floor. He grinned. "You're the spitting image of your momma." He meant it as a compliment because he had always liked Kay, but Dallas reacted by jerking his head in Floyd's direction and Dolly turned away as if wounded.

Floyd said to Dallas, "Saw a few of your calves. Look good. Strong. Healthy."

Dallas nodded. "Yep, doin' fine."

Floyd once again spoke to Shasta. "Dal says you're writing a piece on termination."

"I am."

"Strictly for school or hoping to have it published?"

"Mainly school. Both I guess." Dallas had mentioned to her in passing that Floyd and Tillie might come over sometime and it would be good for her to get their take on things. He said Floyd knew more about Indian history than the Indians did.

"What kind of information you interested in?" Floyd asked.

"I'm going in with an open mind, not limiting myself to facts that will prove a certain point of view. I want to tell the story about termination and its effect on the people."

"So far, what have you learned?"

Shasta leaned toward Floyd. "I've learned there is a lot more to it than I ever considered. Termination affects not only the present, but also the future and the past. It's like a wave washing across the reservation and beyond, touching so many lives, Indian and white alike. It even touches Dad." She had not called Dallas Dad in years and saying that word made her all the more aware that she and Floyd were not the only two people in the room.

Floyd nodded. He was not of Indian blood but he was married to a tribal member and to him that was the same as being Indian. When he spoke, it was with an intensity and passion normally reserved for the square dance floor. "The important thing to remember is that the government has terminated us. We never asked to be terminated. They pushed for it and over a number of years succeeded in driving wedges between the various factions of the tribe. Divide and conquer. That's how the government won this war and they never fired a shot."

Floyd turned to Tillie. "Hon, tell them about the treaty. Tillie's grandfather was one of the chiefs who put his mark on the treaty."

Tillie was a big woman, her features were muted under pounds of surplus flesh, but she retained an implicit attractiveness. When she spoke, her words were delivered with a slow, steady cadence. She said, "It was fall of the year. The aspen and cottonwood were turning color. The Klamath, Modoc and some of the Snake Indians were camped at Council Grove, near where the Agency is now. There were a thousand Indians. The soldiers came from up north and the cavalry regiment was sent from Fort Klamath.

"A group of twenty-seven chiefs and sub-chiefs met in the grove. Huntington, he was superintendent of Indian Affairs for the state of Oregon, spoke first. His words were interpreted for the Indians. He said what the boundaries of the reservation would be, what the government would do. And then each of the chiefs spoke and when they were done they made their mark on the treaty. That was October 14, 1864." It was obvious that Tillie had recited only the facts as she knew them.

Floyd spoke again. "Basically the Klamaths relinquished twenty million acres of land in exchange for peace with the white man, a million-acre reservation and other considerations such as addressing medical needs, food, blankets, clothing. Those promises were never kept. The reservation was to be set aside as Indian land for all time and no white man was to take up residence there. Every last promise has been broken. I've got an extra copy of the treaty. I'll give it to you before you leave.

"One of those who made his mark that day was Keintepoos, a Modoc who the whites called Captain Jack. The

Modocs were a faction of the Klamaths who had split away. They were blood enemies. Putting them on a single reservation was a critical mistake, a terrible injustice to both tribes. But for several years they were able to live side by side as neighbors. Then the Modocs left the reservation and returned to their homelands along Lost River. Settlers had taken up residence there and conflicts between the races triggered the Modoc War, which lasted more than six months and involved a ragtag band of fewer than fifty warriors successfully holding off the U.S. Seventh Cavalry. The military suffered a great number of losses including the death of General Edward Canby, the only United States general ever killed in the line of duty. The tribe could not remain hidden in that forlorn wasteland of the Lava Beds forever, and eventually the Modocs were forced to surrender. Six tribal members were tried before a military court. I might add they were tried without benefit of council. All were found guilty. Two had their sentences commuted to life imprisonment at Alcatraz Island. But Captain Jack, along with three of his sub-chiefs, were hanged at Fort Klamath on October 3, 1873. The remaining Modocs were exiled to Oklahoma."

Dallas interrupted, "You're gettin' sidetracked, Floyd."

When it came to recounting the history of the Klamath nation Floyd would often lose the main topic and meander aimlessly down interesting side trails. He now made a conscious effort to limit his diatribe to the Klamaths who had remained on the reservation. He said that in addition to giving up the majority of their land they were forced to give up their way of life.

"The white man said the Indian religion, based on the supernatural powers of the shaman, was wrong. It was replaced with Christianity. A medical doctor began treating the sick with medicine. Men were not allowed to travel, to hunt, fish, or go to war as they had before. They were forced to tend livestock and grow crops. Families were split apart; the children were taken away and educated at boarding schools two hundred miles away in the Willamette Valley. The wickiups were burned. Houses were built. The tribe's social fabric was ripped apart. The Indian agent, backed up by a garrison of cavalry troops, became the supreme authority figure. His decisions were final and could not be questioned.

"Ever since the reservation was established it has been chipped away at—land was stolen through faulty surveys and for public easements. Then in the 1920s the Congress passed a law allowing reservation Indians to take title to lands on the reservation that they occupied. What resulted was wide-scale sale of those lands. Dallas, maybe you can add a little to this part."

"You're doing a fine job."

"You might tell how your father picked up his first hundred and sixty acres."

"That's not important."

"Yes it is. You've bragged to me that it cost him two bottles of watered-down whiskey. Am I right?"

Dallas crossed his arms defensively. "That's the way business was conducted in those days. All the land I bought I paid fair market value, in cash. You've gotta remember, back a few years ago no white man in his right mind wanted ta live on the reservation."

Floyd continued, "That law fractured the reservation into lots owned by individual Indians and whites alike. And then in the 1950s, during the Eisenhower administration, the general policy was to 'get out of the Indian business.' Individual tribes were enticed with promises of money to vote themselves out of existence.

"The wording the Klamath tribe voted on was ambiguous at best. If a tribal member was casting a vote in favor of termination he checked a box, and I quote from memory, 'Termination of federal supervision over the trust and restricted property of the Klamath Tribe of Indians . . . for the disposition of federally-owned property acquired or withdrawn for the administration of the affairs of said Indians, and for a termination of federal services furnished such Indians because of their status as Indians.' That was what they voted on. What in the heck does that say? Tribal members thought they were voting to get the federal government off their backs. They wanted to keep getting their per capita payments, about fifteen hundred to twenty-five hundred a year, for the reservation timber that was sold and processed into lumber at the reservation mill. They sought control over their lands, self-determination and the right to harvest their natural resources as they saw fit. Representatives of the federal government promised if they voted for termination they would get a substantial settlement. As an added inducement, the Klamath people were to retain all customary hunting and fishing rights on the historical reservation lands. Some tribal leaders spoke out in favor of termination. I don't know if they were taking cash payoffs from the government, but I suspect some of them might have been. And what is the government going to do with that land? Turn it into a national forest, harvest the timber and the money will flow into the government's coffer."

"How many are entitled to the money?" Shasta asked.

Floyd nodded. "Interesting point. Of the sixteen hundred

sixty on the rolls about seven hundred are minors. Their money will be put in trust and when they turn twenty-one they can draw that money out. That is, they can draw it out if any money remains in their accounts. The system is rife with corruption. Lawyers will take a cut for administering the trusts, as will the bankers. There are no checks and balances. The administrators of the trusts have the final say as to how much they will charge for the supervision of those trusts.

"Of the remaining members almost half have been determined to be incompetent. Individual trustees, approved by the Bureau of Indian Affairs, will manage their money. They will find themselves in the same boat as the minors. The lawyers and bankers will steal the bulk of the money and in most cases it will all be perfectly legal because that is the way the white man conducts his business. It is permissible to steal from someone if you have the law on your side.

"With that said, it boils down to this: probably no more than three hundred individuals will get the money with no strings attached. They will be able to buy cars and houses, equipment, land. Or they can blow it all on booze and good times. It is strictly up to them and their discretion.

"Once the money has been disbursed, the Secretary of the Interior will issue a proclamation announcing, in effect, that the Klamath people no longer exist in any legal sense. And the federal government will have broken yet another promise it made to the Indian."

"Jesus Christ," exclaimed Dallas. "Quit your bellyaching. You went to town, cashed the check and pocketed the forty-three grand. Open your eyes, Floyd. You made off like a bandit."

"No matter what I say, you'll never understand the

gravity of termination. The devastation this has caused will continue for generations."

"Hell's bells. Ya didn't come here until after the war. Ya married into the tribe. Here in America we're all suppose ta be equals. What makes ya think you're entitled ta more than me?"

Floyd completely ignored Dallas. He said to Tillie, "Come on, hon, it's getting late. We best be going."

★ ★ ★

The dogs milled around Pokey as he leaned against one of the support posts on the front porch. He was nursing a Pepsi, listening to the music and watching through the window as shadowy figures stirred around in a boozy cloud of smoke. They were entwined like a ball of snakes coming out of a long season of hibernation, moving slow and lethargic. They were drinking, grumbling, cursing, wrestling and taking turns pouring bourbon, wine and beer on each other's crotches. Laughing, giggling, shrieking.

Pokey felt like one of those snakes, but a snake that was in the process of shedding his outer skin and adding a new one. He was not drinking, and would not be tempted to drink, even though tonight was the start of the party to end all parties. It would last as long as there was money. And when the party was over there would be no more: no per capita payments, no subsidized housing, no medical or dental benefits, no surplus food, no college tuition for students who might want to attend school, no more handouts of any kind. No tribal status. No independent nation. No land. They were losing it all.

★ ★ ★

Ah-ooga! Ah-ooga! Ah-ooga! The noise wailed from the direction of the bridge, and a few seconds later crazy headlights scampered, dipped, ducked and reflected off puddles and standing water to send arrows of light dancing through the trees. *Ah-ooga!* somehow discovered a path between haphazardly parked cars, brand-new cars fresh off showroom floors, and *Ah-ooga!* squeezed through narrow openings, dragging with it a sleek, bloodred 1959 Cadillac Eldorado convertible. Ragtop down. Fins tall and flashy. White sidewalls splashed with mud.

Ah-ooga! Ah-ooga! Ah-ooga! Chief behind the wheel, head flopping side to side like a chub working a bobber as it nibbles the bait. Chief holding a champagne bottle at arm's length and pouring the contents over himself, bubbles cascading onto the white leather of the Eldorado. The radio amplifying the nasal twang of Larry Verne singing his novelty tune about a soldier's comical plea to avoid having to go into battle against the 3,000 Sioux warriors loyal to Chief Sitting Bull: ". . . I had a dream last night, about the upcomin' fight . . . there I stood with an arrow in my back. Please Mr. Custer, I don't wanna go. Forward, ho—"

Partygoers spilled outside as if the house had suddenly caught fire. Chief grabbed bottles of liquor from the back seat of the Cadillac and nonchalantly tossed them in the air toward the milling crowd. Men and women fell all over themselves in their haste to claim one of the prizes. Chief picked out Pokey, standing off to one side, and shouted, "Come on, I'll take ya fer a ride."

Pokey walked to the car, opened the passenger door and climbed aboard. Creek came on the dead run, dove onto the wide back seat just as Chief threw the Cadillac into gear. Spinning tires splattered mud on the depraved pile of humanity still fighting over the bottles. The Cadillac carved a wide loop across the marshy area below the house, kicking up a tremendous rooster tail before returning to the road, just in the nick of time, floating up and over the bridge.

Ah-ooga! Ah-ooga! Ah-ooga!

Chief threw back his head and laughed. "Had 'em put that horn on special." He backed off coming through town, explaining, "Don't wanna spend no more time 'n jail, ain't it."

"I called. They said you were out," Creek lied.

"Poke, what ya think 'bout my car, aye."

"Nice."

"Ain't much ta say."

"Guess I never figured you'd buy a Cadillac."

Chief laughed. "Said I would. Never owned one 'fore. Went 'n' did it. Easy as pullin' a trigger. Got the one with the biggest fins. All I wanna do is ride 'round in a showboat with the top down. Paid thirty-nine hundred. Wipe-ass money. Gave 'em the Impala. It was beat ta shit anyway. What kinda car ya get, Poke?"

Pokey shrugged. "Never made it to town."

"What the 'ell?"

"I got a 'vette," Creek said from the back seat.

"Squeak, nobody pulled yer goddamn chain. Shut the fuck up."

As they sped through the night Pokey tried to comprehend why Chief would feel compelled to buy a Cadillac. He grasped the basic philosophy: a Cadillac was a symbol, solid proof that its owner had attained a material milestone of exaggerated splendor, shouting to the world that he had reached the top of the heap. He supposed it was for the same reason Elvis, when he made his first splash in the big time, splurged on a pink Cadillac. And when Elvis got filthy rich he bought Cadillacs by the dozens, gave them away to family and friends and once even tipped a Cadillac to an especially cute waitress at an all-night diner.

Chief's red Cadillac slashed through the black night, headlights illuminated flashes of stately pine trees, shiny-leafed manzanita and the occasional jackrabbit that dashed across the road in front of them. Chief tried to run over the rabbits, jerking the wheel left and right, always missing, until he found one that became confused and did not know which way to turn. Pokey felt it hit and lifted himself up in the seat as the rabbit thumped against the metal under him. In the side mirror a blur of soft fur rolled in the glow of the amber tail lights.

They reached the top of the grade and Chief pulled over at a wide spot. He turned off the engine but left the lights on. And while he and Creek relieved themselves, Pokey sat in the quiet and heard coyotes, so far away their barking sounded like the thin yapping of puppies. Crickets added to the treble and bullfrogs to the bass. Music of the night.

It began to rain again but Chief did not bother to raise the top, and when he got back inside he kicked the transmission into gear and hunched over the wheel so that he was mostly out of the wind and rain. The dash lights illuminated his brown eyes, hazed by alcohol, and they were delirious and ruthless.

Chief drove until the high beam reflected a pair of yellowish-green embers, tiny luminous planets floating in a great black void. As the Cadillac braked, the ghost image of a deer, with a basket of velvet antlers crowning his head, became visible standing a hundred yards up the road.

Before the car had stopped Chief was reaching under the seat, bringing out a model 94 Winchester 30-30. He kicked open the door, got one foot on the ground, and leveled the short-barreled saddle rifle at the buck. It stood broadside, blinded by the bright headlights. Chief took a quick gulp of air and held it as his index finger curled. Pokey shuddered ever so slightly and looked away. A terrible surge of fire spit from the end of the barrel followed by a deafening report. The reflective eyes collapsed inward and disappeared.

"You got 'im. Good shot," squealed Creek from the back seat.

Chief jacked the lever, advancing a fresh round into the chamber, eased the hammer down into the safety position and tucked the rifle back under the seat. With the door still open he drove until he was within a few feet of the buck and, without touching the brake, he slammed the transmission into park. He called for a drink. Creek handed him a bottle of bourbon. Chief cracked the seal and drank while the deer, in the throes of death, flopped around, kicking violently with its hind legs. The buck was having a hard time dying. Chief slid off the seat, dug around in his pocket for his knife and when he found it he opened the blade, stepped over the deer, grabbed one of the majestic antlers, leaned down and with a quick, well-practiced swipe he cut the deer's throat. Bloody froth and air gushed from the severed jugular and windpipe. The deer gave a final few spasmodic kicks and lay still.

Pokey stood in the glare of the headlights. His hands were shoved in his pockets and he watched Chief's knife slice open the deer's hide and underbelly, exposing the paunch and curled intestines. They should be colored grayish-white but under the harsh headlights they looked almost blue.

Every time Pokey shot a deer he always felt remorseful. He tried to imagine the animal at birth, in the protection of a thicket; imagine all the deer must have gone through in its life to reach this point, the bad winters with little food, running to escape forest fires, outwitting predators; imagine the last few hours that would bring it on a collision course with his bullet. He performed the same ritual when he caught a steelhead or salmon, visualizing life in the ocean, avoiding sea lions and seals, imagining various rapids that stretched from the ocean to the upriver spawning grounds. He figured the least he owed the living spirit was a few quiet moments of reflection. But Chief, blood up to his elbows, seemed to savor, even relish the slick tactile sensation as he cut loose the entrails and pulled them onto the edge of the roadway. A thin wisp of vapor rose from the pile into the dank night air. Chief straightened, waved the knife and the deer's heart overhead and went crazy, kicking the carcass, raging, "Who's king of the forest? I am, ain't it, I am."

Pokey grunted and turned away. He walked up the road in the dark. For the life of him he could not figure out why Chief acted the way he did. The only excuse he could think of was that Chief had been born in the wrong era. He belonged back in history, in a time when the very survival of the tribe had rested on the shoulders of the most brutal and savage warriors. If he had lived in that time Chief would have been respected, honored, perhaps even proclaimed a real chief. But in the last half of the twentieth century he was nothing more than a bully, a criminal and a contemptible drunk.

Pokey recalled a story Grandma told, about the time a group of miners from the Rogue River country went looking for gold on the flank of Mount McLoughlin. They were attacked by Indians and several miners were killed. When the survivors returned to Jacksonville, word was sent to Chief La Lakes of the Klamath tribe that the guilty parties must be brought to the settlement to stand trial. La Lakes promised that justice would be served. Several days passed before an envoy of Klamath warriors appeared in Jacksonville. They were dressed in buckskin, strips of red cloth were braided in their hair and their faces were daubed with paint. They carried something wrapped in a blanket, suspended between two poles. The miners thought the chief had sent them a gift, a bribe that would allow the guilty to go free. But when the braves lowered the poles three Indian heads rolled onto the ground. One of the Indians spoke, "La Lakes keep word." And the warriors departed.

Chief dragged the deer, hair and velvet antlers scraping on the asphalt, to the back of the Cadillac. He opened the trunk, lifted the two hundred pounds, tossed the carcass into the wide trunk, twisting the head around so it fit, and slammed the lid shut. He went to the roadside ditch, where he washed his hands and arms in the muddy water, wiping them dry on his pants. He slid behind the wheel. The Cadillac made a U-turn, spurted forward, stopped, Pokey climbed in and away they went. A coyote stuck his nose into the wind and followed the scent toward a free meal.

★ ★ ★

Marg answered the telephone on the second ring, listened for a few seconds and replied, "He's right here. I'll let you speak to him." Covering the mouthpiece with the palm of her hand she turned to Red and told him, "It's the sheriff. He wants to talk to you."

Red took one last bite of mashed potatoes and gravy, laid

the spoon aside, wiped at the corners of his mouth with a paper napkin and went to the phone.

"What can I do for you, Sheriff?"

"We've had a little problem with a couple of your boys. I thought you ought to know about it."

The sheriff did not speak right away and Red felt compelled to ask, "What kind of problem?"

"You know better than me who's poking who, but the way I got it figured, Joe Buck's been throwing the wood to Candy Anderson. After they got their money they were drinking pretty heavy. Joe passed out at the Pastime. Tommy George sees his chance, makes a move and he and Candy have themselves a little roll in the hay. Joe wakes up, finds his gal missing. About that time she comes strolling in with Tommy and they sit together at the bar. Well, Joe goes to his car, comes back with a .44 S&W, six-inch barrel."

There was a long pause and Red asked, "So, what happened?"

"Tommy is sitting on a stool at the bar. Joe walks up, points the pistol level at his head, doesn't say nothing at all, pulls the trigger. Tommy, he either hears something or sees a reflection in the mirror. He throws himself backward off the stool.

"Now Tyler Thompson has been sitting there minding his own business. He's the one who takes it. Bullet in the temple. Hell of a deal."

Again there was a pause. Red was thinking and did not jump right in.

"We got Joe Buck in custody. Figure the grand jury will indict him for manslaughter. Thought you ought to know. One less to worry about. Still there, Red?"

"Yeah, I'm here. Are you sure that's the way it came down, that the accidental shooting ain't some cock and bull?"

"I doubt it, Red. The bartender seen the whole thing. What makes you wonder?"

"Something happened the other day. I didn't think much about it at the time. If I had put any stock in it, I would have let you know right away."

"Tell me."

"There was a vigilante death list posted here in town, names on a sheet of plywood. Three names. Now two of them are dead. Probably just coincidence."

"Probably. Nothing to indicate foul play here. Was the other the car wreck north of town, or am I missing one?"

"That's it. Only thing remotely suspicious was no skid marks. More than likely he passed out and drove off the road. Nothing to worry about but I'll take a look. Make sure the brake line wasn't cut."

"Who you figure put up the sign?"

"I have no idea."

"Let me know if you find out anything. Say, just curious, but who was the third name?"

"Rollin Pitsua. Chief."

"Had him as a visitor in jail a little earlier today. Made bail out of a paper bag full of money. Damnedest thing. Thirty-three grand in a paper sack. He's one big son of a bitch. What do you suppose he goes, six-six, three hundred, maybe a couple beers more?"

"Pretty close."

"Every time he goes on the warpath I have to call in reinforcements. He's got more enemies than brains. For sure. Say, Red, got a joke for you—know the difference between an elephant and a squaw?"

"No idea."

"A bar jacket and about fifteen pounds."

Sixteen

The Chewaucan Grocery was closed. In the adjoining apartment Steve slept in his La-Z-Boy lounger while the television sparkled a vacant test pattern. Debbie, six months and eleven days pregnant, lay awake in bed. She was restless and wanted Steve to join her. Then maybe she could sleep. She got up, walked into the living room, turned off the television, started to awaken Steve and realized she was hungry for something sour and salty.

She stepped into the store. The interior was dark except for an opaque glow from the night light that hung outside on the power pole. A floorboard creaked beneath her pink, furry slippers as she concentrated on her goal, the jars of imported olives, the green ones stuffed with red pimentos. She could almost taste their sharp sourness, and the salty brine.

A shadow, a human form, moved a short distance away, took several awkward strides, paused near the wine rack. Debbie froze. She tried to give the human silhouette a reasonable explanation. When she had turned off the television Steve was in his chair. It would be impossible for him to have gone past her, but Debbie did not listen to the soft voice of reason and called out hopefully, "Steve, that you?"

Nothing—no movement, no sound. An electric motor in one of the coolers kicked on and hummed inharmoniously. Still nothing. But the man shadow remained. Debbie breathed urgently. "Steve." The baby kicked at her tenseness and Debbie crossed her arms over her stomach to protect her unborn child. She took a few blind steps backward. The shadow suddenly moved, reeling toward the door, throwing it open.

"Stop!"

Debbie turned; saw her husband framed in the light from the apartment, arm extended. Fire sprang from his fingertip. A sharp pop bounced off all four walls and echoed against the shelves of canned goods. Debbie saw the shadow lurch, stumble, spin and fall over the threshold.

★   ★   ★

When Red arrived at the Chewaucan Grocery he found the front door wide open. He walked toward the light seeping from the adjoining apartment and was acutely aware of everything; his footfalls resonating against the floor, the residue of burned gunpowder, the fear that hung in the aisle like an angry cloud. Upon entering the apartment the first thing he saw was the small-caliber pistol on the coffee table. Debbie was lying on the couch. Steve was kneeling beside her, holding one of her hands.

"Who got shot?"

The sound of the voice startled Steve and for a fraction of a second Red thought he might make a grab for the pistol.

"Red. God, am I ever glad to see you. Someone broke in. He was trying to rob us."

"And what?"

"I shot him. I had to. Maybe he had a gun. What if he had—"

"Slow down. Start at the beginning. Give me the blow-by-blow. Tell me everything that happened." Red moved closer.

"Debbie was out there alone. He could have killed her."

"Where's the body?"

"I don't know."

"What do you mean, you don't know?"

"It was dark. I told him to stop. I guess I pulled the trigger. It went off. I didn't even know it was loaded."

"You're sure you hit him?"

"I think so. He fell down."

"Did you see anyone else?"

"Yeah, he had accomplices. They took him, carried him off, put him in a car. It had big, round tail lights. That's all I saw."

"What make? What year?"

"I don't know. I wanted to make sure about Debbie."

Debbie continued to sob quietly into a hand towel. Red went to her, leaned down and asked, "Are you all right?"

She nodded. Red turned to Steve, "How many were there?"

"Two, and the one, the one I shot."

"Did he have a gun?"

"I don't know. It was dark."

"Where was he when you fired?"

"Right by the front door."

"I'll take a look." Red stooped to retrieve the pistol.

"You can't take that."

"I have to. It's evidence."

"What if he comes back?"

"He won't."

"Are you sure?"

"Guaranteed. Where'd you get this?"

"I traded for it."

"Traded who?"

"That old logger, Lefty. He wanted to get rid of it."

"Okay. Sure she's all right?"

"You're all right, aren't you, honey?"

Again Debbie nodded but her eyes, like those of a bobcat caught in a leg-hold trap, flickered fear.

Red said, "I'll poke around, see what I come up with."

He pulled the clip from the grip of the .22 Colt Woodsman, slid the action open to remove the live round from the chamber and slipped them into his coat pocket as he moved across the room. Back in the store he clicked on his long-handled flashlight and played the light around the room. On the floor, just inside the front door, the pool of light revealed a few small splatters of something dark. Red dropped to one knee, reached with his left hand and touched one of the drops with the tip of his index finger, testing its consistency between thumb and forefinger. The slick, sticky feel— blood. He wiped it off on his pant leg as he moved onto the landing, following a drop of blood here, a drop there. Down the steps. He lowered himself onto his haunches to examine the evidence. In the wet dirt and loose gravel at the base of the steps were two miniature furrows running parallel for a short distance and then ending.

So: A man was shot. He fell half in and half out of the doorway. Two others carried him away, face down, the toes of his boots scraping the ground. They lifted him into a car. Steve said the car had big, round tail lights. The new Ford Thunderbirds had big, oval tail lights. Maybe an Indian driving a T-Bird.

There was the hollow sound of someone walking on the landing. Steve called out, his voice weak, "Find anything?"

"A little."

"I don't think I killed him. I'm sure I didn't. Did I?"

Red could have told Steve that from the few drops of blood the wound did not appear life threatening. But he did not. It always peeved him when people took the law into their own hands. It was a personal thing, like he was not doing his job or something. And then he relented, "If he's hurt bad he'll show up at the hospital. If not, and I figure it's not, then he'll lay around for a few days like an ol' hound dog got into a bag of poison. Heal up on his own. Either way he won't bother you no more. You made your point."

★ ★ ★

After hanging the deer in the woodshed, and skinning it so the meat would cool quickly, Pokey, Creek and Chief returned to the party. Pokey found a spot out of the way near the stove, slid down the wall and sat on the floor. A heavy-set gal, the butt of a smoking cigarette dangling from a ghastly slash of purple lipstick, scooted near and affixed herself to him like a leech. She pushed an open quart of strawberry wine in his direction. Pokey declined.

"You Klamath?" she demanded.

"Yeah," he told her, not bothering about the white half.

"I'm Paiute." She tried smiling, "How old you think I am?"

Her face was bloated from booze and the party life. Her nose was runny. She was missing several teeth.

"I don't know."

"Come on, guess."

"I can't."

"Come on."

Pokey shook his head.

"Please," she was rubbing his thigh with the hand not clutching the bottle.

"Thirty-seven," he said.

She spit on the floor, "Piss on you. I'm twenty-one."

Pokey stood and moved away from her. He watched bottles make the rounds and breathed in the stench of the cigarette smoke that fouled the air. To his left the door opened, and into this rank assemblage appeared a dark, hulking mass, a wicked-looking woman wearing tennis shoes with no laces and stretched out green sweat pants with gaping holes in the knees. Fat jiggled on the back of her arms. She pushed her face in front of her as if it were a war shield. Her flat nose barely provided a resting spot for dark brown sunglasses. Her expression was dour—no, rancid—and one dreadful scar ran from her scalp across her forehead, through an eyebrow and down one cheek almost to her neck. It was made years ago by the sharp end of a can opener. She wore the disfigurement as a badge of toughness.

Creek saw her coming and tried to step aside, but in his inebriated state he was not quick enough and she shoved him away as she passed. She marched up to Chief, snatched away his bottle of Black Velvet and took a long swig. A few drops dribbled down her chin and onto her sleeveless sweatshirt. She backhanded the dribbles, belched in Chief's face and announced, "Couple guys with me. One of 'em's been shot."

Chief shrugged and took back his fifth. "So, what's that gotta do with me?"

"Maybe Grandma can fix 'im up."

"Don't need no dead men here."

"I'm your mother," Puggy said, and she slugged Chief in the shoulder, a mean knuckle punch.

"Like I need remindin'," Chief told her.

"He ain't dead. Help carry 'im in."

Chief and several others followed Puggy to her blue Thunderbird hardtop coupe. Two men were propped up on the passenger's side. Puggy abruptly opened the door and one of the men fell onto the muddy ground. He groaned, rolled over, got to his feet, but lost his balance and fell into Puggy, knocking her glasses to the ground. She grabbed hold of his arm to steady him. "This here's my old man. Owen. He's Yakima. Been livin' together up ta Toppenish." She smacked the side of his head.

"How come you do that?"

"Felt like it." Puggy nodded in the direction of the man who had fallen over and was lying across the seat. "Get 'im outta there. I don't want 'im bleedin' on the leather no more. Take 'im ta the house."

★   ★   ★

Shasta, relaxed and drowsy from her shower, trod bare-footed down the hallway with a bathrobe covering her and a white towel wrapped around her head. She lowered her-self onto the couch, tucking a leg under her. She removed the towel and began combing out the tangles from the ends of her long, black hair.

Dallas peered at her over the top of his reading glasses. Kay used to do the same thing, comb out her hair in front of him. Dallas closed the newspaper, laid it on his lap, and in a quiet voice, since Dolly had already gone to bed and he did not want her to hear, he asked, "How's your momma doin'?"

"Fine."

Shasta had forced herself to come out and sit with Dallas. If this was what he wanted to talk about, she was sorry she did; then she reprimanded herself, knowing she must work at getting to know her father. No one said it would be easy. She added, "Still working for the state. She wants to put in another eight years and retire."

"I forget. What's she do?"

"Motor vehicle department, license division. The job isn't much fun, I guess, but she likes the people she works with."

"She's probably still a good-lookin' woman."

Shasta had never really considered whether men found her mother attractive but she supposed they did. She nodded.

"How come she never got remarried?"

"I wouldn't know."

"If things had been different . . ."

Shasta felt a pinprick of vindictiveness. "You could have kept in touch." She had wanted to say that for a long, long time.

"Never was much of a letter writer."

"You could have called."

"Maybe so. Well, let me put it like this—I took it kinda personal when she pulled out and took you with her. Then I got remarried. Ain't makin' excuses. That's just the way the ball bounced."

"Any regrets?"

"Not really. We was at each other's throat all the time. She wanted things I just couldn't . . . Ah, hell with it. Water under the bridge." Dallas removed his reading glasses, folded them, and laid them on the stand where he kept his tobacco and papers. He banked the fire in the woodstove, turned and told her, "Well, g'night." For a fleeting instant she thought he might want to give her a kiss, a peck on the cheek, and maybe he did, but if so, he changed his mind.

★ ★ ★

In her dream a fresh limb was tossed on the campfire and sparks flew away like a flock of golden songbirds. A cool wind rustled the aspen leaves and made them whisper. Then the drums began to throb, throats opened to sing and dancers swayed, shuffling their feet, raising dust as they moved, little bells on their buckskin shirts and pants jingling, reinforcing the tempo. Around and around. Faster and faster. They danced until they became a swirl of brown leaves caught in the rising draft of a whirlwind.

Puggy threw open the bedroom door, sending a shaft of intense light toward Grandma. The old woman had difficulty seeing, but she thought the large woman standing over her had brown leaves pushed in where her eyes should be. She thought this was an extension of her dream. Puggy took hold of her shoulders and shook her.

Grandma squinted, finally asked, "Why you come home?"

"Hell of a welcome," Puggy boomed.

"What you want?"

"Friend got shot. Take a look. Fix 'im up."

"How he get shot?"

"Don't matter, ol' woman. Do what I tell ya."

Puggy cleared a path across the front room, shoving people out of her way, to where the wounded man lay sprawled on the floor. Grandma followed behind and when she reached the man she bent over, touched her fingers to his forehead and felt the fever that was beginning to burn within him. She lifted up the tail of his bloody shirt to reveal a purple patch of skin on the side of his abdomen. There was a small-diameter wound in a roll of protective fat. The bleeding had nearly stopped.

Grandma stood and offered, "Take him see doctor."

"No doctor. Do what ya can. Leave it at that."

The frail old woman gathered her shawl around her bony shoulders, tottered back to her bedroom where she rummaged around before finding a small medicine pouch. When she returned to the patient he was awake and Puggy was having him drink from a fifth of Chivas Regal. Grandma waited her turn.

"Hurt much?" Puggy wanted to know.

"Naw," grimaced the man. "Gimme another drink."

Puggy handed him the bottle and moved to the side. Grandma was well practiced at saving people and she went to work, taking pieces of dry leaves from the bag, crumbling them in the palm of her hand and pouring the gray powder onto the wound as she spoke a guttural language in a melodious cadence. As Grandma worked to draw out the poison Puggy paid little attention and continued to drink and talk.

Pokey sat in the far corner, eyes closed, listening to his mother's repulsive voice and the way she used the consonants to squeeze the vowels out of her words. Good became *gd* and money *mny*. Her words chugged along in a singsong chant. When Pokey could no longer stomach the sound of her, he slipped outside into the night. The dogs followed him toward the woodshed. He opened the door and they wanted in to lick at the blood under the deer, but Pokey kicked them out of the way, turned on the light and pulled the door closed. He crossed the room, untied his sleeping bag, lay down on his cot and pulled the bag over himself without bothering to get undressed. He listened to the wind whistle through the slats of the woodshed. It fluttered his drawings and made the bare light swing and shimmy. Shadows swayed. He reached up and pulled the string. The light glowed for an instant more and then the room went dark.

★ ★ ★

Dolly, hair in rollers, was lying in bed reading *Sweet Barbarian*. "Lance rolled his motorcycle to a stop. He looked at her with eyes deep-set, hazel, surrounded by a thicket of bronze-colored lashes. He smiled and it was the warmth of his smile that melted her heart. She would give herself to him willingly but he did not know that, not yet. . . ."

When Dolly heard Dallas banking the fire in the woodstove she closed the book and set it aside, quickly flipping off the lamp. She closed her eyes and listened intently as Dallas quietly opened the door and pulled it closed behind him. She could hear each pop as his cowboy shirt was unsnapped, the rustle of his pants coming off and the clank as his silver buckle came in contact with the hardwood floor. He climbed onto the bed and turned his back to her. She could smell the nicotine and whiskey on his breath. Tears welled up in Dolly's eyes. Dallas never knew.

Seventeen

The party was erupting around, over and through Creek. He took a few weak breaths and the small muscles between his ribs twitched. The arm on the record player lifted and the machine turned itself off. Creek could hear Puggy's voice and wished like hell he could talk. He wanted to thrust words at her knife-like, tell her how much he hated her, and she would take their sharp bite and never feel a twinge of pain or remorse. Creek knew that if he lived to be a hundred he would never possess enough meanness and hostility to pay her back for abandoning her children and allowing herself to become a whore to alcohol.

Puggy kicked Creek in the side, "Hey asshole, ya dead?" Creek did not, could not, answer. Puggy moved on, ignoring Owen, going to Clarence, whom she had known for twenty years. He was sitting on the sofa and was one drink shy of passing out. She flopped down against him, kissed him, drew back and smacked a fist into his chest. The two of them carried on, alternating affection and spite, and after ten or fifteen minutes of this foreplay Puggy dragged Clarence into the boys' bedroom. She flopped on a bed, tugged down her sweat pants and kicked one leg free. Clarence tried to consummate the good time but failed. After a while Puggy gave up, bucked him off, pulled up her pants and returned to the party.

Creek felt sick to his stomach. He pushed himself onto all fours, tottered and then managed to get his feet under him. As soon as he tried to stand he lost his balance and stumbled sideways into a wall. He tumbled through the doorway but managed to catch himself on the porch railing. He leaned over and began vomiting.

Afterward he felt better. He looked up and was aware of all the new cars illuminated by the porch light. He saw his Corvette, moved in that direction. The single thought in his mind was to go, to get away, but he only made it as far as the open door on the driver's side of Chief's Cadillac. He fell backward onto the wide seat and passed out, again.

★　★　★

A shrill whistle, slashing through the night like a whirling ripsaw, announced to all within hearing distance that a small forest of graded lumber from the mill in Bend was approaching the Chewaucan curve. A pair of diesel engines, hooked in tandem, rumbled with power and seemed to growl out the warning, "Get the hell out of my way."

Danger lights winked on and off and Red, stymied by this mechanical monster, sat in his patrol car at the crossing and patiently waited for the train to pass. He poured himself a cup of coffee, took a sip, lit a cigarette and noticed the odometer registered 122,097 miles.

★   ★   ★

Along the river a coyote flushed a pintail from her nest. She left squawking and drumming her wings against her breast. The coyote bit into one of her warm eggs and licked the contents into his ravenous mouth. On the ridge a buck, preparing himself for future battles, rubbed velvet antlers against a sapling. A doe and her twin fawns moved deeper into a thicket. And on the apron of Klamath Lake the wind, a distant cousin of the wind that long ago had blown against the squat wickiups of the Klamath camp, scissored the tall marsh grasses and made the long stems of the cat-tails bow their brown caps and release seeds to the whimsy of the swirling current of air.

★   ★   ★

The music, voices and sounds of unsteady passions, anger and gaiety, crashed and buffeted the river house, rattling the windows, reverberating and leaking out to pulse into the gloomy night. With terrifying clarity a mirror over the kitchen sink reflected the sinuous complexity of the frenzy and the lethargy of the distorted faces.

Puggy took bottles away from those around her. She drank from one. "Whiskey." She stole another. "Vodka." And yet another. "Scotch." When she spoke, her words were delivered with a rhythmic punch, the cadence rolling along almost tunefully. "Drinkin's it." "Whiskey's it." "Booze's it."

★   ★   ★

Creek remained on the exposed front seat of the Cadillac, unaware of the light rain that had begun to fall. He was lost in a dreamless state, drifting along the deep canyons of loneliness and despair.

And then Chief was shouting, "Son of a bitch. Ya stealin' my money!" He was pulling at Creek, manhandling him, trying to drag him out of the car.

Creek fought back, grabbing the steering wheel, hanging on, squealing like a jackrabbit clutched in the spiked talons of an eagle.

Alcohol and anger charged through Chief. His only connection to reality was his distorted and illogical compulsion to protect his paper sack chock-full of money and stuffed under the front seat of the Cadillac. He was so far gone that he could not even distinguish who was trying to steal his money but he was willing to fight, hell, he was willing to die for that money. As he struggled, his hand reached under the seat and pawed around; but instead of his fingers closing around the sack, they wrapped around the stock of the short-barreled 30-30. He pulled the rifle free. And as he did, by habit, he yanked back the hammer with his thumb.

Creek felt a dull stab of pain as the end of the rifle barrel bit into the thin layer of skin stretched over his sternum. His response was to raise a hand, to feebly wave that hand as if it were a white flag. "Don't, don't, don't kill me," he pleaded.

All the brilliant colors in Creek's field of vision became profoundly clear: the light from the porch illuminating the surroundings in a surreal, lactic yellow glow; the cool blue of the rifle barrel; the soft brown of the wooden stock. But the focal point of Creek's vision was the hulking mass above him and, in particular, it was Chief's eyes. They were devoid of any color whatsoever.

All Chief had to do was pull the trigger. And for an instant Creek thought the rifle had discharged because Chief's mouth suddenly flopped open, he blinked several times and then a strange, haunting expression crossed his face. It was almost as if Chief had had a sudden revelation, and what he saw in that thin sliver of time was absolutely unmistakable and emphatically clear. He jerked the rifle away and took a jolting step backward.

★　★　★

The sharp crack of a gunshot, and the wave of the concussion, awoke Pokey from a sound sleep. Oddly, his first thought was of the priest at the Catholic church. When they were young Grandma used to wake Pokey and Creek early on Sunday morning and march them across town to attend Sunday school and mass. After the service the priest would take the two boys shooting. The priest said target practice helped him to relax after a difficult morning of hearing confessions and preaching. They shot tin cans and bottles off stumps. For several years, during fair-weather months, shooting was a Sunday tradition.

Echoes of the single gunshot ricocheted off the ridge, touching the delicate mist and making the raindrops that clung to the thin fingers of the pine needles tremble. Reverberations bounced, blended and finally bled into the night. But this gunshot would never completely die. It would last through eternity. And the gray squirrel that lived in the lightning-struck pine tree popped her head out of her nest for a quick look-see, and hastily ducked back inside.

* ★ *

There came a scream and it was as if some invisible force were yelling, wailing, shrieking and moaning all at the same time. It was such an unearthly sound it seemed to ignite the dark, and at first Pokey was not sure whether to jump up and fight or to run away from it and hide. He found himself outside, where a wet wind slapped him fully awake. He took a quick breath that stung his lungs with its coolness. He heard an eerie moaning sound and he turned toward it and saw movement, saw Creek under the big pine tree, arms wrapped around the tire swing spinning in meaningless circles.

People poured out of the house and Pokey watched them crowd onto the porch and spill like water down the stairs. He heard a distant melody that did not seem real or relevant and noticed a form on the ground, near the Cadillac. It was Chief. He was stretched out, lying face up. Pokey moved forward and it seemed as though his legs had difficulty keeping up with his forward momentum. He was the first to reach the body and he dropped to one knee. Chief's eyes were wide open, unblinking, staring blankly as if they were seeing everything, or seeing nothing. Pokey instructed the others, "Stay back," and placed three fingers across Chief's neck, probing for a pulse.

Creek broke from his futile dance, pushed away from the tire swing and walked in an unsteady line toward the house. The subdued revelers parted for him. He went inside and, overcome by a sudden compulsion, he began washing his hands in the kitchen sink while the record spun on the turntable. Johnny Preston sang, "Running Bear dove in the water. Little White Dove did the same. And they swam out to each other; through the swirling stream they came. As their hands touched, and their lips met, the raging river pulled them down. Now they'll always be together in their happy hunting ground. . . ."

★ ★ ★

The dogs ran in a wide circle that took them back on the ridge and down along the river. The leader slipped on the wet stones and went down. The other dogs seized on his moment of weakness and turned on him in a snarling mass of flashing teeth and flying fur. The fallen dog scrambled to his feet and quickly regained his dominance.

★ ★ ★

When Red saw a line of headlights snaking their way over the bridge and down the dirt road toward town, he knew something bad had happened. Indians never leave a party unless serious trouble is brewing and by then the pot has usually boiled over and someone is dead.

"Didn't hear any shots," he muttered to himself, then realized the car had been running, defroster on high to keep the windows clear, and probably he would not have heard gunshots unless it was a goddamn war. "Christ," he lamented. He allowed the traffic to clear and in an odd way he was relieved and thankful he would not have to face a drunken crowd while he conducted his investigation. He dropped the power glide into gear and started over the bridge.

Red eased to a stop. The tire swing was still moving in a tight circle like a plumb bob, Grandma was peering from behind the screen door, Creek was sitting on the porch with his head between his knees, Pokey was leaning against the fender of a red Cadillac convertible. The driver's door was wide open. There was a body nearby on the ground. Red supposed it was Chief and that he was dead.

A mangy white dog, that seemed to have been awaiting his arrival, padded over and pissed against the back wheel of Red's car while Red adjusted his spotlight on the body. He left the motor running. This was going to take a while and he did not want to run the battery down. He flung open the door, pulled on his coat and moved to center stage. As he approached he removed his hat, backhanded his brow with his sleeve and, before shoving the hat back on his head, directed a rhetorical question in Pokey's direction. "Dead?"

Pokey nodded.

Red saw blood seeping into the wet ground and blood on Chief's shirt. Five feet away lay a rifle. He leaned over the body and made mental note of the hole in the ten-X spot, directly over the heart. The material was pock-marked with powder burns. It had been an extremely close shot. Carefully Red opened the top two buttons of Chief's shirt. There was a small, circular entry wound and a thin trail of blood leaking from it. He knew the exit wound would be a gaping hole. He rebuttoned the shirt, rose, shook his head as a sympathetic gesture and asked Pokey.

"When did it happen?"

"Five, maybe ten minutes ago."

"Anybody touch the body?"

"I checked for a heartbeat. That was it."

"He fell right here?"

"Yep."

"You didn't pull the trigger, did you?"

"No."

"Anybody see it?"

"I don't know. I was sleeping."

"Where?"

"In the woodshed."

"Why were you sleeping in the woodshed?"

"Got a spot fixed up there. It's where I bunk."

"So you were passed out?"

"I haven't been drinking."

"Well if you ain't, you're about the only sober joker on this here reservation." As soon as he said it Red remembered this was no longer a reservation, but that way of thinking was going to take some getting used to. He looked in Creek's direction. "Why did Creek shoot him?"

"Don't know he did."

"How many shots?"

"One."

Red told Pokey not to touch anything, walked over to his car, reached through the open door, pulled the hand mike out. "Car one to base."

"Base."

"Marg, call the sheriff. There's been a shooting. Chief's dead. And Marg, send a meat wagon over here to the river house to pick up the body, but tell them to take their time. The sheriff will wanna have a look-see."

After replacing the mike Red went to where Creek was sitting on the porch. Red draped a meaty arm around the boy's shoulder. He could sense Grandma somewhere behind him, like a sparrow hawk, circling, circling. Red spoke in a low tone meant only for Creek. "Well, son, wanna tell me what happened here tonight?"

Creek looked up at him. Tears stained his mahogany-colored cheeks. His eyes were red. "I don't know what you want me to say."

"Try the truth."

Creek began to cry. Between sobs he related, "I woke up. I was on the front seat."

"Of the Cadillac?"

Creek nodded and continued, "He was yelling at me."

"Yelling what?"

"Something about money. He thought I was stealing his money."

"Then what?"

Creek rubbed at the tears with the heels of his hands. "We were fighting."

Creek fighting with Chief was so ludicrous that Red had to distract himself or he might have broken into uncontrollable laughter. He removed his arm from around Creek.

"He was trying to pull me out. I grabbed the steering wheel, wouldn't let go. Then he had the gun. He pushed it into me, right in my chest. I was scared. I thought he was going to kill me."

"What else?"

"He smiled. I remember that. He never smiled that way before. It was strange. The look on his face. He backed up. That was when he must have gotten shot."

"How did it happen?"

"I don't know. Maybe he tried to throw the gun away and it went off by accident. I never saw. I know it wasn't me. I never had the gun. I couldn't have pulled the trigger. You know that, don't you?"

"Sure. Anything else?"

"That's all."

The black night drew back and spit rain again. Pokey came over and asked if he could pull a tarp over Chief. Red told him, "Leave him as he lies. Sheriff will wanna send out someone to investigate."

"What happens now?"

"We wait." Red shook loose a smoke. He lit his cigarette and turned to Creek. "Since you've been back, you and Chief had any problems? Any disagreement? Any bad blood between you?"

"No."

"That vigilante thing," Pokey said, "think someone could have shot him?"

"You just never know." Red was fresh out of answers. He pushed himself off the stairs and walked over to the Cadillac, finished his cigarette and tossed it down. He checked under the front seat and pulled out the brown paper sack. He opened it, turned toward the spotlight and whistled under his breath at the wad of crumpled currency.

Red set the sack on the front seat of his car and stood there leaning against the door. Rain gathered on the brim of his hat and ran off in a tiny rivulet. Each time he drew on his cigarette the tip glowed hot and his face emerged from the darkness and blushed an orange color that quickly faded to black. And while he smoked and waited he rolled over in his mind that the most logical explanation was that Chief had killed himself. But why? Why this particular night? But then again, why not? Chief never did put much value on life. It all pointed out to Red that no one ever knew just what would trip another man's trigger, make him act different than he normally did; mix in alcohol and the line blurred even more.

Eighteen

The radio squawked. Red picked up the mike and told Marg to go ahead. She said she had Steve Atwood on the telephone. "He's concerned about his wife. She's in a lot of pain and he thinks maybe she's gone into labor. It's way too early. He wants to know what he should do."

"I'm tied up here, no way I'm gonna get away. He can call an ambulance, but tell him it would be faster if he made the run to Klamath. Have him tuck a blanket around her, keep her warm and as comfortable as possible. Tell him to get going, don't waste no time."

When Red first saw Debbie, after the incident at the store, he realized she was shocky but he thought she would snap out of it. Apparently not. And now she had taken a turn for the worse. He shook out another cigarette, lit it off the butt of the last, and thought to himself, "Why does everything have to happen at once?"

★ ★ ★

Lefty, having heard the gunshot, had gone out on the porch and watched the parade of departing cars. After they passed one rig went in. He figured it was Red and that someone had gotten killed. A half hour, maybe forty minutes later, two vehicles with flashing overhead lights drove over the bridge and up the lane. By then it was raining hard and difficult to see much of anything.

Lefty told himself he should go inside but sat where he was, even though the coolness of the night was chilling him to the bone. He drank to warm himself, the crimson wine radiating an illusion of heat from his belly outward.

He said aloud, "Damn them. All that money and they go around killing each other. Why bother giving it to them? If the government was gonna throw money away they should've throwed some my direction." After that he went in, stoked the fire and stood by it. He continued to drink the sweet, warm wine.

★ ★ ★

Pokey left the law with their notebooks, measuring tapes, cameras, cigarettes and two-bit cigars. He went to check on Grandma, found her sitting in the kitchen, in a straight-backed chair, wearily rocking her body back and forth. He asked if she needed anything. She said nothing as she stared at the pinpoints of light seeping from holes in the woodstove. The campfires of long ago flared. "Pile sage brush, it burn hot, pile high."

Pokey dropped to one knee in front of her and looked at her, really looked at her, and for the first time he comprehended that he knew nothing about her. She had been someone to cook and wash for him. Someone to tend the chores. She had been there when he needed her. He watched her face and her eyes, eyes that had seen too much. They were open and staring straight ahead like Chief's eyes as he lay dead on the ground.

"White man say no burn body. Say bury him. One sun come. Two sun come. You bury. No tomorrow. Day after."

"I'll see to it," Pokey reassured her, and mentally he was already making the arrangements for Chief's burial. When he stood, it seemed as if the walls rushed inward, closing in on him. To avoid being crushed he knew he had to get away.

★ ★ ★

Steve lifted the glass, bourbon neat, gulped it down. He closed his eyes as it hit bottom and then nodded for a refill.

"Bad day?" asked the bartender.

"You can't begin to believe how bad."

The first drink had been to stop Steve's headspinning free fall and the second was to fortify himself, pump some hope back into his depleted system. Indeed, it had been a rough few hours; the shooting at the store, rushing Debbie to the hospital, and finally the premature birth of the baby, a son. The doctors said Deb was doing fine but they had been less than positive about the baby. They said the first twenty-four hours were critical and had put the odds for the baby's survival at no better than 30 percent. That did not seem fair; a tiny baby should not have to buck the odds just to live.

If the baby had been a girl they were going to call her Leslie Anne. A boy, Sean—Sean Michael Atwood. And now little Sean was fighting for his life. Bitterness burned a hole through the pit of Steve's stomach. He blamed everything on the robber. He was the one who was responsible for all of this. Steve figured he had to be an Indian and vowed he would hunt the bastard down. He was going to make him pay.

The bartender asked if he needed another. Steve shook his head, pushed himself off the stool and made his way outside. The cool air relaxed him. It was still raining. He stood there wondering what he was supposed to do now. By reflex he made his decision. He would return to the hospital and sit beside Debbie through the night. That was preferable to returning to Chewaucan and having to face the cold store and the lonely apartment.

Nineteen

With the coming of dawn the wet soil and cool air provoked a thin layer of ground fog that stretched across the green pasture like cotton candy. Here and there faint outlines of robins could be seen hopping, pausing to listen, bobbing their heads and pulling worms from the ground. High overhead, in the Pacific flyway, an oblong V of Canada honkers passed, traveling north like a long sigh. The dogs chased away a black raven that flew on loose wings over the brushy thicket and across the river toward Lefty's shack.

One of the young dogs, its hair loaded with burrs shaped like arrowheads, turned its attention to a butterfly and chased after it, coming close to a killdeer's nest in the gravel. The killdeer cried out in alarming notes, "Kill-dee, kill-dee, kill-dee, kill-dee," pretending a broken wing as a ruse to lead the dog away from her camouflaged eggs.

★   ★   ★

If Chief were making the decision he probably would have chosen to have a backhoe dig a big hole and have himself buried in the Cadillac. But as Pokey walked through the display room of Whispering Pines Funeral Home in Klamath Falls he reasoned that Chief's termination money should buy him a fancy casket for the hereafter. He pointed to a clear-grained Port Orford cedar casket with brass-plated hardware and handles, telling the funeral director, "I'll take that one." The director, a thin man with a sympathetic voice, praised the decision and talked about the service, inquired what he could do to accommodate the family's wishes. Pokey said there would be a gathering at the burial site, no traditional service, and that he wanted the funeral the following day. The director protested, said he would not have sufficient time to make all the necessary arrangements. Pokey offered more money. Tomorrow would be fine.

When Pokey emerged from the funeral home a gentle breeze was blowing the storm away and the sun winked down from a slot in the clouds. He drew a deep breath of fresh air and squinted at the fickle sun. His gut ached. He walked the short distance to the Cadillac, opened the door and sat. He idly watched the sporadic traffic and waited for Grandma.

She had insisted on coming to town with him. He had dropped her off at the bank. She was going to cash her termination check and then she was supposed to walk the two blocks to the funeral home. That was the plan. Pokey had not been to the bank and was not sure he wanted to go. In the back of his mind he thought that maybe by not taking

the money he was somehow still entitled to his Indian heritage and to the reservation land.

★ ★ ★

Once he left home Dallas rarely returned until evening.
But when he stopped for gas that morning Floyd told him
about Chief's death, the shooting at the store and Debbie's
premature baby. Dallas knew Dolly would want to know,
and so would Shasta. When he reached home he found
them in the kitchen, seated at opposite ends of the table,
sipping coffee. They wished him a good morning. He
returned the greeting, went to the coffee pot and poured
himself a cup. He leaned against the counter so they would
have to turn to face him and said, "Li'l excitement last
night. Someone broke into the store. Got shot. Wasn't no
body ta be found. Guess they crawled off ta die.

"Couple hours after that, Debbie," Dallas directed his
attention to Shasta, "she and her husband Steve own the grocery, he's the one done the shootin' but anyway, Debbie, she
done goes inta premature labor. Steve gets her ta the hospital
in Klamath Falls. She has the baby. Boy. Guess he only
weighed like four pounds an' a handful a pocket change."

"How are they doing?" Dolly asked.

"Don't know 'bout that. But that ain't even the biggest
news. Nope. Bigger news 'n that," Dallas paused, giving
Dolly a taste of her own medicine.

"What is it?"

"Trouble down ta the river place."

Shasta's first thought was of Pokey, and then Creek.

"Seems Chief done got hisself shot dead by his own rifle.
An' Creek's the one they think done it."

The news blindsided Shasta. "Where is he?"

"Red's got 'im locked up down ta the jail."

"Pokey," she said and then didn't know what she wanted to ask. "Is he all right?"

Dallas shrugged, "Far as I know he weren't mixed up in it. But who knows 'bout them wagon burners? Once they get ta drinkin' any little thing might set 'em off. Sometimes nothin' at all an' 'fore you know it someone ends up dead."

★ ★ ★

Creek lay on the lumpy sag of the jailhouse bunk, staring at the dingy gray ceiling. Even in the morning light there remained a pale reflection of the four-way caution light blinking yellow, yellow, yellow. Time stretched like taffy. Somewhere in the free world a dog yipped and a voice commanded, "Shut up." The yipping continued.

He could see Chief's face above him, could feel the rifle pressed into his breastbone, see those anthracite eyes and their raw meanness, see that goddamn smile that came to Chief's face just before the end. Creek tried to make sense of that smile and wondered if Chief had somehow foreseen his own death. Was the smile a wave of relief washing over him? But that made no sense, no sense at all. None of it made any sense.

Red walked into the small jail carrying two cups of coffee, handing one through the bars. Creek, smelling the rich aroma, got up and took the cup, using both hands. He offered a weak, "Thanks," went back and sat on the bunk.

"I make a point to always try to treat the boys who stay with me like human beings. You know, anyone can make a mistake. How you feeling?"

"Like a pinball machine flashing tilt," Creek said.

"Well, just so you know, I've got a decent library of westerns. Luke Short. Tom J. Hopkins. Stuff like that. You like westerns?"

Creek shrugged. Red pulled a paperback book from a hind pocket. Pictured on the cover was a white man kicking a knife away from an Indian. "This is my all-time favorite." He read from the back cover, " 'He was a big man, wide-shouldered, with the lean, hard-boned face of the desert rider. There was not an ounce of softness to him. His toughness was ingrained and deep without cruelty, yet quick, hard and dangerous. Whatever gentleness that might lie within him was guarded and deep. He had been sitting motionless and still on his buckskin for more than an hour. Patience was the price of survival, he knew that, and often the first to move was the first to die.'

"Not bad, huh? Makes it seem like you're there. Hell of a good story. Course, Zane Grey was the best writer of all time. I've got most of his: *Rainbow Trail, Thundering Herd, Twin Sombreros, West of the Pecos, Wild Horse Mesa, Riders of the Purple Sage*. If you want to try Zane Grey let me know. Got them all at home."

Red tapped the cover of the pulp western. "Good one." and although he did not say it, he just supposed he was cut from the same bolt of cloth as the hero. He reached through the bars and flipped the book onto the bunk. Creek just sat.

Red stared hard at him. "You been to college, maybe you don't cotton to westerns. Like something a little more intellectual?" He made the last word sound vaguely contemptible.

Creek sipped his coffee. "I just don't feel up to reading right now, that's all."

"You change your mind—"

"Why did this have to happen?"

Red said nothing but he grinned as if the answer was obvious and Creek should know it.

"I didn't do anything wrong, except get drunk. You haven't even arrested me. You can't keep me locked up."

"Forty-eight hours. Forty-eight hours without charging you. Don't blame me. That's the law. Sheriff said to hold on to you. I'm holding on."

"I have the right to make a phone call."

"Sure. Who you gonna call?"

"An attorney, have him get me out."

"Save your dime. He ain't gonna be able to do nothing, not for forty-eight hours. By then the grand jury will have convened. They'll let you go. They ain't got nothing to hold you on."

"Think so?"

"I know so. You say you never touched the rifle. Who the hell's gonna dispute it? No witnesses. No evidence to the contrary. I could pull a couple dozen names off the top of my head, people just itching to pull the trigger on Chief. Let's face it, Chief wasn't up for winning any popularity contests."

"Do you think he killed himself?"

"It's mighty hard for a man to shoot himself in the heart with his own rifle. But Chief was a big man and the model ninety-four is a short weapon. That's a definite possibility."

Creek said, "Why? It doesn't make sense. He had all that money."

"Money's not everything."

"Maybe if you think you're going to lose it."

Red shrugged. "Who the hell knows. Could be that. Could be he just snapped, suddenly saw himself for who he was, like looking at his reflection in a mirror and hating everything he saw. Could be something even simpler than that. Maybe Chief just got tired of living." He let that sink in, then added, "By the way, Marg says she's fixing chicken for dinner. Her chicken melts in your mouth. And mashed taters and gravy. She'll have a vegetable—peas, corn, carrots, I don't know which. Dinner's a ways away, but it'll give you something to look forward to."

★ ★ ★

A couple of hours later Red returned to the cell. He had another man with him. He introduced him as State Police Detective Springer and said the detective had driven over from Salem. Detective Springer was wearing civilian clothes: dress pants neatly pressed, a gray sports coat over a blue shirt, open collar. His shoes were the imported kind that slipped on. With a jangle of keys Red unlocked the cell door, left it open and returned to his office.

The detective sat on the bunk beside Creek. His tone of voice was almost fatherly as he asked what happened the night before. Creek explained; he had arrived at the party late, drank for several hours, left the party and stumbled to the Cadillac. He said he passed out on the front seat and awoke with Chief trying to pull him out of the car.

"What did you do?"

"I tried to fight him."

"Your brother was a big man. By comparison you're just a skinny kid. You want me to believe you fought him?"

"Not like fight him. I was just trying to keep him from pulling me out, onto the ground. I grabbed the steering wheel, wouldn't let go. I was kicking him with my feet."

"Did you grab the rifle?"

"No."

"You're sure. What if your fingerprints are on it?"

"They won't be. I never touched it."

"According to your earlier statement he pushed the barrel into your chest and then for some reason he pulled it away and stepped back."

"That's right. That's exactly what happened. He just smiled and that's. . . . Wait, I remember now. He stepped back and started to turn the rifle around so it was pointing at his own chest."

The detective stood. "Bullshit."

Creek was close to bursting into tears. "He killed himself. He did. I know it, now. I really do."

"You want me to believe you just now remembered that he killed himself on purpose? How goddamn convenient."

"I never saw the gun go off. But then, you know, I might have had a premonition of what was going to happen and closed my eyes. That would be a normal reflex. Wouldn't it? He turned the gun on himself. And from that moment, until the shot was fired, was just a split second."

The detective grabbed Creek by the front of his shirt, jerked him to his feet and slammed him against the bars. His face was only inches away from Creek's. "You Indians are all the same; a bunch of worthless, lazy, lying, murdering bastards. You get drunk, do something crazy, and try to cover your ass by throwing the blame on someone else. You killed your brother. You shot him dead." He pulled Creek forward and slammed him against the bars once more, even more violently, hissing, "Admit it!"

Red was there, moving fast, pulling the detective away, spinning him across the cell and lifting and pinning the man to the outside wall. Hanging up there, on the end of Red's arm, the detective looked like a moth pinned to a piece of cardboard. "While this young man is in my custody it's my job to protect him. You ever pull something like this again, I'll squish you like a bug."

★ ★ ★

Steve had gone out for breakfast and then stopped by a florist shop. He returned to the hospital with a dozen, long-stemmed red roses in the crook of one arm. He walked along the sterile hospital corridor, and was passing the nurses' station when a man's voice called out to him, "Mr. Atwood. Oh, Mr. Atwood."

Steve stopped, turned slowly around, and found himself face-to-face with a man dressed in the white collar and the black garments of a clergyman. He requested, "Please follow me, Mr. Atwood."

Steve dutifully fell in step, moving down the long hallway, taking notice of inconsequential things; a janitor wringing a mop that smelled strongly of disinfectant; an unseen patient's dry, choking cough; a visitor sitting on the foot of a patient's bed; a television blaring an advertisement for Bruno's Photography Shop, "Wouldn't Mother love a portrait of her family on Mother's Day?"

The clergyman led the way into a chapel; a tiny room with a wooden cross dominating one wall and the sides adorned with imitation stained-glass windows. Steve found himself thinking, if there truly was a God, he would reside in a magnificent cathedral and not some back-pocket room like this.

The reverend faced Steve. His eyes appeared icy and

glazed. He had made this speech a hundred times, several hundred, and it was just a job, although it was one of the more unpleasant aspects of saving souls. He cleared his throat in preparation for the business at hand and it occurred to him that if this young man were an Indian, he would lay it on the line without much, if any, sentimentality because Indians were used to death. They took that sort of thing rather well. But the preacher could sense that the young man standing before him with a handful of flowers was sensitive and emotionally fragile, and so the preacher folded his hands piously, bowed his head and eased his way into the deliver. "Life is a very sacred thing. Only God can bestow that precious gift upon us, the gift of life. And only God can take it away. . . ."

Steve thought that if he could trade punches with this man of the cloth, that might even the playing field, they might get along fine. But Steve knew that was not the way this was going to play itself out. In this scene he was going to have to stand with his arms at his sides and the preacher was allowed to hit him with his best shot. Steve looked away, diverting his gaze to a scuff mark on the floor. He concentrated on that spot and tensed his muscles. He wanted to shout, "Get to it. Just do what you have to do. Say what it is you have to say."

"Sometimes it is difficult for us to know what God has in mind when he calls home one of his children. I think that is the hardest thing for any of us to accept, the loss of a child."

"My son, you mean he's dead?"

Twenty

That Chief should meet a violent death came as no real surprise to Shasta, and yet she found herself distressed that she could not muster even a trace of compassion for him. But Creek—she felt it was a total injustice that he was in jail. He would never take another person's life.

Dallas set his coffee cup in the sink and shuffled toward the door. "Can't dilly-dally 'round all day. There's work ta be done." He slammed the squeaky pickup door and started the motor. As he drove away Shasta asked Dolly, "Would it be okay if I borrowed your car, just for a little while?"

Dolly, who was wondering why no one had called her this morning and was itching to find out whether or not the phone was out of service again, replied, "Oh sure, dearie. But I've got bridge club today. We're meeting at noon. Be back, say, no later than eleven thirty."

As soon as Shasta went to the other room Dolly tried the

phone. The line was dead. When Shasta returned, Dolly asked, "Suppose you could stop at the service station and ask Floyd to call the phone company for me? Tell him my line is dead, again. I need it fixed. This is the third time this month. It is so exasperating. If you or I tried to run a business like the phone company does, with such poor service, we would all go bankrupt."

★   ★   ★

Grandma wanted to pick up a few necessities at the feed store. She bought rolled oats and chicken feed, adding a bag of oyster shells to the list because lately the chickens had been laying eggs with thin and brittle shells. Oyster shells would firm them up. She also bought a mineral block for the cow and then she splurged on herself, buying wool socks and rubber milking boots. Grandma paid for the items she had purchased with a crisp hundred-dollar bill while Pokey helped load them into the trunk of the Cadillac.

Returning home Grandma went directly to her room. She was tired and sat in her rocker, oblivious to all but her rocking. She knew enough about life to be ready to die.

★   ★   ★

Pokey drove to the barn, where he unloaded the feed, oyster shells and the mineral block. The cow rubbed her neck on the gatepost and bellowed she wanted to be milked. Pokey obliged, taking the lazy way by turning in the calf to do the job. After that he headed uptown, driving straight to the municipal building, parked and took the dozen steps to Red's office two at a time.

* ★ *

His head throbbed and his body ached, he was sick to his stomach, he got the cold shakes, and memories haunted him. Every bit of the suffering Creek now had to endure could be traced back to that single beer Chief forced on him. That drink followed by two days of drunkenness, ending on the front seat of the Cadillac with Chief lying dead on the ground.

When Shasta appeared behind the wall of metal bars, it caught Creek off guard. He had not heard nor seen her come in, she was just there and she was as unexpected and as welcome as a rainstorm on the desert.

"How you doing?" she asked.

He got up off the bunk. "Okay."

"Anything I can get you?"

He looked up. "A hacksaw, maybe." He tried to smile. "Red says I won't be here long. Says they don't have anything to hold me on. Maybe tomorrow I'll get out, next day for sure." The flame of expectation flickered unsteadily.

"Will you go back to school?"

"Where else could I go?"

Shasta recalled what Pokey had said about Creek, that one day he would sell his soul to the highest bidder and measure his success against the goals of the white man. Maybe Creek would talk about that with her someday, after all this was behind him. Creek's forearm rested on a bar and Shasta took his hand. His skin was as cool and clammy as the jailhouse.

"Tell me what I can do."

"Just having you come helps a lot. Knowing you haven't given up on me."

"Of course not. I never would."

After she was gone Creek felt even more isolated. He turned contemplative and thought about growing up on the reservation, where he had always been an oddity. However, in the outside world his differences were overlooked and his intelligence admired. At college his classmates and friends gave him support, and above all a sense of belonging. But Creek had difficulty embracing that fellowship. He often thought of himself as an interloper and an imposter. None of the people he knew in Eugene had ever set foot on an Indian reservation, and therefore they could not recognize the humiliation Creek felt in his Indian blood, his family background and his heritage. Nor could they see below the surface—to Creek's primary fear—that he would be found out and that he would no longer be liked and accepted in the white world.

★　★　★

When Pokey walked through the door Red looked up from a pile of paperwork on his desk. "Just the man I wanted to see."

"Why's that?"

"We had a visitor here, a detective from OSP," Red said. "I'll spare you the details, but when he left out of here he wasn't none too happy."

"What's the problem?"

"I just hung up on a call from the detective's commanding officer. He tried to throw his weight around. Since the reservation is no longer under the protection of the BIA, the State Police think they have jurisdiction. They want to make an example out of Creek."

"An example of what?"

"Draw a line, let folks here know who is in charge. They are threatening to push this as a murder one case, with all the trimmings."

"Not the gas chamber?"

"Something like that," Red said. "The important thing is that they aren't buying suicide. They say nobody in the history of the state has ever shot himself through the heart with a long-rifle. Blow their brains out, sure, but never through the heart."

"Don't they realize it was a saddle gun, short-barreled?" Pokey said. "Chief was a big man. That rifle was like a six-shooter to him."

"They're looking at the overall picture," Red claimed. "They've backtracked and know all about Creek driving that Corvette through the showroom window. They figure he's crazy when he's been drinking, and there's plenty of witnesses who will testify he was drunk."

"What's the motive?"

"Money."

"Jesus Christ. Creek cashed his check. He had plenty of his own money."

"I know that, and you know that," Red said. "But their line of thinking is that he was reaching under the seat and trying to steal the paper sack of cash. Chief tried to take it away. Creek pulled out the rifle and shot him."

"Horseshit."

"Then you tell me what you think happened."

Pokey sighed. "What I think happened—I think Creek was passed out in the Cadillac just like he said. Chief found him, went ape, and when he realized he had come that close to killing his own brother he lost it. Boom. What did he have to live for, one more drink? I hate to say this, but he was an asshole when he was drunk, and he was drunk most of the time. With all that money it was just going to get worse."

Red reached for a cigarette. "That's about the way I see it, too. Now, just so I have it straight—where did Chief keep his rifle? Where was it just before the shooting?"

"In his rig." Pokey kicked back a braid with his hand. "I didn't see him move it when we got back."

"Back from where?"

"Riding around. Chief was showing off his Cadillac. He shot a deer."

"Jacklighting?"

"Naw. He just happened to pick it up in the headlights."

"That was the venison hanging in the woodshed?"

"Yeah."

"Was the rifle lying on the seat?"

"Under it."

"Driver's side?"

"Yep."

Red thought aloud, "Okay, so the rifle was under the front seat on the driver's side, which means Chief leaned down and pulled it out. When he did, he should have been able to feel the sack of money. So then why accuse Creek of stealing it? It doesn't make sense."

"It doesn't have to make sense. You know Chief, the way he was, he could go off the deep end for no reason at all. Might have come across the rifle first. Hell, I don't know."

"If Creek didn't pull the trigger—and I have no reason at all to believe he did—and if Chief didn't do it himself—any idea of who might have done it?"

"Not the foggiest. All I know is I heard a single gunshot, got up, ran outside. Chief was on the ground and Creek was over under the pine tree with his arms wrapped around the swing. He was crying. People started coming out of the house. I told them to stay back. I went to the body and checked for a pulse. There wasn't one. I don't know anything else. Period, end report."

"Okay. One last thing, after Chief shot the deer, did he eject the spent cartridge?"

"I suppose so."

"He usually did?"

"Yeah."

"You sure?"

"He was always ready. He would have jacked in another round. What difference does it make?"

"I'll be perfectly frank. I'm concerned—three names on a vigilante list, same three get kilt. Odds of it happening on its own, mighty slim. Just speculating whether someone might have lent a helping hand."

Twenty-one

Shasta shouted over the roar of the Jeep engine, "You took off the top and the doors, why?" The wind was sharp and cool enough to make her eyes water. She grabbed at her hair and tucked it down the back of her coat.

"Want you to have the full effect." Pokey was wearing his black reservation hat pushed down tight and Shasta thought it looked rather good and yet odd, as if he could not quite make up his mind whether to be an Indian or a cowboy.

After visiting Creek, Shasta had driven around for a while and then stopped by the grocery store for something to drink. She was sipping a bottle of Coke and unlocking the door of Dolly's station wagon when Pokey drove up, stopped, and got out of the Jeep.

"I heard you visited Creek. How do you think he's holding up?" Pokey asked.

"When I asked him if there was anything I could bring him he suggested a hacksaw." Shasta smiled. "He said they didn't have any evidence to hold him on and that he would probably be released by tomorrow. That's what Red told him."

"Could be more serious than that," Pokey said. "Law enforcement jurisdictions are jockeying for position. There's talk a murder indictment could be handed down."

"But how could they?"

"Easy as throwing mud against a wall. They figure something is likely to stick."

The Jeep rattled across a long stretch of washboard and then Pokey let off on the gas and steered down a potholed lane leading to a cluster of abandoned buildings. He leaned close and said, "The old Parker place."

The deserted ranch was a little over a mile from town. Boys often came there for their introduction to cigarettes, beer and the fine art of writing nasty words on walls. Once in a while they coaxed a girl along and copped a feel, got her naked or maybe more than that. The house was in shambles; the pine flooring was etched by years of sand and shuffling feet, windows were broken, copper pipes had been carted away, holes had been kicked and punched in the Sheetrock, and the doors were falling loose from their hinges.

Pokey passed the house and drove to the barn. It stood skeleton-like, rafters sagging and shingles missing. The big door lay flat on the ground with weeds grown through curled boards. The barn, which had once held the sweet fragrance of hay, was empty and stank of the sourness of desertion. There was a wary stillness. Sunlight sliced through gaps in the roof. As her eyes adjusted to the dim light Shasta could begin to see hames and lines hanging on wooden pegs, and old collars with the padding sticking out through holes in the leather. A rusty currycomb sat on a shelf. The stall boards were polished from where horses had rubbed against them. Cobwebs were strung across the corners.

Pokey climbed onto the manger, reached high and removed something from one of the stringers. He handed it to her. "I wanted to show you this."

It was a thin box, once covered by stamped leather but chewed on and pecked at over the years until bare wood showed through in places. Shasta opened it. Behind protective glass, and framed by gold filigree, was a photograph of a boy. He appeared to be an equal mix of Indian and Caucasian. He was dressed in an ill-fitting suit and tie; his left forearm rested on a table and the thumb of his right hand was tucked in his belt. He looked uncomfortable, solemn, unhappy, posed.

"How old?" Pokey asked.

"Eight or nine."

"No. How old do you think the photograph is?"

"Old." Shasta said, "Maybe from the '20s. Who is he?"

"I have no idea. I found it here a long time ago. I asked around, but nobody could tell me anything except that the Parkers were a white family. They built the place, stayed a dozen years or so and moved away. I've always wondered if old man Parker had something going on the side with an Indian girl and this was their child. You know about researching and that sort of thing. How could I find out?"

"Did you ask your grandmother?"

"Yeah. She told me old man Parker ran Hereford cattle. That's about all she would say."

"You might go to the county assessor's office, see if they were listed on the tax roll. Find out which years they paid taxes. How about tribal records? Mr. Parker might be listed as the father. The county library or the museum might have a list of births. If you find a date you can look it up in the newspaper. Their name would be listed if they bought or sold property, if they were arrested or won an award. All that information is part of the public record. It is amazing how much you can discover about someone if you spend a little time following the leads."

"Sort of like tracking a deer, just stay with the sign left behind."

"I suppose that's a pretty good analogy." Shasta handed back the photograph. She wondered why this photograph would have such meaning to Pokey and why he would feel compelled to share it with her. Was it because he identified with the half-breed boy? Was it because he wondered what it would be like to have grown up in a white family? She tried to draw a mental picture of Pokey as a boy, off the reservation, living the American dream with a bicycle and a baseball mitt and a dog named Freckles, but she could not.

★　★　★

Pokey drove back to the road and turned right, following a scraggly fence line with rotted posts dangling from strands of rusted barbed wire. He downshifted and the Jeep climbed a steep hillside as the road dodged stately ponderosa pine and clumps of manzanita, madrona, wild plum and white thorn. The tires kicked loose rocks and chunks of mud that thudded against the underside of the Jeep. Shasta held herself on to the seat with both hands so she would not be bounced around, or out.

Near the top of the grade they clattered across a shale flat, coming to an abrupt stop on the summit. Pokey shut off the ignition. The view extended from Mt. Shasta, standing like a soft petal torn from a white rose, north to Mt. Scott. Klamath Lake stretched from the base of the hill west to the Cascade mountain range, and mirrored snow-capped Mount McLoughlin. There was absolute stillness. And then one noisy bird warbled joyfully. A lizard scurried across the face of a boulder.

Shasta scanned the panorama to the southernmost mountain. "Dad said even when he was away at college he could close his eyes and still see Mount Shasta. That's why he insisted on naming me Shasta. Mother wanted Kimberly Ann."

"Shasta, it's a good name. A strong name. No matter where you travel, you always carry something of this land with you."

"After we moved and I started going to a new school, Mother told the teachers my name was Kimberly. But I refused to answer unless they called me Shasta." Saying this made Shasta feel as if she were divulging too much. "I asked you before, but you never said, what are your plans? What are you going to do now that termination is final?"

"I was thinking about becoming a cowboy, gave it considerable thought, until I realized all the cowboys I know have to wear rubber boots, pack irrigation pipe, sit on the seat of a tractor and put up hay. They only get to ride a horse every now and then and when they do, they're likely to get bucked off. Come Saturday night they feel compelled to get drunk and crawl home. Naw," he laughed, "Forget being a cowboy."

"Seriously."

"Don't know." He fingered the straight brim of his hat. He was remembering the accident last fall that killed his girlfriend and unborn son. Indian philosophy held it was best to live in the here and now and never worry about yesterday or tomorrow. Yesterday was gone and tomorrow would take care of itself.

"What sort of things do you enjoy?"

"Fishing, hunting, playing basketball. Summertime I ride bareback and saddlebronc, mostly at All-Indian rodeos. I don't carry a professional card, never wanted to hit it that hard a lick. I do it for fun. Once in a while I'll dance."

"As a Klamath Indian, what do you think is the most important thing to preserve?"

Shasta was surprised by the quickness and vehemence of Pokey's response. "The land. If you have land you have everything. Without land you have nothing."

The wind intensified, blowing up the face of the incline, making the crevices in the rocks moan. Shasta watched a flight of pelicans, wing tip to wing tip, wheel overhead, close enough she could see their large pouches and orange feet. They maneuvered as if perfectly choreographed, circling lower and lower, until they skimmed to a landing on the water.

"We've got miles to go." Pokey started the Jeep. They traveled downhill and passed between brown ridges interlaced with outcroppings of basalt and clay deposits. A few miles farther they entered the confines of a dense pine forest, interspersed occasionally with open meadows, pockets of aspen and thickets of lodgepole. On the north side of the highest ridges, patches of melting snow leaked water that dribbled, trickled and gurgled.

Pokey braked. "We have to walk from here. Maybe a half-mile. It's worth it."

He led Shasta through a low marshy spot where mud sucked at the soles of their shoes. They rounded a side hill littered with loose stones and came to the base of a massive rock wall. Pokey stopped. The sun ducked behind the wings of a wispy cloud. Deceptive light and strange shadows played across the face of the cliff.

Shasta slowly became aware of another presence—ancient art adorned the rock wall. These symbols from the spirit world caused her jaw to go slack and her eyelids to open wide in amazement as she gazed up and up, then side to side. There were mystical markings that looked like human figures, outlines of birds and plants and animals, the sun, moon and dots that could have been stars. The pale colors of these pictographs were taken from the earth, from berries and lichen and animal blood. They were muted yellows, blues, reds and shades that mixed the primary colors.

Conflicting emotions caused Shasta to feel simultaneously threatened and exposed and then strangely calm, as if this were the most profound yet tranquil place she had ever been, and, when she spoke, she thought her voice seemed tiny and insignificant. "This is almost too much to comprehend, what this represents: The passing of time, lost people, a way of life that is no more, all this history that will never be told." She felt her stomach go queasy, as though she had been yanked around an unexpected curve. "It's so hard to fathom all this."

Pokey asked, "You okay?"

"I think so. It's just that I don't know if I belong here."

"You do, because you see it for what it is, you appreciate it. I know that when I stand here I feel as though I crawl inside myself. These drawings show what it really means to be Klamath. Maybe modern man should take a lesson—leave the land like it was intended to be, don't carve it up, build on it, slap asphalt over it. He should learn to live in harmony with the land instead of always trying to conquer it. What are the chances people in this day and age could live anywhere for fourteen thousand years and leave behind only a few drawings on a rock wall?"

From silence came a recognition: The Klamath Indians were being required to sell more than just the reservation, the magnificent land and its natural resources. They were selling everything that being a Klamath Indian encompassed. As Shasta's painted fingernail lightly traced over lines on the rock she asked, "Do these represent mountains?" She touched tick marks and wanted to know, "Is this rain?"

"Grandma said that particular drawing is pretty new, within the last few hundred years. According to Klamath legend, thirty-four men with white skin and bushy beards rode horses here from the direction where the sun rises. They stayed in winter camp along the river, on the flat below where our house sits. In the spring, thirty-two men continued on over the mountains, traveling toward the setting sun. They were never heard from again. You're right, those marks represent the Cascade mountains. But the marks you thought were rain, count them, there are thirty-two. Over here are two other marks representing the men who stayed. They took Indian brides and started families."

"And that was the first mixing of white and Klamath blood." She turned to Pokey who was standing with his cowboy hat pushed back. "You're half Indian, half white. How do you feel about that?"

"Hard to say."

"Come on. Aren't you a different person than if you had been born all Indian or all white?"

"Yeah, well I guess if I was white I wouldn't even be here. I'd live in Portland or Seattle, somewhere like that."

"What do you get from your white blood?"

"I never wanted to be white."

"Why not?"

"The white man gave us smallpox, diabetes, tuberculosis, syphilis, alcoholism."

"I saw the crucifix in your grandma's bedroom. It made me wonder why an Indian woman would have that. Is she Christian?"

"Grandpa Sam was. Grandma was a convert. Catholic. But she never completely let go of the old beliefs. She talks about K'mukamtch, the creator of life, and she talks about the power of Raven. Personally, I feel closest to the Creator when I'm out in nature. I believe in the Church of the High Blue Sky. If you want to see God all you have to do is look around. The mountains, rivers, lakes, the birds, animals and fish. God is everywhere.

"Have you read the Bible?"

"Bits and pieces. Grandma tried to make us Catholic, but we never fell for it."

"Does it come down to the fact you refuse to accept the white man's concept of God?"

Pokey nodded. "Maybe."

"Is there anything the white man has that the Indian needs?"

"You're asking if our lives are better, more fulfilled and richer than the lives of the Ancient Ones? I don't know. Do we live easier? Yeah. Do we live more comfortable? Yeah. Do we have more choices? Yeah. But do we live better? I don't know the answer to that question. All I do know is that we can never go back to the way it used to be. We can never live like before. That time has passed." Pokey moved away from the wall. "Come on, I want to show you Sycan Marsh. We'll have to hurry or it'll get dark on us."

It was hard for Shasta to walk away and break the bond between herself and the mighty wall of ancient art. What would it have been like to be in the party of thirty-four? Why would two have stayed? And why would the Indians take them in?

★   ★   ★

The Jeep ground along in low gear, front wheels hitting chuckholes, rear wheels bouncing through and jarring again. They bisected timbered islands, sprinted across sagebrush flats, rattled over loose scab rocks and forded washes and creeks. Shasta caught transitory impressions of a beaver pond with its lodge of sticks jutting above the water line, a covey of quail scattering, a magpie looking like a crow dressed for a formal ball, blue lupine, ruddy Indian paintbrush, the delicate white blooms of wild strawberries. Once they stopped to watch a doe and a fawn cross the shoulder of an open meadow. After they had disappeared Shasta said, "I was just thinking about something you said—that sometimes you dance. You mean like with feathers and bells and beaded leather things?"

"Yeah, but I don't do it often. I've got a good set of buckskins, Grandma made 'em for me, brain-tanned leather, hand-stitched. She did all the beading. They're authentic. It pays good but I don't know, it makes me feel funny because the dances are all stolen from other tribes, Plains Indians mostly. Not much of our culture has survived. Grandma and a couple others are the only ones who can speak our native tongue. Basket weaving is a lost art. So is the traditional way of making arrows and chipping arrowheads."

"What do you mean, how does it make you feel funny?"

"How do I explain it? Okay, it's like this. Sometimes I hear the drums beat and it fills my head, takes me over and it's like I've gone back in time a thousand years—then something breaks my trance and I look around and the drummers are sitting in lawn chairs and most of the dancers are wearing sun glasses. Afterwards, I feel like we are kinda cheating. No, that's not quite right—its like we're a bunch of kids pretending to be Indians."

"You mean it makes you feel dishonorable?"

"Not really dishonorable. Just sort of bogus. You know, fake."

They continued on and passed an oval lake that, with the green hills around it, appeared like a precious drop of dew collected within the curled edges of a leaf. They came to a clear-cut, an ugly man-made clutter of stumps and colorless rocks. Above the clear-cut the road dwindled to ruts in white clay. They crossed a patch of dark green kinnikinnick, a low-growing plant used in the past as Indian tobacco. Above were towering, cinnamon-barked ponderosa pine that dated to before the coming of the first Hudson's Bay trappers. Black scars on the tree trunks gave mute testimony to lightning strikes and fires that had swept through the forest. Hidden away behind the layer of bark were growth rings that recorded cycles when the rains came early and years when the rain never came at all.

Pokey made a sweeping motion with one hand. "On old maps all this land, everything east of the Cascades, was marked as 'uninhabitable wilderness.' But it wasn't wilderness at all. It was populated with Indians who lived here. Guess the mapmakers didn't figure we counted for much."

★   ★   ★

Shasta sat on a windfall that had been uprooted and had shed its bark. She reveled in the warmth of the late afternoon sun and wished this day would go on forever. But shadows were already beginning to lengthen. Sycan Marsh was spread out in front of her, a huge meadow of lush marsh grass. Here and there wildflowers provided bursts of colors. Cows grazed and calves kicked up their heels in play. Very slowly the landscape was suffocated by an extraordinary glow as the sun moved behind a wispy, mare's tail cloud. The outer rim sparkled gold. It seemed to Shasta as if the world took a long collective breath; the birds were hushed, the air did not move and even the cattle stopped grazing. The only movement was in the soft edges of the clouds where the gold changed colors, bleeding into a brilliant red that became as full-bodied as a port wine.

Pokey was on the ground, sitting cross-legged, Indian style, alternately glancing at Shasta and sketching with a pencil on a sheet of paper. Eventually the coolness of evening crept in and Pokey got up, grabbed a blanket from the Jeep and wrapped it around Shasta's shoulders. He went back to his work while a chorus of tree frogs filled the evening with their vibrations. Crickets joined in. And for a time it seemed each individual component of life hung in a fragile balance of sights, and smells, and sounds.

The long shadows had melted into the nondescript gray

of twilight by the time Pokey finished his work. He walked to Shasta and sat beside her on the log.

"You look sad."

She forced herself to smile. "I was sitting here, drinking in how incredibly beautiful the world is, when it hit me that Creek is there in that dingy little cell. I feel so terrible for him. None of this was his fault."

"He got caught up in things."

"I know but it seems like there is something we should be doing."

"There isn't. Not unless they charge him."

"It's so frustrating, doing nothing."

Pokey handed her his drawing. "This is for you. I want you to have it. Every time you look at it, remember today."

"I'm flattered. You made me look like a magazine model."

He grinned. "I just draw what I see."

Twenty-two

Steve broke down the spare bed and carried it, piece by piece, from the apartment into the store. He reassembled it near the oil heater and gathered around him objects that gave him strength and reassurance—flashlight, rifle, cartridges. Then, not bothering with sheets or even kicking off his shoes, he lay down, propped his head up with a couple of pillows and drew an old wool Army blanket up to his waist. He squinted in the direction of the front door like a man who was expecting trouble and knew from which point of the compass it was most likely to arrive.

Steve had vowed to avenge the death of his son. If he were forced to, he would shoot every Indian and sort out the guilty from the innocent once they were dead on the ground. If that was the way it had to be, so be it. But for now he was content to sit and wait. The man who was responsible would return. Steve was sure of it. Just let the son of a bitch try to break in. He touched the rifle barrel. Power and confidence radiated from the cold steel.

★   ★   ★

Lefty stood spraddle-legged, limp penis in hand, waiting for the pressure in his bladder to build enough so he could piss. He swayed.

"You bag of bones," he told his moonstruck self. He talked drunk. He smelled drunk, too, and he backhanded a little spit from the corner of his mouth. "Nobody wants you. Even I don't want you." Then he pissed.

Afterward he stared into the night with hollow eyes. His wrinkled old skin hung like spoiled beef on a meat hook. God, was he ever tired of having to try to live on social security and no hope for anything more. Hell, the monthly check was barely enough to keep him in booze. So tired of the fight. Would there be another gray dawn? Maybe God would have mercy on him and just allow him to die. Finally, Lefty went in, sat on the couch and listened to time seep through his veins.

★   ★   ★

As long as there was a prisoner in the Chewaucan jail the interior light remained on, glowing like a vagrant sun glued to the ceiling. Creek pulled a blanket over his head and drifted off to sleep. But in a dream he saw Chief's face and that scared him awake. He searched for solace in the glaring light, found none and finally picked up one of the books Red had brought in, a western, and was able to momentarily lose himself in a story about a Texas ranger named Luke who rode a black gelding. One afternoon, with a bad thunderstorm threatening, Luke took refuge in a deserted cabin. A girl came galloping up on a high-strung pinto. Luke invited her in, out of the rain. Creek's eyes drooped as if they were greased, but he fought sleep long enough to find out whether or not the girl's ripe breasts popped out of her silk blouse. They did and, according to the author, they resembled "two plump moons."

★   ★   ★

That night Sam spoke to Grandma in a dream. He said many things. Finally he reached his hand toward her, urging her, "Take hold. Come with me." In response Grandma summoned every ounce of energy she could gather, but no matter how valiantly she tried, her bony old hand always remained a few agonizing inches shy of touching her husband's outstretched fingertips.

★   ★   ★

Clouds rolled up against the flank of the Cascades. The mountains proved only a temporary dam and a great raft of clouds began a slow, steady flow across the basin sky. When Grandma awoke with Sam's words fresh in her mind, the eastern sky was turning a warm color and lighting the fawn-colored hills. Magpies came to perch on the roof of the river house waiting for handouts and a blue jay screeched from a hidden perch in the pine tree. The dogs growled, snarled and fought furiously under the house.

Sam had told Grandma what she must do. Slowly she pulled herself off the cot. She tugged on her tennis shoes and her overcoat and went out the door. She threw a pinch of tobacco into the air for the spirits and headed down the lane. Overhead, clouds were beginning to overrun the sky.

The dogs tried to follow. "Go back," Grandma scolded and they obeyed. Out in the pasture the cow gave forth a long, sad moan and moved toward the gate. But Grandma shuffled past the barn and as she approached the bridge she sang an old Indian song. In her mind others joined in and she could distinguish the individual voices that sang with her. She could feel the drums vibrating the air and the dancing feet keeping beat, lightly tapping the skin of Mother Earth.

Grandma was aware that all the Indian songs were old and that everything old was being forsaken. The last vestige of the Klamath culture had been buried under a thick layer of government money. No more buckskins, moccasins, eagle feathers—replaced by Levi pants, tennis shoes, baseball caps. No more wickiups—houses. No horses— automobiles. No digging camas in the spring, picking huckleberries in late summer, gathering wocus, collecting tules and pine needles, weaving baskets, grinding grain with rock pestles, smoking mullet and salmon, feasting on venison and elk. Mighty K'mukamtch was standing in wait at death's door.

Sam, more than any other man of his era, had been the beacon of this transmutation, the journey from what the white man viewed as savage to a so-called productive member of civilized society. Perhaps it was easier for him because he owed his life to a white soldier. Whatever the reason, it was his domesticated ways that attracted Grandma to him. She recognized that the fastest way to the new life was with Sam. But even with him she had never been able to completely untangle herself from the past.

"Sam. Sam. Sam." Grandma muttered as she plodded along the lane, avoiding the puddles by walking on the berm between worn tire tracks. She crossed over the bridge. On the other side she turned down the pathway following the river, the trail that led to Lefty's shack.

As she drew near to the shack, a cloud slid across the morning sun and sent down sprinkles of rain. She trudged up the steps and her knuckles, misshapen by merciless arthritis, rapped on the wood door. Nothing. She knocked again. A stirring came from inside; the unmistakable clatter of a bottle falling over and rolling across the floor.

★   ★   ★

Lefty's stomach growled like a flathead six about to lose its main bearing. He told himself he ought to get up off the couch and have a bowl of mush, but he could not move. What was the use? He would sleep a while longer and maybe later, when the store opened, he would hike up and get a bottle. He might swing by the bar, drink wine or maybe grab a beer, listen to the jukebox, smoke, hear the dead laughter of the same drunken Indians. Another notable day. To hell with it.

Lefty wondered how the average workingman ever survived: getting awakened by an alarm clock, jumping out of bed, brushing his teeth, combing his hair, dressing, fighting traffic to get someplace where he made money for a boss who bitched and moaned if his employee was two minutes late. Some other poor asshole's world, not Lefty's. He built himself a cigarette, and after smoking it his mind drifted and he dropped off to sleep once again.

Lefty was awakened by a rapping on the door. His head

ached and his stomach was sour. All the vital signs. He reached for the bottle on the floor but it squirted out of his hand like a wet trout and the last of the wine puked onto the linoleum.

"Christ on a crutch."

More knocking. Lefty rolled on his side, pushed off, sat, and groaned to his feet. He went to the door, opened it and was greeted by Grandma's face, looking as dry and craggy as a rotted stump. He squinted, woofed, "What ya want."

Grandma retreated a couple of awkward steps. He followed her and pulled the door closed behind him.

"K'mukamtch make mountain. Make forest. Make deer. Make elk. Bird. Fish. Give to Indian. Say forever Indian keep. White man take."

"What the hell you talkin' 'bout?" Lefty studied her with skittish eyes. One of her hands was in her coat pocket. Instinct told Lefty she might have a gun.

In all the years he had lived across the river from Grandma's house he had rarely spoken to her but had often seen her shadowy form, catching a glimpse of her through the willows, on her way to the barn, to the outhouse, hiking along the road going to or coming from town. She had stopped by Lefty's place only one time before, and that was to ask him to be a pallbearer at Sam's funeral.

Sam had been an all right sort, not like most of the others. When Sam was alive, he and Lefty had hunted and fished together. They had been good friends.

"Why'd you come?"

"Me want go where Sam go. Him live up heaven. Me go heaven."

"If you're fixin' to drop dead, don't do it here. Go back over home." Lefty tried to recall Sam's funeral and could not. Now there was hardly anyone alive who even had a memory of ol' Sam. Dead and gone, how many damn years had it been? Twenty-some, maybe more.

Lefty had always considered himself fortunate to be born white. But really, what difference did it make? Did he not voluntarily live on the reservation? And he was worse off than the Indians because the government never gave him charity, except for social security, and he had worked his butt off for the little dab they bestowed on him every month.

"Sam, him say you good man." She withdrew her hand from her coat pocket and handed Lefty a thick, round bundle of bills held together by a stout rubber band. Lefty took the money, allowed his thumb to flip through the corners of the crisp currency as though this were a fresh deck of playing cards. He absently made an effort to count this wad of hundred dollar bills. Hell's bells! There had to be every bit of forty thousand dollars. It hit him where the money had come from. It was Grandma's termination money. His heart fluttered, missed a beat or two. He felt light-headed and to steady himself he leaned against the wall of his shack.

"Why are you doing this?"

"Sam, me talk him. Him say give you."

Her eyes were dull, faded, watery, weary. He wailed, "What the hell am I suppose to do with this?"

Grandma turned, stepped off the porch and slowly retreated. Lefty glanced at the money, again flipping through the crisp bills. The next time he looked she had disappeared. He moved his mind around with the ponderous effort of a homesteader digging out a stump and then suddenly his ravaged face broke into a wide grin.

"By God, how lucky can a feller be."

★ ★ ★

Steve stood guard over the store until after the first light of dawn blushed through the front windows. In that moment time became an object, as smooth and lovely as old glass. The cooler droned monotonously. Tranquil dust swirled and settled. And even though the store should soon be opening, Steve was overcome by the urge to sleep. One hand searched for reassurance along the tight grain of the rifle stock.

The body on the bed was not the same cautious person who, all his life, obeyed every stop sign, even when there was no traffic; the consummate organizer who sorted his record albums in alphabetical order; the young man who insisted on adding up the tab in his head before paying the waiter. That young man had played out, had been replaced by a thin shell of a man crammed with grief and guilt and remorse. Steve dreamed he was standing on a mountaintop screaming, "God, why did you take my baby? God damn you, God."

There came an electrifying shiver as the front door rattled against its lock. Steve was jarred awake. What time was it? How long had he slept? Five minutes? Five hours? Time lacked an absolute point of reference as the rattle again shook the door. Something there, a stoop-shouldered figure in the gray light. Trying to break in. Baby stealer. Steve sat upright in bed. The rifle butt fit snugly against his shoulder. He aimed down the sight and jerked the trigger.

Foot-pounds of energy drove the bullet, and air whooshed in to fill the hole made by its passing. The impact of the slug was ugly, like the dull thud of a faller's axe driven into punky wood, and a fraction of a second later the hallucinating crack of an angry rifle walloped off the walls and left Steve with a ringing in his ears. And yet he wondered if this was not some vivid nightmare and he had just awakened with the rifle to his shoulder. He dropped it beside him on the bed. He could have opened the breech and known for sure whether a round had been fired, but he did not. A light rain began to fall and the room was so quiet that a good listener could have heard the temperature drop a few degrees. Tiny droplets collected, ran down the corrugated metal, fell through space. Drip. Drip. Drip. These subtle noises provided a hushed backdrop to Steve's raspy and irregular breathing.

The Supreme Being spoke in a booming voice, "You have come to the foot of the cross."

Steve, still sitting on the bed with the rifle beside him, whispered, "Give me peace, Lord."

"Peace is not something that is bestowed. It is something you must attain. Accept Me into your soul. Only then can you realize eternal peace."

"Oh God, I've made a terrible mess of my life. Lord Almighty, forgive me. Grant me the courage to turn my life over to you."

It was at that moment, the turning point in Steve's life, that he became reborn. He made his commitment. "Lord, I accept you into my life. I give myself to you."

For Steve it was like Dorothy transported from Kansas to the land of Oz.

Twenty-three

Lefty hunkered over his glass of tepid red wine while an occasional drop of blood dribbled onto the floor. Around one leg of his barstool was a thin pool of crimson. He ignored the pain. How had he ever lasted all those years felling timber—crawling over deadfalls, surviving kickbacks and chased to hell and back by widow-makers. He cheated death a thousand times, more, and it had come down to this. For the first time in his life he had a piss-pot full of money and, to go along with it, he was packing a slug in his leg. He was convinced he was dying, and although it did not seem fair, he accepted it.

Lefty did not realize that the slug had traveled through the front door of the Chewaucan Grocery and lost most of its wallop before it grazed his outer thigh. But hit by the scorching metal and surprised by the report of the rifle, Lefty believed he had been fatally shot and lurched from the store, across the street to The Tavern. The blood beneath him was all the proof he needed. He told himself if he were a dog he would crawl off, dig a hole and die alone. Now he sat in the smoky room with those who were adding on to the night before and the early birds who were in dire need of an eye opener. Music and voices washed over him. He waited to bleed to death, took a drink of his wine and listened to the small talk around him: reservation killings, an attack dog named Gunner that had ripped apart a cow dog, fish runs, deer hunts, drinking, parties, poontang. Lefty sank deeper, submerging himself, relaxing in his self-pity as if the room were a deep tub of warm bath water.

He knew that a man could give up on life over a period of time, or do it quick. Pull the trigger. If you've got the guts. Guts was all it took. Back in his prime Lefty had backbone and courage. Sometimes, to show off, he would tap a stake in the ground opposite the lean of a tree and take bets he could bring the tree around a full 180 degrees and drive that stake clear out of sight. One time he won $500.

The years, the long hours on the end of an axe and pulling a misery whip, later running a power saw, had taken a terrible toll. The work had worn him out. Chunk by chunk. He always figured he would go fast, have a tree fall on him, a saw cut him in two. But no, it was not to be that way. He took a sip of wine and concentrated on dying slowly.

Back in the old days the timber faller was king and his domain was ten feet in the air, balanced on a flimsy springboard. Hanging there on the side of a big yellow-belly pine caused some sort of special bond to form between the lumberjack and the tree. Chop the undercut one axe-stroke at a time and then, on the opposite side, draw the crosscut back and forth to meet the open wedge. The hinge creaked, groaned and uttered a final prayer as high overhead the top began to wobble and move in tight little circles. On its descent, the tree picked up speed as it arced downward, slamming into the ground, kicking up a great cloud of dust and duff. For the faller it was hard to explain but somehow, after working on dropping a tree, it seemed that the destinies of the man and the living wood were intertwined. When the tree finally did go over, a faller always felt a little bit contrite.

Before WWI the east side forests were full of show-off timber. Ponderosa pine grew eight feet thick on the stump and the clear vertical grain, "ladder stock," ran for 200 feet. There was plenty of timber to go around and no need to spare it. When the country went to war Lefty joined the army, was issued a tin hat and a gun and went half a world away to fight the Germans. When he finally returned to the Oregon woods, he discovered that technology was turning the world of logging on its ear. Power saws had been introduced and the big trees were falling like stalks of grain before the blade of a sharp scythe.

"Gas burning sons-a-bitches," he would swear, and then go to work early and try to drop fifty or sixty thousand board feet before the sun went down. He sat on his barstool and recited the history of logging according to Lefty: "First pop-saw was a Mercury, weighed one hundred and forty pounds. I was the one took the beating. Had the noise, the stink of the exhaust, the scream of the chain, the terrible vibrations, all that weight. Get a tree 'bout ready to go, tweak the trigger a little, try not to kill it, but usually it was all or nothing, and then she starts over and my partner better act fast to protect me or else the engine will come back and crack me so damn hard across the shins it'd make my eyes tear up. All them saws, the Mercury, Diston, Titan and Mall, were all terrible for kicking back."

The power saws were to blame for the tendinitis in Lefty's elbow, his white-finger disease, and the constant pain in his wrists and hands that made him suffer every waking hour of his miserable, rotten existence. At the moment his neck felt as though someone were driving a hot railroad spike into it. His back ached and his muscles were beginning to go into spasms. If God would only end his suffering, stop the pain, he would gladly jump off and let this old world keep right on spinning.

Lefty lifted his good arm to sip the stale wine and the movement caused his nerves to tingle with an electric shock that traveled from his neck across his back and through both shoulders. More unpleasant chainsaw residue. How much longer did he have to endure all this? He leaned to one side to have a look-see under the barstool. He was hoping the puddle had spread but it remained about the same size as the last time he looked.

"Damn you, God," he muttered, "you're gonna make me live, ain't you."

Cap heard Lefty and called down the bar, "Ready for another, old timer?"

"Gimme a bottle to go."

Cap brought the bottle wrapped in a paper sack and Lefty paid with a hundred-dollar bill, waited for his change. And then, very deliberately, he slid off the stool, limped out the door and headed down the trail leading to his shack. On the way he noticed that the mix of rain and sunlight had brought out the buttercups. He bent to pick one, held it close and nearly grinned. From only a few feet away came a burst of noise that startled Lefty until he saw it was only a woodpecker tapping the bark of a bull pine, working for bugs. He tossed the flower aside and hobbled toward home.

★   ★   ★

Grandma sat on the edge of her cot waving her bony hand at a persistent fly that circled and landed, circled and landed, circled and landed. Where had she put her Saint Christopher medal?

She believed in the spirit of Standing Rock and the unlimited power of K'mukamtch. But she also believed in Jesus Christ and the Virgin Mary. Which religion could be trusted? If only she could find the Saint Christopher. She wanted Chief to have Saint Christopher as well as the medicine pouch she had prepared for him. Then, in the afterlife, Chief could decide for himself whether to go to heaven or the happy hunting ground.

Years ago Grandma had purchased two Saint Christopher medals. One of them she tucked in the casket with Sam when he died. The other she kept. Where could it be?

She saw Sam, a wispy Indian man wearing blue-striped overalls and a brakeman's cap. He was holding a railroad lantern burning bright red. The train started up. Sam climbed onto the bottom rung of the caboose ladder. The rustling wind smelled of wood smoke. Steam hissed. Rumbling shook the ground. The train moved away. A whistle tooted, wafting clear and lonely. Sam waved the lantern.

Memories washed over Grandma. She had always liked Sam to tell the story about the massacre. The renegade whites inviting the warriors from the Klamath village to a feast. The white leader holding a peace pipe aloft, but instead of peace he signaled treachery. His men leaped to their feet and began firing weapons, at point-blank range. And after the warriors were killed, the whites traveled to the Indian village. Women and children were pulled from the wickiups and slaughtered. The younger women were saved for sport, and after the men had satisfied their appetites, they killed them, too.

That terrible day Sam's mother, with Sam still inside her, was shot. As she lay dying her last act was to expel her newborn. When the detachment of soldiers from Fort Klamath drove the white renegades away, the baby was discovered among the pile of bodies. One of the soldiers was going to bayonet the infant to put it out of its misery, but another, a man who had children of his own, stopped him. His name was Sam Preston. He took the baby boy, tied off the umbilical cord and severed it with his knife. He held the baby to his mother's breast, allowed it to nurse. He wrapped the boy in a blanket, carried him to the fort and gave the infant to a barren Indian woman. She named the baby after him, Sam Preston.

The woman raised Sam near the fort. The boy grew up with the soldiers, running errands, peeling potatoes, washing dishes. They taught him his first English words. Young Sam was soon proficient at cussing. When he was sixteen years old, Sam used the money he had saved doing favors for the soldiers and bought a horse. He moved to a log cabin along Wood River and began working for the railroad. In almost every way, except the pigmentation of his skin, Sam was white. He dressed, smoked cigarettes, talked and swore like a white man.

Thinking about her dead husband always made Grandma feel a chill creep into her bones. She gathered her shawl around her shoulders and lay back on her cot.

She dreamed of the journey she would soon take, the journey to be with Sam. In this dream she was young again, the aspen leaves were shocking yellow, the vine maple brilliant red and the various animals came out of the forest and led her along a well-worn trail. Towering firs formed a canopy overhead to keep out all but slanting rays of saffron light. Ahead, in a tiny clearing, a noisy waterfall cascaded into a pool. There, in the reflective surface, was the image of a handsome young Indian man. Sam. He was smiling.

★   ★   ★

It had never much mattered to Pokey before, but it mattered to him now. He could not go on hating his white blood forever. It was a part of him. Shasta had made him aware of that. Pokey entered Grandma's room, sat on a corner of her bed and when she came awake he asked her, "Grandma, tell me about my father. What kind of a man was he?"

She told him some of what she knew. His name was Jimmy Weston. He was the son of a basin potato farmer and had worked at Modoc Lumber Company mill, pulling lumber off the green chain. It was said he was a hard worker and a man of his word. He died in a car wreck before Pokey was born.

That was all Grandma shared with Pokey. But she knew more. Knew that Pokey's father had been a drinking man, and when he drank he liked to fight. One night he and another fellow got in a scuffle over who was going to take Puggy home. Back then she was young and good-looking. After the brawl the two men threw their arms around each other and decided they ought to be friends. They bought a half-gallon of whiskey, got rip-roaring drunk and awoke the next morning in bed, with Puggy lying between them.

Nine months later Puggy gave birth. She named her baby boy Pokey because she had endured eight hours of hard labor when all she really wanted to do was to have the kid and split, go somewhere and get drunk. At least she had the presence of mind to bring Pokey, just as she had his two half-brothers, and deposit him at Grandma's house. It fell to Grandma to raise the three boys.

Grandma had drifted back to sleep. Pokey gently tapped her shoulder, "Grandma. You need to get up. We have to be going."

Grandma came awake. Her eyes fluttered. Lips trembled. "Saint Christopher. Need Saint Christopher."

Pokey reached to lift the Saint Christopher medal and chain off a nail on the wall. He handed it to her.

"Raven him trickster, him hide."

"Don't think so. It was right here where it's always been."

"Raven, him show you where find."

"Okay," Pokey said, not caring to argue. "You ready to go?"

"Where go?"

"The funeral. For Chief. Told you last night. Got the car warmed up. We're taking the Cadillac."

"No." She shook her head emphatically side to side.

"You've got to."

"No go. You take Christopher medal. Take medicine pouch." She handed him a small leather pouch with the drawstring pulled tight. "You put with Chief. Him choose."

"Put these in the casket?"

She nodded, yes.

"How come you don't want to go?"

She dismissed him with a wave. The big veins on the back of her hand were as blue as new denim. "Me sleep."

It was then he noticed her tennis shoes by the bed. They were wet and sitting in a small pool of water. He asked her if she had been out. She did not answer.

★   ★   ★

A few drops of rain splattered the windshield as he herded the gaudy red Cadillac along the highway leading up the canyon carved by the Chewaucan River. Shasta sat close to the door on the passenger's side, seemingly a mile away from Pokey. She wondered what it would have been like to have had a brother and wondered, too, if it would be akin to the bond she shared with her mother. Probably not. There were feelings and emotions she and her mother had never shared, would never share, secrets that only a brother or sister could understand.

Kay was content to live in a manufactured world of work, luncheons, gardening, knitting, reading, cooking—little things to consume her time and keep her busy. Occupied but never satisfied, or fulfilled.

Shasta looked at Pokey. Both his hands were gripping the steering wheel. He was staring straight ahead. "I can't begin to imagine," she said, "how hard this must be for you."

"I don't suppose anyone was very close to Chief. It's kind of tough to feel sorry. There was only one way for it to end. It should have happened a long time ago. I'm more sad for him than anything. Sad he wasted the time he had coming."

The Cadillac slowed. Pokey steered onto a wide turnout. Gravel ground beneath the tires. After they stopped he pushed open the door and said, "Come with me."

They dropped off a short embankment to the level of the

river. A great blue heron stood knee deep in an eddy, feeding on minnows. It gave a startled, guttural laugh and launched itself into awkward flight, the long neck folded back and the legs extended. In flight, the ungraceful, blue-gray bird became dignified and stately. It disappeared around a bend in the river.

Pokey looked down, noticed a coyote track in the mud. "Grandma says coyotes used to be scarce. Back in the old days. Since the white men took over there are a lot more."

"I read," Shasta said, "in Los Angeles coyotes lose their fear of man and come right into people's backyards. They eat garbage and kill pets."

Pokey smiled. "When this world blows itself into smithereens, and nothing is left, there is liable to be one mangy coyote sitting on top of the rubble heap baying at the moon."

Coyotes had never come prowling around Shasta's suburban neighborhood, never visited her sorority house. All she knew about coyotes was that they were the subject of Indian legends. "Aren't coyotes supposed to possess supernatural powers?"

"Grandma says, 'Remember, the coyote that laughs is the same one that bites.' "

"It surprises me that your grandmother didn't want to come."

Pokey reached to make sure the Saint Christopher medal and the medicine pouch were still in his coat pocket. Then he bent and picked up a fist-sized rock. It had been rounded by the tumbling action of the current, until a few hundred years ago, when a flood rolled it above the high water mark. Now pastel lichens were slowly eating at it. Lichens were patient; if they did not finish their work in their lifetimes they had confidence their descendants would do so in the next few millenniums.

"Grandma used to be big on telling stories. I remember she said when someone died, family and friends would start a rock pile and any time they passed that way they would add another rock. The size of the pile would show how much that person was thought of and respected. Chief deserves that much."

Shasta listened to the river gurgle and the wind moan through the canyon. She thought about Grandma. The old woman had tried to hand down the oral traditions of the tribe, but with her passing there would be no more stories to tie the past to the present. No clear path to yesterday. No sense of where the journey began or where it might lead. Shasta supposed that for the white race to comprehend such a devastating trespass it would have to endure the loss of its governmental structure, laws, borders, holidays, traditions and religious beliefs. Society would be required to reject as false everything that had previously been learned, or was known as fact, and people would be compelled to communicate forever after in a foreign language. If all that happened, only then would the white race appreciate what had come to pass for the Klamath people.

Twenty-four

Pokey was in a talkative mood as he steered the Cadillac through sharp corners and down straight-aways. He told where friends and acquaintances had been drinking and driving and wrecked, got themselves messed up or killed.

"Do you drink at all?" asked Shasta.

"I used to," Pokey said. "But I looked around and decided the cost was just too high. And I don't mean money."

They passed quick bursts of pines, aspens, cottonwoods and willows; white water braiding and unbraiding itself through the rapids; black basalt ledges, rounded boulders and steep rock slides. All these blended together like a watercolor wash, impressions without hard, defined edges.

The Cadillac swung away from the river, climbed over the lip of the canyon and descended to a high, treeless plain. Pokey slowed, rolled down his window and breathed in the aroma of sage while a cool wind licked the left side of his face. "Look at the deer," he said. About thirty head were working their way off the barren summit toward the incandescent green of the valley floor. "When they get to that grass I bet it'll taste as sweet as sugar."

A few miles farther Pokey steered off the oil road and followed a pitted path that led between two round buttes. The tires galloped over the washboard and splashed though puddles until, after a mile, they arrived at the Indian cemetery. It sat on the sterile shoulder of one of the buttes and was defined by a fence. Of the twenty million acres that had long ago comprised the Klamath nation, the original territory they had held against marauding tribes, it had come down to this: three measly acres of Indian bones surrounded by rusty barbed wire. And in reality even this now belonged to the government.

Fancy cars and pickup trucks were parked alongside the graveyard fence. Two days earlier they were waxed and shiny and new. Now they were dusty and dingy with scrapes and scratches and crumpled skin.

Manhattan Island had been stolen from the Indians for a handful of colorful trinkets. Shasta thought this latest landgrab was no different, just more expensive. When the Cadillac came to a stop she stepped out, pulled on her coat and walked with Pokey to a configuration of posts sunk in the ground, arranged to keep cattle on the outside of the fence but allowing humans to squeeze through the narrow opening. Within the compound she was transfixed by the graves—crude wooden crosses tilted at odd angles, small headstones and piles of loose rock. Some graves were decorated with plastic animal figurines, fake flowers, faded American flags, Christmas tinsel, a model car, a whirligig, dishes, a kid's bicycle. Scattered everywhere, like leaves after an October windstorm, were bits and pieces of broken glass and silver and gold bottle caps.

Indians were gathered around a roaring fire built beside a mound of dirt and a gaping hole in the ground—solemn profiles of a few old Indian women wearing long dresses, hair confined in netting and blankets drawn tightly around their shoulders; old men standing, slump-shouldered, wearing drab, wrinkled suits and ball caps. The young people favored bright colors—red, blue, purple, pink, orange, gold. They drank beer, wine and liquor straight from the bottles. Just another moment in the regrettable life span of the termination party. At some point it would end for them all. It had already ended for Chief.

A sudden wind came up, gusting and blowing sand around. Shasta's eyes burned. She used two fingers to rub and massage one eyelid at a time.

A man holding a fifth of Johnnie Walker Red said to Pokey, "We get done here an' we're gonna party over ta Duck's place. Hafta come on over." Pokey nodded. Shasta moved away. Pokey watched her through the heat shimmers and smoke of the fire as she circled the outer fringe of the group. The wind lamented and the eager fire snapped and popped. Pokey gazed past Shasta and followed the confining outline of the cemetery fence. In comparison to the broad sweep of the open landscape the three acres shriveled until it was no larger than a jail cell. Pokey looked back into the fire.

A dark-skinned woman took a drink from a quart of *vin rosé* and told no one in particular, "Let's get him planted, get the hell outta here." Her voice was harsh, without the slightest hint of emotion.

The wind fluttered a flag above a grave. The whirligig

clattered and spun. A tiny black speck on the horizon moved closer and, in time, became a hearse. The driver stopped at the fence, puzzled over the access gate, then took the post and the wires in a wide arc, laid them on the ground and drove inside. He backed around so the rear of the hearse was pointed toward the hole in the ground.

The driver was the same thin man with the sympathetic voice Pokey had dealt with at the funeral home. He was wearing a long black raincoat over his suit. He gave a glance at the sky and nervously scurried about preparing the contraption for lowering the casket into the grave. He avoided eye contact with anyone and when everything was in place, including a chunk of green carpet to cover the mound of dirt, he announced, "Ready for the pallbearers. Will the pallbearers please assist me."

The cedar casket with brass-plated handles was placed on top of the mechanical hoist. Pokey moved forward. The funeral director recognized him and extended his hand. Pokey shook it and then instructed the man to open the casket.

"That's not something I can do. I'm very sorry."

Someone woofed at him, "Ya talk like a man with a tin ass."

Another ordered, "Do what you're told."

"But legally I'm strictly forbidden, I just can't."

"Yes you can," Pokey assured him, "you will, or we'll get a pry bar and break it open."

★   ★   ★

The casket was unsealed. Shasta, rather than look at Chief, turned away and allowed her gaze to search across the gray-brown panorama, beyond the sagebrush and the wind-twisted junipers, to where the Chewaucan River appeared as flat as a band of pounded metal. At the far edge of the valley was a line of crumpled hills covered with dark green pine trees. Behind those hills were taller ridges cloaked in timber and as they receded into the distance, they changed color and ended in a pale shade of gray that welded itself to the sky.

Shasta concentrated, not on this strange drama that was down to the final act, but something from memory, the familiarity and security of her sorority room in Eugene: an image of the framed photograph of her mother on the dresser, the way the drawers were laid out with each item of clothing in its proper place, hearing the sounds of traffic rustling past on 18th Street, Connie Francis singing *Everybody's Somebody's Fool* on the radio, the muffled voices and laughter coming from the hallway.

She felt the wind tug at a loose strand of her hair. A drop of rain slid down her warm, white cheek. The damp sand acted as a conductor and she felt the restless souls from vanquished generations moving around, drifting aimlessly beneath her feet.

★ ★ ★

Standing in front of the open casket, Pokey broke the government seal and uncapped a half-gallon of Black Velvet. In a voice that was firm and steady he made a toast. "Chief, I'm sorry your time on this earth has come to an end. Here's hoping that in the afterlife you find peace and contentment." He clenched his hand around the neck of the bottle and held it high. "To you, Chief."

He handed the bottle to his right and each of Chief's friends, in turn, drank. The last bit of whiskey remaining in the bottle was tucked in the casket with Chief. It seemed only fitting that he should take the final dregs to eternity.

A light rain sprinkled against Chief and stained his leathery skin a darker shade of brown. Pokey took the medicine pouch and the Saint Christopher medal from his pocket and placed them in the casket. His breath made a little cloud of fog around the words as he said to the funeral director, "Let's get him buttoned up."

After Chief had been lowered into the ground, the elders, a few walking with canes to aid their balance in the uneven dirt, filed off the hill to their vehicles. The younger crowd split up, some to get booze from their cars and others after more wood.

The fire licked at the dry fuel and flames leaped into the air. There was laughter and swearing; stories made the rounds attesting to Chief's prowess at fighting and drinking. Glass broke with sharp pops as empty bottles, flung against rocks, shattered.

"She ain't suppos' ta be here," grumbled an Indian screwing up his mouth, showing off rotten teeth from too many candy bars, too many Pepsi's.

Pokey said nothing. He took Shasta by the arm and led her away. They walked to the far side of the cemetery and at the fence he held the wires apart so Shasta could duck through. Then he stepped over. They hiked to the top of the butte. By then the rain was slanting down and opening slits, like tiny eyes, in the white sand.

"This was the crematorium ground," Pokey told her. "One time I was here after a big storm and found a cavalry button. The rain must have washed it to the surface. I suspect it came from an army shirt and that it was some warrior's prized possession. He was probably cremated wearing it."

"What did you do with the button? Did you keep it?"

"Naw, dug a hole and buried it."

Pokey and Shasta stood at the summit of the butte, gazing down on the scene below and none of it seemed quite real: the fancy cars appearing counterfeit, the capricious wind pushing smoke on an oblique path, between, over and around headstones and whimsical decorations, drinkers laughing and passing bottles around their tight circle, the funeral director shoveling wet dirt into the open grave. A fresh breeze blew cool on Shasta's face. Her breathing was slow and shallow. She became aware of a confusing dampness on her cheeks. It was not the rain.

Pokey noticed her tears. He took her by the shoulders, turned her, and, using the flat part of his thumbs, he gently dried her cheeks. Shasta moved that last small, half step that separated them and wrapped her arms around him. She rested her head on his chest. Standing there on top of that butte, with the storm blustering around them, they could have been the last man and woman alive in the world.

Lightning was using up more of the sky and thunder was booming. Finally Pokey pulled away and said, "Probably not the safest place to be." He led the way down off the butte. A long-eared jackrabbit stopped to watch them pass. "One year, I must have been nine or ten, there was an infestation of jackrabbits, so many that everybody on the reservation got together and we had a rabbit drive."

"A rabbit drive?"

"Yeah, the women and children spread out and drove the rabbits toward a corner that was fenced in with chicken wire. The men clubbed the rabbits to death. Hundreds, maybe thousands. It never really seemed to cut down on the number of rabbits, but it was a hell of a party. The next winter was really cold. Got down to thirty below. That's what finally killed off the rabbits."

"A winter like that is hard on wildlife, isn't it?"

"The worse the weather, the greater the winterkill. But what's bad for some is good for others. The coyotes and foxes, eagles and hawks, ravens and crows and magpies had a picnic feeding on the carcasses. That's nature's way. Grandma said there used to be wolves around here. Said there were grizzly bear, too."

As they neared the car Shasta asked, "Could you help me with something?"

"Sure. What?"

"I told you I tried to talk to your grandmother. She won't tell me anything. I would really like to learn about the things she remembers. Maybe if you were there."

"Fine," Pokey said, pleased that it was something so simple. "First, I have to—I'll just be a second."

Pokey took the rock off the front seat and jogged back up the hill. The bonfire blazed and the party continued. The funeral director was using the flat side of the shovel to pack the dirt on the grave. The rain came down hard. Lightning flashed and thunder rolled across the valley floor.

Twenty-five

Grandma, a blanket covering her legs, was seated in the rocking chair. Shasta sat on a corner of the bed, a stenographer's pad balanced on her knee, pen poised. Pokey lowered himself to one knee in front of the old woman and said to Shasta, "I'll ask about K'mukamtch. He's the Great Spirit." And then speaking in a loud voice, "Grandma, tell about K'mukamtch."

Grandma rocked. The floor creaked. Grandma's tiny voice was in rhythm with her rocking. "K'mukamtch live sun. Him greedy like raven. Him sneaky like coyote. Him trickster. Wife moon. Name Le-tkakawash. Le-tkakawash tend fire. Papoose on back. Fire leap in sky. Pull in papoose. Papoose gone. K'mukamtch him say, 'Knee hurt bad.' Le-tkakawash pull baby from knee. Baby cry, cry. K'mukamtch name baby Aishish. Baby cry no more."

As Grandma spoke Shasta tried to write notes but she had difficulty spelling the names. She did not want to interrupt and tried to write phonically. "How long ago was that story told to you?" she asked, making sure each word she spoke was loud and distinct.

Grandma ignored her.

Pokey picked it up. "When was that story told?"

"Told lot a times."

"When was the first time she remembers?" Shasta asked Pokey and he repeated the question as an interpreter. Grandma just rocked. Slowly her head came forward and eyelids closed. It appeared she had fallen asleep, but then she began talking again. "Beaver dam block Chewaucan. K'mukamtch want loon dive, break dam. Want see him break dam. Spit chalk on back. Make white spot.

"Beaver dam good place fish. Indian want keep dam. Cut hair. Put pitch on head. Call K'mukamtch. Him come. Make loon break dam. Turn Indian stone. Put Indian in river. Make water go over Indian. Raven see Indian in river. Raven him laugh."

Pokey told Shasta, "That's the story of Standing Rock. It's below the house here, a rock ledge that the river flows over. A short falls. She didn't mention it, but Standing Rock is supposed to be protected by what they called the Spell of Laughing Raven. Sometimes the spell can be very powerful, making good things happen out of the clear blue, or just as likely something very bad can come to pass. I don't know, the old stories, they're strange, hard to make any sense out of them."

★ ★ ★

Grandma told many other stories. Finally she came to an event she remembered when she was a small girl. "Sucker fish come Standing Rock. K'mukamtch send Sucker fish. Indian spear fish. Smoke fish. Plenty fish. Plenty fish.

"Soldier Fort Klamath come. Bring big net. Take horse. Pull net. Many, many fish. Great pile fish. White man take. Indian take. Still fish. Fish spoil. K'mukamtch mad spoil fish. Stop fish run."

Grandma seemed to run out of breath. She flinched in pain, chest swelled, tears appeared, fists clenched and unclenched, eyelids snapped wide open and her body became as rigid as a rubber glove pumped full of air. Her lips trembled. She panted. Her forehead was shiny with perspiration.

"Grandma. Grandma." Pokey scooped her up in his arms, carried her and gently laid her on the cot. She shuddered. Gasped. And then her breathing stabilized and became more normal.

Shasta laid aside her pen and pad and moved to check Grandma's pulse. It was difficult to find the main artery that ran down the inside of the old woman's bony wrist and, when she did locate it, the pulse was shallow and weak. Shasta glanced at her wristwatch, began counting heartbeats. The timeless heart muscle continued to pump blood and oxygen in a slow, perfect cadence. A good sign.

Pokey moved to cover Grandma's legs with a Pendleton blanket. Shasta brushed away a fly that landed on the old woman's hollow cheek. She lowered her voice to just above a whisper. "I think she's either had a stroke or a heart attack. We've got to get her to the hospital."

★　★　★

Lefty came to his senses, saw the sun had somehow succeeded in popping through a small gap in an ocean of clouds. The temperature warmed and the air began to stir. Pine needles swayed, thin shadowy fingers played across the trail and Lefty realized he had been standing in one spot for God knows how long. He felt something in his right hand. A book of matches. Odd, because he did not know where it came from, could not remember having picked it up. Words appeared to be printed on the matchbook cover. He tried to read, but the letters wiggled deliriously.

If the letters had held steady, Lefty would have read, "Make Something of Yourself—Get Your High School Diploma," and a telephone number to call. Lefty strained to see, moving the matchbook cover closer to his eyes and then farther away. A raven cawed and the letters of a single word burst into sharp focus. That word was "School."

Lefty remembered his last day of school. It was in the spring of the year, a warm afternoon, and the teacher, Miss Abbott, was droning on about reconstruction and carpetbaggers sweeping into the South after the Civil War. For Lefty school was boring, a total waste of time. He made a snap decision, rose and walked from the classroom. Miss Abbott called after him but he ignored her, walked home, threw a few things into a knapsack, went to the rail yards and hopped the first train that passed. It happened to be heading west. By the end of the week Lefty was living and working in a logging camp on the east side of the Cascade Range.

"School." Lefty said the word out loud. It had a ring to it. He had a sudden inspiration that he might have amounted to something if he had stuck it out long enough to get his high school diploma. Hell, he might have carved out a better living for himself, been bull of the woods and run the logging show, or at least had his own gypo outfit.

"Never too old to go back to school. Never too old to get your diploma," called the raven's voice.

Lefty drew a deep breath. Him go back to school? He laughed. But drunken laughter could not hide the possibility that Lefty's guardian angel had finally caught up to him and planted a seed in his conscious brain. Or should the Spell of Laughing Raven be given the credit? Either way, if that small idea, that possibility were allowed to germinate, and grow, there would be no telling what might come to pass.

The chance at a new beginning, no matter how slim a chance, seemed to shove aside Lefty's bitterness, depression and heartache. He felt invigorated and found himself grinning, actually grinning, and it occurred to him that the real trick to being happy was all in the way a feller looks at things.

Lefty started to move and a stab of pain reminded him he had been shot. But the pain was only part of it, like the tip of an iceberg. There was not a snowball's chance in hell he would go back to high school, let alone get his GED. And then a brilliant thought occurred to him. "At least they could dry me out. Maybe give me some medicine ta stop my hurtin'."

He looked out over the spot where the Chewaucan River ran over a short waterfall, the place the Indians called Standing Rock, and then an impulse nudged him. He turned and started back toward town, gimping along on his bum leg.

★ ★ ★

Red sat in his office, feet propped on his desk, watching the old logger limp up the street. He felt a jolt of pity, but when Lefty reached the bottom of the stairs and began to slowly mount them, Red wondered, "What's that sorry old coot want now?"

Lefty reached for the doorknob and found it was not easy to open. But he managed. He stepped inside, dragging his bloodstained leg as though it had suddenly turned to wood. He shuffled forward to Red's desk, stood there unsteadily. "I've been sick a long time. I wanna get well."

"What are you talking about, Lefty?"

"Things," Lefty said. He could still call it off, back out, buy a bottle, get drunk.

"What kind of things?" Red really did not have time for aimless bullshit.

"My drinking for one."

"What about your drinking?"

"In a minute. But first I wanna make a deal with you. I heard you been asking around about that vigilante deal. Investigating the matter. Well, I know who put it up. I'm willing to make a trade."

Red swung his feet off the desk. They made a loud thump when they contacted the floor. He snapped upright in his chair. "Old man, I'm all ears."

"It's kind of complicated."

"What isn't?"

"I need a favor."

"If it ain't immoral or illegal, I'll see what I can do."

"I wanna go on the wagon, go to one of them dry-out farms. I got money to pay for it."

"Lefty, you don't got squat."

"Do, too," Lefty pulled the money Grandma had given him from his pants pocket.

Red whistled through his teeth, "Which wahoo you steal that from?"

"There wasn't nothing stolen. I got this fair and square."

"If you say so."

"So, we got ourselves a deal or not?"

"You better not be lying about the money."

"Swear to God, I ain't."

"Okay. I give my word, we'll get you some help. Now tell me what you know about the vigilante crap."

"I gotta have me a drink." Lefty's hands were shaking. "Then I'll be fine. That's all I need. One little drink."

Red pulled a bottle of Early Times from a drawer and set it on his desk. Lefty had to come and get it. He swept it up, held it close to his body to reduce his shaking and unscrewed the lid. He took a satisfying swig, gulping the amber liquid down. Almost instantly his shattered nerves began to repair themselves. He screwed the lid back on and returned the bottle to the desk. He backhanded his mouth with a sleeve. "A week or ten days back, Cap cashed my social security check. I paid my tab. Put the rest in my pocket. Had me a few drinks. On the way home I got jumped, hit over the head. They stole my money. I followed them. I seen who done it."

"Who?"

"Was Chief and Tyler and Nathan." From the look that crossed Red's face, Lefty knew Red had added two and two. "Yeah, I'm the one tacked up the sign. Did it just to worry them. Never thought you'd concern yourself about it. Never thought the three of them would up and die."

Red reached out, took the bottle and had himself a drink. He offered it to Lefty but the old boomer shook his head.

Twenty-six

With a jangle of keys Red unlocked the cell door and pulled it open. Metal screeched against metal. Creek lay stretched on the bunk. He did not move right away, did not want to get his hopes up just in case this was a false alarm.

"What I tell you? Everything worked out. Grand jury took a look at all the evidence, went over every last detail, and failed to indict. They determined there was only one person who could have killed Chief. And that was Chief. It's official—died at his own hands. Suicide."

Creek kicked his feet off the bunk, placed them on the floor and sat erect. His face flushed. "I can go?"

"You're as free as a bird. Here's your car keys and the other things you had in your pocket. Money's all there. Twenty-one thirty-seven. Count it if you want."

"I trust you."

"You need a lift somewhere?"

"Naw." Creek bolted through the door, leaped down the last few steps and hurdled a puddle. He began skipping, the way a boy will do coming home from his last day of school. He shouted, "Free!" His whole life was now in front of him. All he had to do was get to his car. He remembered he did not have a title or plates. He would take care of that later; right now nothing was going to stop him, or even slow him down.

Overhead a bastion of clouds, the chocolate color of a plowed lake bottom, wheeled and collided. A deluge of rain tumbled from the sky, soaking Creek, but what did it matter? He trotted over the bridge and passed the barn as rain pounded against the tin roof. A loose board banged in the wind. The dogs barked, but the weather was so blustery they did not come out from under the house. When he reached his Corvette, Creek ran his hand over the wet fender and gave thanks that the soft top was in place even though he could not remember having put it up. He rushed up the steps to the porch and through the door. "Anyone home? Pokey. Grandma." He checked Grandma's room. "Where the hell is everyone?"

Even though Creek rarely smoked, he felt a compulsion for a cigarette and urgently picked through the debris scattered around on the floor until he located a partial pack. He found a book of matches, lit the cigarette and drew a satisfying cloud of smoke into his lungs. But the gratification was short-lived. He looked around and wondered how such a familiar place as home could seem so offensive and detestable. He darted into the bedroom and quickly changed clothes, stuffing things in his duffel bag. He made a conscious effort not to glance at Chief's bunk.

On the way out he grabbed a six-pack of Pepsi, tossed the butt of the cigarette in a puddle and lowered himself into his car. There was a church key on the key ring and he used it to pry open a Pepsi. It spurted foam. "Damn it." He wiped at the crotch of his pants while his left leg depressed the clutch. He kicked over the starter and the engine roared to life. The rumble of the exhaust pleased Creek and his right hand searched for first, found it, and the Corvette began moving down the rutted lane. He switched on the radio. Del Shannon's falsetto voice sang, "Run-run-run-run-runaway." Creek was gone.

★　★　★

Lying on the hospital bed Grandma gave the appearance of a tiny, damaged sparrow. An IV bag dripped a saline solution into one bony arm, while another bag hung on the bed's framework, capturing the liquid wastes. She was hooked to a machine that recorded her heartbeats, showing them on an oscilloscope as a series of faint red dots that echoed a slow but steady ping-ping-ping-ping.

At one point during the early morning hours Grandma sighed to herself, "K'mukamtch come. Lay bone shore Klamath Lake. Him go. Come next day. See many smoke. Him smile, talk self, say, 'Live well my people.' That how Klamath Indian come be made. That is end."

The past played like transient shadows racing across a desert landscape. "Indian sign treaty. White man give Indian name. Say you Jim Joe. You John Joe. You Jim George. Some get name—Scar Face Bill. Bad Leg Charley. One-Eye Frank.

"Indian agent take children. Make children live boarding school. No see mother. No see father. Make stay. Make go school. Teacher say no speak Klamath. If speak Klamath punish. Make hold up stick, hold up high. Make girl hold willow. Make boy hold fence rail. Hold up hour, two hour, three hour. Whip boy. Make boy take shirt off. Whip bad. Make boy bleed. Boy never get over. Me say we whip teacher, see how he like. We make noise, take away food. Get hungry, no make noise.

"White man come reservation. Kill bear. Kill wolf. Kill deer. Take fish. No food left. Indian go Fort Klamath, beg food, beg blanket. White man shake head. Him say no. Indian die."

★   ★   ★

A pale green moth caught a wing tip on the water and dropped onto the dusky surface of the Chewaucan River. It struggled to free itself, wiggling its body but unable to lift its water-soaked wings. An alert trout accelerated from the deep pool beneath Standing Rock and, nearing the surface, dropped its lower jaw, inhaling the moth. The fish continued up and out of the water. At the top of its arc, a quick flip of its tail sent a shower of diamond-like water drops to mingle among the stars. The fish smacked the hard veneer of the river and Pokey looked in that direction, watching the spiral rings march outward from the point of impact.

He heard a chorus of tundra swans. They sounded somewhat like geese, except their distinctive song was mellower and more melodic. Pokey searched the sky and found them just as their black shadows passed over the white face of the moon. They traipsed noisily down the sky and Pokey tried to imagine how remarkable it would be to fly with them—the basin unfolding below, the burnished skin of Klamath Lake reflecting the night sky, the ridges extending like ribs off the snow-capped peaks of the high Cascades.

A primary feather dropped from one of the tundra swans. It fell lazily through the night near where Pokey stood at the edge of the river. Waves, sounding like tiny hands clapping, were breaking against the shoreline. How could this gentle water know of the journey that awaited it? That a few miles downstream was the placid lake, and beyond the outlet was a river that plunged in a series of frothing rapids for two hundred miles and spent itself in a tidal pool, mixing its fresh waters with the brine of the mighty Pacific Ocean.

A woman's voice spoke softly; her tone was delicate, tender, affectionate, alluring. "Pokey, I need you. Come to me." The river goddess was seducing Pokey. He obeyed, moving toward the voice, stepping into the river.

He was knee deep in the water, and moving forward, when Grandma's shrill command stopped him. "Pokey, you get home." He obeyed her, just as he had when he was a boy and she had called him home. He stepped out of the water, onto the shore. If Grandma had not called him, the river temptress would surely have wrapped her arms around him, entwining him in her tight embrace, and drowned him.

How many times had Grandma warned the boys of the Spell of Laughing Raven? This time the trickster had been up to one of its cruel deceptions. As he moved away from the river Pokey heard a raven back in the willows give a scornful caw.

A sympathetic breeze brought the white swan feather to Pokey. It fell at his feet and he scooped it up and held it. A white feather from heaven. What could it mean? Grandma would know. In her absence the shadows around him grew all the more strange, sullen and mysterious.

★ ★ ★

Shasta could not sleep. She lay on the feather mattress between sheets line-dried and smelling of pine and wild-flowers, and thought about what Floyd had said. He told her the white man had done everything in his power to civilize the Klamath Indians. A sawmill and a flour mill had been built on reservation land. The government had provided a blacksmith, a carpenter and a wagon and plow maker. The treaty stated: "This document is intended to promote the well being of the Indians, advance them in civilization, and especially agriculture, and secure their moral improvement and education."

Shasta had also read Floyd's copy of the legislation terminating the Klamath reservation. In it the Interior and Insular Affairs Committee of the 82nd Congress reported: "It is the belief of the committee that all legislation dealing with Indian affairs should be directed to the ending of a segregated race set aside from other citizens. It is the recommended policy of this committee that the Indians be assimilated into the Nation's social and economic life."

The government had come up with the perfect word to describe this heavy-handed social experiment. Termination. It occurred to Shasta that the word annihilation was interchangeable with termination and she wondered how a group of individual Indians, loosely knit together in the fabric of a tribe, could ever stand up to the federal government? Especially considering that all the Indian leaders throughout history, who had fought the government for what they believed was right, had been discredited or killed. Geronimo exiled to Florida and forced to become a farmer. Sitting Bull gunned down at a ghost dance by police. Crazy Horse killed while supposedly attempting to escape. Captain Jack hung. Chief Joseph forced to live and die in exile. The white man had intentionally destroyed all the Indian heroes. Was it the government's intent to have the Klamath Indians, and every other Indian in America, merely slink into obscurity like useless grains of sand slipping through history's hourglass?

★ ★ ★

The cold bluish tinge of shadows on snow, the lushness of grass in early spring, the noisy hum of insects over a slough, the golden sparkle of aspen leaves, the rank smell of a hot springs bubbling from the ground, a ruffed grouse drumming its wings, an osprey diving for a fish, smoke wafting around a campfire, the tart taste of huckleberries, the sleek curve of a pine needle basket, raven calling—Grandma slept.

Twenty-seven

A great horned owl had taken up residence in an elm tree adjacent to the Klamath Memorial Hospital. For the past several weeks she had been bringing in mice, kangaroo rats, pieces of rabbits and even skunk meat to feed her two babies. At night she sat on a dead limb and serenaded the patients and staff with a variety of hoots, bizarre shrieks, and weird screeches.

A nurse swept into the room, speaking as she entered, "How we feeling tonight?" not expecting a response. She cranked open the blind and stood for a moment staring at the ruddy moon.

"Whoo-who-whoo."

"Our owl is back. He's right outside your window. Aren't you lucky." The nurse moved around, efficiently checking medical contraptions. When satisfied they were functioning properly she exited the room.

"Screech!"

Grandma shivered ever so slightly. She always shivered when an owl called. Owls could be ghosts of the departed who had come back. Owls were hard to resist. They could also be a shaman assuming the form of an owl. If so, the owl was very dangerous. All a shaman had to do was call your name and you went to the land of black shadows.

"Call my name."

"Whoo-who-whoo."

★ ★ ★

The owl sat on the dead branch, content to wait for the strong juices of her digestive tract to separate soluble portions of the mouse. Over the course of several hours she watched through the translucent window as nurses came and went, checking the old woman, weighing fluids dripping in and weighing fluids dripping out, taking readings, writing numbers on a chart that was hung on the frame at the foot of the bed. These nurses worked diligently to keep the old woman alive for a few more minutes, hours, dollars. Grandma was kept quiet and made comfortable. The morphine guaranteed she would not suffer. The Great Spirit and God waited in the wings to claim her soul.

The owl was away hunting when Pokey slipped into the hospital room in the early morning. He stood beside the bed and removed his hat. He held it respectfully over his heart, the way he did when the Star Spangled Banner played at rodeos. Grandma lay motionless between clean yellow sheets. Pokey spoke to her. His voice quavered, "I don't want you to die, Grandma." His eyes were moist.

Grandma was beyond temporal boundaries, floating somewhere on Klamath Marsh. In the old days the marsh was vital to the survival of the Klamaths. The deep water provided fish. In the shallows grew the lily called wocus and the beds of tules. Both plants were used for food, clothing, shelter, and woven into rafts, hunting blinds, sleeping mats, containers, and vessels. The marsh was alive with the calling of coots and the strange, wonderful cry of the loon. Turtles. Dragon flies. It was noisy with life. Bull frogs. Snowy egret. Sandhill cranes. Trumpeter swans. Blue-winged teals. Buffleheads. Scooters. Mergansers. Wood ducks.

The mouth of the frail old woman trembled as it fought to form the boundaries of words, but the only sounds were utterances as muted and insignificant as tumbleweeds grinding against a barbed wire fence.

Twenty-eight

As Leland Campbell boarded the corporate airplane in Portland the sun was not much more than a pink glow in the sky behind Mt. Hood. Campbell, the U.S. West Bank Vice-President of Operations—Northwest Region, was dressed in a conservative charcoal business suit, a starched white shirt and royal blue tie drawn firmly around his neck with a perfect Windsor knot.

On the flight south he recognized the various snow-capped pinnacles of the Cascades: Mt. Hood, Mt. Jefferson, Three-Fingered Jack, Mt. Washington, the Three Sisters, Broken Top and Mt. Thielsen. On numerous occasions he had taken his two sons into the mountains to hike and to fish the high lakes and small streams that tumbled down the west side. Some of his fondest memories were of sitting around a campfire, watching the boys roast marshmallows, fixing s'mores, and telling them scary stories. They would sleep so close to him in their canvas tent he was afraid of rolling over in his sleep and smothering them.

He recalled a specific fishing trip; it must have been in April he thought, because snow was still scattered around in patches. Mosquitoes had nearly eaten them alive. He was smiling at the memory of the boys running down the trail, flailing at the bugs as they ran to the safety of the car. Those were fun days. Now the boys were grown, off in college, and in a few short years they would be married and have families of their own.

Flying so high, it was impossible for him to get a real sense of the country down below. The snowfields appeared serene, but on the ground a blustery wind was cold and cutting. The ridges looked like progressively tighter accordion folds but in reality were steep-sided, impenetrable tangles of brush growing through crisscrossed windfalls. The areas that were black and seemed flat as glass were actually rocky lava flows where vegetation refused to grow and few animals could exist. Riding on a carpet of air, Campbell was blissfully content until, near Klamath Lake, they hit a pocket of minor turbulence. But they were through it quickly and into their final approach.

Arny Osborne met him at the airport. Arny was dressed in a blue suit and driving a black Lincoln Continental. A rental. His own car, a Rambler sedan, would not have been presentable to ferry around such an esteemed executive. On the way to town the big car purred and the men engaged in pleasantries about the weather, golf and fishing prospects.

At the bank the two men settled in the pecan-paneled conference room. Arny's secretary delivered coffee and a plate of donuts. Campbell was trying to watch his diet. The week before, his doctor had told him he needed to lose twenty pounds, but the chocolate glazed donuts looked so delicious. He eyed them for several long seconds before taking one, tearing it in two and dunking an end in his coffee. When he had finished chewing he complimented Arny. "You did a commendable job with the termination program, especially considering the complexities that were involved."

Arny grinned. "Thank you, sir. There were a few trying moments there . . . but we were able to prevail."

Campbell took a sip of coffee. "This infusion of termination money really improves our bottom line. What is your assessment for the immediate future?"

"We have an investment fund set up for the seven hundred tribal minors. Those monies will remain with us and will be disbursed as the individuals reach legal majority. We will administer those funds and, of course, will collect our customary fees. And there were an additional three hundred members who had their money placed under guardianship or trusteeships. A few got away, but not many. We retained the majority of the accounts. The remaining members, about three hundred, were paid."

"And how did that go?" Campbell wanted to know.

"For the most part it was rather satisfying to see the number of new accounts opened by tribal members. We worked hard to garner those. The money that was drawn out went to pay off bills and to the purchase of refrigerators, stoves, washers, dryers and other household appliances. They bought rifles and fishing rods. And, of course, there was a real spurt in automobile sales. One dealer sold seventeen new cars the first day, fifteen for cash."

"I hope he's a customer of ours." Campbell chuckled.

Arny nodded. "Yes sir, he most certainly is." He grinned for a moment and then grew serious. "Of course, with so much money floating around, a few individuals got out of hand. We had several who demanded cash for the total amount."

"What did you do?"

"I tried to steer them toward investment opportunities."

"And, were you successful?"

"Not really. One stuffed his money into a paper sack."

"A paper sack?"

"Yes sir, and when I tried to intervene he knocked me down."

"My gosh. Were you injured?"

"Mainly just my pride. He was arrested on the sidewalk in front of the bank."

"What happened to the money?"

"They gave it back to him after he posted bail. Then he went and bought a Cadillac. I read in the newspaper where he killed himself the same day."

"What a tragedy."

"Yes, it was. And there were others. A woman put ten thousand dollars into a checking account and the very next day she was overdrawn. She had to add money from her savings. A fellow took twenty thousand dollars in cash and turned around and handed half of it to a buddy. I heard from a local bartender that an Indian gave him five thousand dollars and told him to keep pouring drinks until the money ran out. One young man is supposed to have driven a new Corvette through the showroom window. Suffice it to say there have been some fantastic stories making the rounds. The sad part is, most of them are probably true."

"I suppose it wouldn't matter, you bestow that much

money on any segment of the population and there are going to be a few wild ones who spend it recklessly. When we spoke on the phone you mentioned there were a few loose ends."

"Probably the most pressing is one that poses an interesting dilemma. Every member of the tribe has claimed his money, cashed his check or established a guardian or trustee account. Every member except one. He sent a note to the bank refusing the money."

"He what?"

"Said he refused to 'sell out.' Those were his words, 'sell out.' "

"Let me get this straight. This fellow has a check for forty-three thousand dollars and he sits on it? That doesn't make one iota of sense. He's not earning a dime of interest."

"I know," Arny said.

"Have you spoken to him?"

"Not directly."

Campbell leaned back. He raised his left hand and used his thumb and middle finger to massage his temples. He heaved an exaggerated sigh and dropped his hand back to the table. "This could be huge. The federal government assigned U.S. West Bank as the financial administrator for this transaction. We represent the American public in what is undoubtedly the biggest land sale since the purchase of Alaska. We cannot, under any circumstances, put ourselves in the position of making any omissions, miscalculations, or oversights. I am extremely concerned about the possible legal ramifications resulting from one party to the proceedings refusing to participate. I have to question—will that, in any way, jeopardize the termination agreement?"

"You're worried?"

"Yes. I'm worried because I don't know the consequences. But I have to assume this individual is either not thinking rationally, or lodging some sort of protest. If he is protesting—I'm thinking out loud here—maybe he doesn't feel the settlement was adequate. If he were to try and sue the government because of inadequate compensation, would that put the bank in a vulnerable position? It could. Absolutely it could—and expose us to a major liability. It might obligate the courts to take action. I'll have to run this past legal council. But we can avoid any potential stumbling block if we convince this lone holdout to accept his payment. Do you know where we could find him?"

"In Chewaucan, an Indian community twenty miles north of here."

"Why don't we drive there and speak with him. What's his name?"

"Pokey Pitsua."

"Strange name—Pokey?"

"As I understand it, he's a young man of mixed blood, Indian and Caucasian. It was his half-brother I had the run-in with, the one who later committed suicide. Maybe his death played a hand in all this."

"Do you know where he lives?"

"I can find out. I spoke with the deputy in Chewaucan, Marion Durkee, to garner information about Mr. Pitsua. I'll give him a quick call." Arny started to rise. He placed his hands flat against the smooth surface of the conference table and on a whim decided to add, "Whether Mr. Pitsua signs off and takes the money or he doesn't, U.S. West has profited from this arrangement, and the lucrative trust arrangement guarantees we'll continue to do well into the future."

Campbell crossed his arms over his chest and looked directly at Arny. "Our fiscal positioning, as well as the necessity to follow the letter of the law, is only a part of this equation. Don't lose sight of the fact we are morally and ethically accountable to our customers. Including every last one of these Indians. If we fail to serve their best interests it could come back to haunt us. To put it bluntly, it is our necks on the chopping block. And I can't seem to shake this feeling that the doo is about to hit the proverbial fan."

★   ★   ★

A doe slipped from the timber, took several tentative steps and reached the shoulder of Highway 97. She attempted to dash across the road in front of oncoming traffic but just as her four hoofs touched blacktop a Lincoln Continental splattered the muscles and bones of her chest to mush. Tail lights blinked a luminous red, elevated, dipped as the big car skidded to a stop. The right front fender was shoved in and was rubbing against the tire.

"Dammit," Arny muttered, trying to recall if he had paid extra for the rental insurance, hoping he had. "Are you okay?"

"That thing almost landed in my lap." Campbell felt strangely calm. He had been anticipating a catastrophe and it came as no great surprise to him when it actually did happen. He pulled on the handle and leaned his shoulder against the door. The door bound against the fender and when it came open, the metal gave a loud popping noise. Campbell stepped to the ground and went to where the doe lay. She spasmodically kicked her legs a time or two and her chest expanded. Then she exhaled, her muscles relaxed and a thin bluish film began to glaze over her eyes. "She's dead."

Arny was down on his haunches, busy trying to pry the twisted metal away from the tire. He was unable to budge it. He stood. "Chewaucan is just a mile or so up the road. Maybe we can limp in and have this pulled out, at least enough to get home."

Campbell picked up the deer's hind legs and tried to drag it off the road. His stomach felt queasy. "Give me a hand."

Five minutes later, as they eased into the Floyd's service station, a funeral wake of meat-eating animals, birds, insects and microorganisms began to break a trail to the carcass of the deer. In time, particle by particle, they would remove and consume everything edible, leaving behind only hair and bone.

★   ★   ★

Dolly was up early with plans to make a quick trip to Klamath Falls for groceries and a few odds and ends. Coming down the hallway she did not look at her reflection in the mirror and instead, once again, imagined herself as that young majorette. The toss went up, the white bulbs on the ends of the baton making flawless circles. Up. Up. Up. Hanging there. Dolly dropping to one knee. Making the catch. Prancing, twirling, throwing, catching.

She walked to her pride and joy, her Pontiac Bonneville Custom Safari wagon. It had electric seats, electric windows, electric everything, tooled Naugahyde, color-keyed vinyl floor mats. It was perfect in every way, except there was no bubble gum stuck to the seats, no little footprints on the dash, no scuff marks on the doors.

Even before she started the motor Dolly could sense the fervor welling up inside her. When it hit she quickly removed a wad of tissue she kept tucked between her breasts for such occasions. She whimpered and dabbed at the corner of each eye, then blew her nose fiercely into the tissue. Sadness overwhelmed her. She had wanted children and now wanted grandchildren. And why, oh why, could she not have stayed that lively young majorette of her youth? Having that taken away, to Dolly, was like a sighted person suddenly going blind. You have it, you lose it, and you miss it more than if you had never known it at all. As she drove away, the cauldron of emotion bubbled over again, even more intensely, and she had to pull over and park.

★ ★ ★

Shasta heard the Pontiac start and idle for a few moments before it pulled away. She got out of bed, pulled on comfortable clothes and took a yellow pad from her suitcase. She went to the kitchen and poured herself a cup of coffee that she diluted with milk and sweetened with sugar. She sat at the table and got down to the business of putting words on paper. She titled the first page "Grandma," and drew two lines under it for emphasis and to help focus her thoughts.

Grandma was born while her tribe was camped on Huckleberry Mountain during berry picking season. She will die in a sterile hospital room.

In her lifetime, nearly a hundred years, her entire world was transformed and the way of life she had known was replaced by the modern world: where food is stockpiled in grocery stores; voices and images are bounced around the atmosphere; light comes from a copper wire strung from home to home; people travel by automobiles, trains and airplanes; and men climb into rocket ships and are blasted into orbit around the earth.

Grandma had a brother who was sent to boarding school in the Willamette Valley. Grandma was too young to know why he had gone away. She was not aware of the proclamation made by Indian Agent L. S. Dyar: "Being fully convinced that a radical change in the Klamath Indian character can only be wrought in childhood and early youth, I would most respectfully urge the co-operation of the Government in the prosecution of this work, of taking the children from their native haunts of degradation, and clothing, feeding, and teaching them the habits and arts of civilization."

Grandma's brother went to school but he ran away. He ended up in Klamath Falls where he got drunk and was stabbed to death in a back alley. He was sixteen years old.

And then it was Grandma's turn. School was difficult for the young girl because she could not speak English. If she attempted to speak her native tongue she was whipped with a willow switch or forced to hold a pole over her head until she was exhausted. Sometimes, late at night, the girls would lie on their cots and whisper back and forth in Klamath.

Grandma's schooling ended the day a teacher demanded she write the answer to a question on the blackboard. Grandma did not know the answer. The teacher told her she was stupid and made the class chant that word over and over until Grandma threw the chalk on the floor and ran away. She lived in the woods until the weather turned cold and then she returned home.

Grandma remembers, as a child, standing beside the road watching a long column of blue coats return to Fort

Klamath with Captain Jack and the other Modoc war-
riors who had fled the reservation. A trial was held and
the sentences handed down. When it came time to mete
out the punishment, the blue coats made the reservation
Indians travel to Fort Klamath and bear witness.

The prisoners, wearing old army uniforms—except
Captain Jack who wore trousers and a bright checkered
shirt with a blanket thrown around his shoulders—were
led onto the parade grounds. The army band played the
Dead March and the Modoc women wailed and cried.
The prisoners were escorted to the gallows. Their arms
and legs were bound with ropes. Black hoods were
placed over their heads. The chaplain offered a brief
prayer, made the sign of the cross in front of each of the
condemned men, and stepped aside. The signal was
given, the trap doors fell open and the ropes jerked tight.

The sight of four convulsing bodies dangling in the
air made a deep impression on Grandma. From that day
forward she knew the old ways were dead. To survive
meant the Indian had to submit to the influences of the
dominant white culture. Grandma returned to school
and graduated. She married and lived in the white
world, but she desperately clung to the traditions and
beliefs of her people. And now, like Grandma, these tra-
ditions and beliefs are nearly gone.

Shasta read it over. It needed work, but it was a start.

★ ★ ★

Dolly returned from town and Shasta borrowed the station
wagon to say good-by to a few people before she caught the

bus to Eugene. After she had gone, Dolly, on a whim, decided to take a leisurely bath and wash her hair. But she felt guilty about being so self-indulgent, cut her bath short and set to work on a pile of ironing.

Dallas came home to check on a sick calf and noticed Dolly's car was gone. He figured she was still in town and thought he probably should stick his head in and say howdy to Shasta. But when he approached the house he was greeted by the noise of rock and roll music. To his amazement he observed his wife, wearing a housecoat and hair in curlers, ironing in front of the television. She was completely engrossed in Dick Clark's *American Bandstand*.

Dallas could feel the explosive music vibrating through the soles of his boots. On the TV screen he caught glimpses of twirling dresses, long legs and bouncing breasts. And there was Dolly moving her hips to the beat. She pulled up the hem of her housecoat, flashed a bare thigh and that was entirely too much.

He yelled, "Woman, what the 'ell ya doin'."

Dolly jumped. She was unaware that anyone else was in the same county. Even the iron spewed steam. "You scared me." She set down the iron, turned off the television and glared at Dallas. "Why did you do that?"

Dallas kept his face from showing any emotion. It prevented Dolly from knowing where she might be picking up, or losing, points. "Where's your car?"

"She's got it." When he was acting like this, Dolly never volunteered information unless it was to her benefit.

"Where'd she go?"

"She had something to do."

"What?"

"See Pokey."

"Why?"

"I suppose to tell him good-bye."

"She's leaving?" Dallas already knew the answer and he was relieved; ever since his daughter had arrived he had regretted her tracking mud from his past into the present. That was the reason he could never show his daughter affection, because it would hurt too damn much if he were to ever let her into his heart. Maybe if she were still a little girl he could hold her in his arms and coo, "I'll bet you're daddy's little girl, aren't ya?" But she was not anyone's little girl, not anymore.

"She has to get back to school," Dolly said, crossing the room to her chair, sitting cross-legged and removing the rollers one at a time while her fingers blindly massaged her scalp.

Dallas licked his lips, and even though it had been cool and raining, they still tasted like dust. He thought to himself he could damn well use a shot and walked into the kitchen. He poured a mug of coffee, complaining loud enough for Dolly to hear, "Christ, this coffee'd float a horseshoe," adding whiskey to dilute it. He heard Dolly walking down the hall and figured she was probably headed to the bathroom to get dressed and fix her face.

That was fine. There were more pressing matters on his mind. For a while he had let this termination thing get him down. He had actually considered selling his ranch. But he was on the rebound. Let the bastards win? No way. He would stay and fight.

He blamed the government, blamed the Indians, blamed everyone but himself for everything bad that had ever happened to him. His view of the future was a black storm rolling across a wide open field, straight at him. All his bravado collapsed. He wavered, hell yes, he'd be a fool not to sell; cattle prices were down and hay prices had skyrocketed. Dolly would love it if he sold and they moved to Klamath Falls. But what the hell would happen to him? He had no desire to end up a ravaged old drunk sweeping out a pool hall. And if he went to work on somebody else's ranch, they would eventually turn him out to pasture, which meant he would sit on a mower and trim the ranch house lawn. No thanks, partner. He finished his drink, set the mug in the sink and went back to work. The swagger was back in his gait. Make the bastards drag him out by his heels. That was his new philosophy.

★　★　★

Dolly heard the door close and muttered, "Thank you," because Dallas was gone. She walked down the hallway to the bedroom. The shades were drawn. The only light in the room was the orange glow from the electric blanket control. She sat on the edge of the unmade bed and rubbed one weary foot and then the other. Without seeing them, she knew the varicose veins were there on the inside of her ankles. That depressed her. She would chase her blues away by squandering the remainder of the day playing bridge with her friends. Yes, that would cheer her and she began to feel better, but wait, the girl had her car. Dolly was not going anywhere, and she started to cry.

Twenty-nine

Pokey stoked the woodstove and busied himself cleaning up the front room. He stacked empty bottles on the back porch and threw loose paper into the fire. The stove lid was hot and a blue enamel pot of boiling coffee confused other, less desirable, smells. He reached for the coffee pot, burned himself, stripped off his shirt and used it as a hot pad, then filled his cup with coffee and tossed the shirt on the counter. He added milk from a can of Carnation to dilute the bitterness, took a sip, wrinkled his nose and looked around for the one-pound box of sugar. After pouring in the sweetener he tried another sip and thought it tasted better. He set the tin cup on a corner of the table and slowly sensed an arcane calmness in the room, like when the wind dies for a few seconds just before the arrival of a thunderstorm.

Suddenly, from under the floorboards, the pack of dogs exploded with growls and barks. Pokey looked, saw Dolly's station wagon bouncing up the lane toward the house, figured it had to be Shasta, and quickly pulled on his shirt.

★ ★ ★

Shasta was thinking that she still had an extensive amount of research to do, and although some of it could be accomplished at the university's library, the problem was that the written word told only the white man's version. The Indian side of history had never been recorded, never would be, and there was nothing she could do about that.

Floyd was a wonderful source of information, but Shasta knew she needed to communicate with a representative of the Bureau of Indian Affairs. Several key questions required a governmental response. The most important: after the termination of the Klamath tribe, should all other Indians living in the United States live in fear of suffering a similar fate? A second question, along the same vein, would be to discover if it were current governmental policy to put an end to every reservation. And finally, if the reservation system were allowed to continue, would Indians ever be given the right to self-determination, or would they forever live as wards of the federal government?

Shasta recalled that a professor once made the statement in class that an author needed to build a story one layer at a time. And that was what she planned to do. She was starting with Grandma, portraying the old woman as the bridge to the past. The fate of her great-grandsons, after termination, was the tie to the present, as well as to the future.

When Shasta reached the Pitsua house she found Pokey waiting for her on the porch. He invited her in for coffee.

She sipped the bitter liquid and admitted to him, "I'm excited about writing this paper, but a little scared, too."

"Know what you mean. Every time I climb down on a bronc in the chute I always get a little anxious. You get that way because you never know the outcome. There's always the risk you might get bucked off. Same thing with you. You're scared you might fail." He was smiling. A horsefly found an opening in the screen. Once inside it noisily bashed itself against the kitchen window in a frenzied but futile attempt to escape.

Shasta blew across the hot liquid in her cup, making tiny ripples. "Floyd told me that the life expectancy of reservation Indians, nationwide, is less than forty years. Eighty percent of reservation dwellers are unemployed. Sugar diabetes and tuberculosis are epidemic. And alcohol is the contributing factor in nearly every problem, from health, to unemployment, to crime. Why?"

"Two reasons I suppose. First, alcohol was not, historically, a part of Indian culture. Our bodies have not built up immunity to it like the European has. And second, for a lot of Indians, alcohol is the only good time to be had."

"Help me understand something." Shasta took a tentative sip of coffee. "The white man is blamed for this and blamed for that, and sure, some terrible injustices have been committed, but isn't the Indian also responsible? At least to a degree?"

"You look real nice."

Shasta was caught off guard. "What brought that on?"

"I saw you in that dress at the basketball game."

"I couldn't bring my entire wardrobe."

"I'm not complaining," Pokey said. "Blue is my favorite color."

Shasta felt heat rising in her cheeks.

Pokey decided to take a chance. "I like you. I think you like me."

Shasta glanced around the room, at the clutter. Most certainly this was not a honeymoon suite in Hawaii. Yes, Pokey was more attractive than the boys at college who tried to impress her with good looks, fancy cars, sweet talk, potential, and promises. But she had formulated a blueprint for her life and a boyfriend right now would only complicate matters. How could she explain that in words?

Under the house the dogs came alive, kicking around bottles and turning on each other in their haste to reach the head of the driveway, where they stood barking and growling. They were announcing the arrival of a car and Pokey moved to the window.

"Christ."

"What is it?"

"She's back."

"Who?"

"My mother."

Thirty

When Puggy was young she had a slim waist, flawless complexion and a hint of innocence about her. But she started drinking in her teens and when she went on a toot she would horse around with any man who kept her in booze. Men lined up for the privilege because she was a fun gal to party with, and when she was drunk she had no inhibitions whatsoever.

For Puggy, the parties rolled together into an endless stream of alcohol and now, a thousand years later, Owen was the latest man in Puggy's life. When he was younger Owen had been a promising bronc rider who, it was said, had a legitimate shot at winning the world championship. He had squandered his talents on alcohol but continued to live under the illusion he could still ride. After Puggy cashed her termination check he talked her into staking him his entry fee in the saddle bronc event at the all-Indian rodeo in Red Bluff, California. They were headed in that direction, along with Owen's best friend Louie, who was healing up from his gunshot wound, when Puggy heard on the car radio that her oldest son had died. She tried to wake Owen, telling him, "Gotta line on gettin' more dough." He was too drunk to respond.

At Red Bluff, when it came time for Owen to crawl on his bronc, his name was called but he never showed. His horse had to be turned out. Puggy went looking for him and found him passed out behind the chutes. She gave a couple cowboys twenty bucks each to haul Owen and Louie to her T-Bird and stuff them inside. She drove north to Chewaucan where she spent several hours in The Tavern before getting around to the business of collecting her dead son's money.

Puggy burst into the house and stood glaring at Pokey and the white girl. Her hands were braced on her wide hips and she was swaying. She started to lose her balance and wobbled to the wall. By holding a hand against it she made her way to an impressive mound of glass bottles. It had been Pokey's intention to pour out the contents but he had not finished the task. Puggy grabbed a bottle, opened it and drank. When it was empty she tossed it on the floor and the bottle flipped, twirled and skittered, finally wedging itself under Chief's chair. All was quiet except for the whine of the horsefly and Guy Mitchell mournfully singing in the distance on the car radio: "Heartaches by the number, troubles by the score, each day you love me less, each day I love you more . . ."

There was a commotion on the porch and then Owen and Louie staggered through the doorway. It appeared as if they were trying out for a part in a slapstick comedy. Owen was falling-down drunk and Louie, still wearing the blood-splattered shirt with the hole in it, was in just as bad shape. Puggy watched them dive into the pile of bottles and flounder on the floor. Then she grabbed herself another bottle, took a drink, and this time the alcohol seemed to stiffen her mouth and open her eyes. She wanted to know, "Where's Grandma?"

"In the hospital," Pokey said.

"What happened?"

"Heart attack."

"Die yet?"

"Not yet."

"Where's da money? Ya got it, ain't it?"

Pokey shrugged. "What money?"

"The goddamned money. Chief's money. Don't play games, ya son of a bitch." She took another swig from the tequila bottle and her eyes narrowed to dangerous slits. "I ain't screwin' 'round. Give me the money." She threw the bottle against the far wall but not with enough force to break it.

"Red's got it. Took it as evidence after the shooting."

"Bullshit. You're lyin'."

Pokey shook his head.

"I'm gonna get my gun." She turned away. In her wake the screen door slapped the frame.

Owen was on all fours on the floor. "She'll kill ya," he warned.

Louie offered, "She's crazy."

Shasta whispered, "What are you going to do?"

"The only thing I can," Pokey said and he stepped to where a rifle was leaned against the wall.

★ ★ ★

Grandma appeared before the Subcommittee of the Committee on Public Lands during their 1947 testimony hearing held in Chewaucan. She told the senators: "Indian put on reservation. Agent say him be Chief. Want Indian plant garden. Say no gamble horse race. No play bone game. Say man only have one wife. Must go Agent house marry. Pay five dollar. No money pay five horse. White Chief say Indian god no good. Give us bible. Want us have his god. Agent make Indian just like white man.

"This our reservation. Make home here. Live here long time. Build good house. Build good fence. Raise cattle. Raise horse. Want keep land. This where live. White man try make Indian take money. Klamath no want take money. No want sell land."

★ ★ ★

Pokey slid the bolt forward, advancing a live round into the chamber. He moved in front of Shasta. When Puggy stuck her head inside, the first thing she saw was the .308 rifle pointing directly at her. She was cradling a 12-gauge, automatic shotgun. "I gotta right ta that money."

"You've got a right to turn around and leave, that's all."

"I was his mother."

"You were never a mother. Not to him. Not to me. Not to Creek." Pokey glared at her. His heart thumped against his ribs. He despised her, but he could not kill her. Slowly, very deliberately, Puggy swung the shotgun into position, until it pointed directly at Pokey's chest. There was no question, unless she got what she wanted, she would pull the trigger.

★ ★ ★

Debbie had borrowed lipstick, eyeliner and a hairbrush from one of the nurses and had fixed herself up. But worry furrowed her brow as she waited for Steve. She feared that when he did visit, he would hold her responsible for the death of their baby. She had told one of the nurses that very thing. The nurse had tried to reassure her, "Oh no, he won't, honey. He loves you."

"Then he will think we're being punished." Debbie had cried softly, dabbing at her eyes with a corner of a washcloth.

And again the nurse told her, "No, he won't."

And then Steve swept into the room. His face was radiating brilliance and optimism and passion. He took Debbie's hand and held it. "It's going to be all right. Everything is going to be all right." He fell to one knee, opening his arms to heaven and announced, "I have taken Jesus into my life. I am born again!" He stood, rushed to Debbie and embraced her. He was laughing and crying at the same time. Debbie just held him. She did not know what to think. A nurse came gliding in, stopped short, smiled as though this was about the sweetest scene she had ever witnessed, and tiptoed out of the room.

★ ★ ★

"Put it down," Red commanded through the screen door. "Do it, Puggy, or you're horsemeat."

Puggy did not turn around. She kept the shotgun trained on Pokey. "You ain't got no gun. You never carry no gun."

"If I did, you'd already be dead."

Puggy found this amusing. She cackled.

"Put it down."

"If I don't?"

"You will."

"What makes you think so?"

" 'Cause, if there's one ounce of trouble, you go to jail."
Red pointed through the screen door toward Louie. "And
you're gonna have to explain that hole punched in your
belly. Breaking and entering is good for three to six." He
pointed toward Owen. "Being an accessory nets you a min-
imum of two." The finger came around to Puggy. "And
you're bucking with assault and attempted murder. Put the
gun down now. Walk away. Get the hell off the reservation
and outta Klamath County."

★ ★ ★

"No problem," Floyd had told the bankers when they drove
the Lincoln into the open bay at the Shell service station and
asked if he could pull the damaged fender away from where it
was rubbing against the tire. "But I'm not a body and fender
man. It'll be functional but not particularly pretty."

Leland Campbell nodded his approval. "All we need is to
be able to drive to Klamath Falls. We'll worry about cos-
metics later." After that Campbell stood beside the roll-up
door. He purposely did not lean against anything because
everything seemed to carry a coating of grease and dust and
he did not want to soil his suit. He watched the small, wiry
man in the blue shirt and clip-on bow tie pound and pull
against the metal with a hammer and crowbar.

"That should do it," Floyd said as he laid the tools on
the workbench and used the rag in his hind pocket to
clean his hands.

"How much do we owe you?" Arny asked as he pulled out
his wallet. He had only twenty-five dollars cash and was
hoping that would be enough, that he would not have to ask
Campbell to pitch in.

"No charge," Floyd said. "Next time you pass through stop for a fill-up."

★ ★ ★

Arny parked the Continental between a Jeep and a red Cadillac convertible. The bankers got out of the car, walked around the mud puddles, and climbed the steps onto the porch. From here they could see an Indian woman through the screen door and she was pointing a shotgun at the belly of a deputy sheriff. The bankers, whose faces had become as blank as farmers in purgatory after spending a long day driving tractors in endless circles, did not move. Finally it was Campbell who forced himself to speak. "We could come back later."

Red grinned. "Stay. The more the messier."

Campbell wondered if this was supposed to be a round-house attempt at intimidating humor. Red was standing there facing a shotgun pointed at his gut and he did not look frightened, or even the least bit concerned. In fact, it appeared as if he found this to be all too amusing.

"This is a bit awkward," Campbell confessed.

Red faced the bankers. "When I saw Puggy here roll into town I sort of suspected she might be up to no good. She couldn't make it past The Tavern but I waited, followed her. Sure enough, she went totin' a shotgun into the house and I pretty well knew things weren't up to Hoyle."

Red turned back to the screen door and the shotgun-toting woman on the other side. "Puggy, either get the hell out of here, or pull that goddamn trigger. One way or the other. I ain't got all day."

Puggy tossed the shotgun onto the sofa. "Wasn't even

307

loaded." She backhanded the screen door, and pushed her way past the pair of bankers. Owen and Louie trailed after her like destitute afterthoughts. Their arms were wrapped around more bottles of liquor than they could carry. Bottles squirted away, hit the porch and rolled down the stairs.

After the T-Bird had gone, and even after the sound of it thumping over the bridge had drifted back to the house, the bankers remained rooted to the same spot. Red surmised, "You fellows must be preachers or salesmen. If you got business here best step on inside." He held open the battered screen door for them.

The two men entered the room and introduced themselves, Arny Osborne first, since he was closest, and then Leland Campbell. Arny talked in a rush, explaining he was the Klamath Falls branch manager of U.S. West Bank and that Mr. Campbell was the vice president of operations for the northwest region. "We had quite a time getting here. We hit a deer and then we had to stop at the service station and have the mechanic pull out the fender. And then that woman with the gun. That was the topper. Boy, oh boy, what a day."

Campbell took over. "Mr. Pitsua, we at U.S. West are always looking for ways to best serve our customers. It has come to our attention that you are the only member of the Klamath tribe who has failed to cash your termination check. Forty-three thousand dollars is way too much money to ignore."

From the poker-faced expression on the Indian's face it appeared to Campbell that the young man might be mentally slow. He tried a slightly different approach. "I am talking dollars and cents here." He reached into his inside coat pocket and withdrew a narrow sheet of paper. He spoke slowly, each word a distinct and separate entity. "This is your check. If you will endorse it, we can open a savings account in your name and put this money to work for you drawing interest. Every day you will make more money."

"You're doing this for me?" asked Pokey.

"Yes," Campbell said.

"I don't believe you. I think you want my money so you can make money. Isn't that the way the game's played? Well, Mr. Campbell, I'm going to tell you the same thing Tecumseh told the white man when they tried to buy his land. He said, 'No tribe has a right to sell. Sell a country. Why not sell the air, the clouds and the great sea?'"

Campbell waved the check and wanted to know. "Don't you want this money?"

Pokey flipped back a braid and said, "Hell no."

Thirty-one

The bus driver slammed the luggage compartment door and walked past Pokey and Shasta. "Let's go," he called.

"Guess this is it," Pokey said. He dug into his pocket, withdrew the arrowhead he had found on the ridge the day before termination and handed it to Shasta. "Take it. It'll give you strength to tell your story the way it should be told."

"Got a bus full waiting," the driver commanded through the open door.

"Thank you." Shasta looked up at Pokey. She did not know how to convey her appreciation for this gesture, and for their friendship. She started to move away, changed her mind, turned back and gave Pokey a kiss on the lips.

The kiss surprised Pokey. The warmth of her lips lingered on his even as she bounded up the steps of the bus. He raised his hand to wave, but she boarded without so much as a backward glance. He dropped the hand.

The driver was beginning to inch forward when a car horn sounded and Red's two-tone Chevy slid to a gravel-throwing stop. He rolled down his window, stuck his head outside and, when the driver cranked open the door, he hollered, "Got one more."

"Hurry it up."

Lefty slipped from the passenger side, hobbled around to Red's window and handed him the wad of money with a rubber band wrapped around it. He told Red, "Hold on to this. If I don't make it back, you keep it, or give it away. I don't give a damn."

He boarded the bus and plunked himself down across the aisle from Shasta. As the bus pulled away, he removed a miniature bottle of Black Velvet from his coat pocket. A deft twist unscrewed the lid. He raised the single shot in a toast, turned to her and winked. "Sweetheart, here's one last one for the road."

Epilogue

From the ashes of the termination party, which lasted until the money ran out, rose all the saints and the sinners, but only one true hero.

Dolly and Dallas reached a compromise and agreed to live apart. Dolly moved to a nice little apartment in Klamath Falls. Dallas refused to budge off the ranch. He visited Dolly, or she visited him, for a weekend every now and then and somehow, they managed to keep the strings of their marriage loosely knotted.

Creek graduated from the University of Oregon and, because of his background in mathematics, was recruited and given a job with the City of Portland Water Bureau. He successfully parlayed his termination money into a small fortune in commercial real estate, never married but shared a house in the Irvington district with a male companion.

Within a year of the termination payoff Puggy had spent all her money and was flat broke. She died a few months later. The cause of her death was listed as "acute alcoholism."

Red and Marg moved to the Oregon coast. Red bought a 38-foot boat and began operating a charter service, taking clients out from Depoe Bay to catch bottom fish, and salmon when the run was on. He swore he was perfectly content being a charter boat captain.

Floyd never retired and remained working six days a week at the Shell station. He and Tillie joined the Sagebrush Shufflers, a square dancing club.

After having bled every last penny he could from the Indians, Cap Andrews boarded up The Tavern and went on an African safari, where he killed an impala, several antelope, a zebra, a cape buffalo and a lion. The last anyone heard, he was working in Montana as a big-game guide.

Steve and Debbie Atwood moved back to California. Steve returned to college and, after graduating, accepted a teaching position at a Christian school in Grass Valley. They had two children, a girl and a boy.

Lefty might have died a hopeless drunk; that miniature bottle of Black Velvet he pulled from his coat pocket on the bus ride north was just one of many. But he dried out, returned to Chewaucan and used Grandma Pitsua's termination money to build the largest logging museum in the world.

Readers with romance in their hearts may fantasize that Shasta and Pokey fell in love, married, and were blissfully happy ever after. That would make a nice fairytale ending.

Not long after Shasta had arrived in Eugene, she received a note from Pokey telling her that Grandma had died peacefully in her sleep. Shasta sent a sympathy card. The two of them continued to exchange notes and letters, but their interchange became less and less frequent, and finally ceased altogether.

Shasta parlayed her term paper on termination into an internship at *The Oregonian,* the newspaper with the largest circulation in Oregon. The following year she graduated from the Honors College at the University of Oregon School of Journalism and found employment as a reporter for the *Boise Spokesman.* She was recruited by the *Seattle Daily Times* to an editorial assistant position and two years later her upwardly mobile climb landed her a job as a weekly columnist with the *San Francisco Chronicle.* She never married.

Pokey became an accomplished artist. He made the pivotal decision to follow his heart and never cashed his termination check. He told the parade of government officials who visited him that his land and his heritage were not for sale. But he offered a compromise, saying he would settle for 160 acres along the river that included Standing Rock, as well as the site where the ancient village of Chewaucan had once stood. He claimed he wanted to preserve the history of the Klamath people and re-create their village as an interpretive site for school children to visit and learn about the Indian way of life.

To back up his demand he had started a ceremonial fire in a pit at Standing Rock. For eight years he tended that fire. Eight years in the wind and the rain and the snow. Eight years feeding the fire and fighting the federal government. He never gave in and never gave up. It would have been so easy to simply take the termination money.

The bureaucrats had taken a wait-and-see approach, figuring eventually Pokey would tire of the fight and simply slink away. But he stood his ground, tended his ceremonial fire, and eventually public opinion, and the influence of a few powerful politicians, helped to change the course of history. Special legislation was passed and finally, in a ceremony at Standing Rock, Pokey was given the deed to 160 acres in lieu of his share of the liquidated Klamath tribal reservation. The ceremonial fire was allowed to die.

Author's Note

Termination is seen by most Klamath Indians as the worst disaster that ever befell them. They say they were tricked into selling their reservation by the federal government and now they want the land returned to them.

In August 1986 President Ronald Reagan, attempting to soften the harsh realities of termination, signed a bill restoring the government-recognized status of the Klamath tribe. Chuck Kimbol, the Klamath tribal chairman, said: "When termination happened we were told we were no longer a tribe, we were even told we were no longer Indians. Psychologically this bill will have a great positive effect on our people."

Oregon Senator Mark O. Hatfield, who guided the bill through the Senate and attended the tribal celebration, where he participated in the traditional Owl Dance, said: "This action is great news for the Klamath tribe. Although it does not return the tribe's historic lands or suggest that the federal government create a new reservation, the restoration will provide important assistance in the tribe's struggle to become economically self-sufficient and to alleviate the health, education and employment problems left in the wake of the 1954 Termination Act."

In 2002 Interior Secretary Gale Norton opened formal negotiations with the Klamath Tribe, which could lead to the return of the former tribal reservation. If this does occur, it would be the largest return of ancestral lands to a Native American tribe and would set a precedent, which could have far-reaching national effects. To date no final resolution has been reached.

Our land is more valuable than your money. It will last forever. As long as the sun shines and the waters flow, this land will be here to give life to men and animals. We cannot sell the lives of men and animals; therefore we cannot sell this land. It was put here for us by the Great Spirit and we cannot sell it because it does not belong to us. You can count your money and burn it but only the Great Spirit can count the grains of sand and the blades of grass. We will give you anything we have that you can take with you; but the land, never.

—SPOKEN BY A NORTHERN BLACKFEET CHIEF
UPON BEING ASKED BY A UNITED STATES DELEGATE
FOR HIS SIGNATURE ON A LAND TREATY

About the Author

Rick Steber was raised in Klamath County and lived on the Klamath Indian reservation. He has won numerous awards and honors for his books and his writing. He is a member of the Western Writers of America and the Outdoor Writers of America and has worked with the U.S. Department of Education to set national education standards and achievement levels for U.S. history curriculum.

In addition to his writing, Rick is an engaging Western personality and is in great demand as a featured speaker at national and international conferences and banquets. He donates many hours to visiting schools, talking to students about the importance of education, helping them develop reading and writing skills, and impressing upon them the value of saving our history for future generations.

Rick lives near Prineville, Oregon, with his wife, Kristi, and his sons, Seneca and Dusty. He writes in a secluded cabin in the Ochoco Mountains.